The Dream of
Santa María de las Piedras

bp

Bilingual Press/Editorial Bilingüe

General Editor
   Gary D. Keller

Managing Editor
   Karen S. Van Hooft

Senior Editor
   Mary M. Keller

Assistant Editor
   Linda St. George Thurston

Editorial Board
   Juan Goytisolo
   Francisco Jiménez
   Eduardo Rivera
   Severo Sarduy
   Mario Vargas Llosa

Address:
Bilingual Review/Press
Hispanic Research Center
Arizona State University
Tempe, Arizona 85287
(602) 965-3867

The Dream of
Santa María de las Piedras

Miguel Méndez M.

*Translated from the Spanish
by David William Foster*

Bilingual Press/Editorial Bilingüe
TEMPE, ARIZONA

ISBN: 0-916950-98-0
Printed simultaneously in a softcover edition. ISBN: 0-916950-99-9

Library of Congress Catalog Card Number: 89-61106

PRINTED IN THE UNITED STATES OF AMERICA

Cover design by Peter J. Hanegraaf
Back cover photo by Luis Bernal

Acknowledgments

This project is jointly supported by a grant from the Arizona Commission on the Arts, a State agency, and the National Endowment for the Arts in Washington, D.C., a Federal agency.

Clarification

Santa María de las Piedras—Saint Mary of the Stones—is in reality only a dream, like the dreams dreamed by the stones. Yet, the desert of Sonora does exist, and there is along the frontier a town with streets and a plaza. Anecdotes and characters match real events in the same way that images reflected by mirrors match. Facts could well be what flickers in the mirrors and reality what gives off reflections. How strange, surely, are our dreams. If there are those who are offended by the context of these dreams because they see themselves in them, they should realize that it is nothing more than pure coincidence.

For years and years Santa María de las Piedras was a place turned in on itself. Other towns around it have the ring of legend and sound like the invention of wild-eyed explorers, even though they are located only a few days' ride away. But it was not the distances that erased the trails; rather it was the sand, so many, many stones, the atmosphere like soaring flames, and the labyrinthine roads wiped out over and over again by the clouds of dust. They were paths retraced by the survivors of other labyrinths to be found in the inner recesses of their minds. Time and space in Santa María de las Piedras are swallowed up by the breath of the desert. Stung by the sun and left with its poison, the inhabitants are abandoned, exhausted and blinded, to the mercy of God, not knowing what's coming or what's going or if everything is suspended in one being. Here in Santa María de las Piedras many times and more than one space flow together. Look down on it from above as though you were a passenger in one of those machines invented by the gringos. See how Santa María de las Piedras is an anthill on the edge of the desert, right in the middle of the Altar district. I realize that the towns scattered along the edge of the open plain or in the middle of the barren desert itself are names known in Sonora and beyond. But Santa María de las Piedras will never cease to be a mystery. Perhaps it is nothing more than the reflection of the desert towns turned by the sun into mirrors irradiating soaring flames and humanity that converge here. The gringos saw this wasteland as a natural frontier. A frontier of cactuses, stones, sand, and fire between Mexico to the south and the United States on the northern side.

Should you want to establish the exact point where Santa María de las Piedras is to be found, you are likely to miss it. There are those who insist that this town is a joke, a dream, and make no mistake, even one of those stories that travel with the dust or float along the washes every time the clouds forget and dump themselves on these burning rocks. If it is true that Santa María de las Piedras did exist, here we are to demonstrate it with our presence, standing on these blurred streets. That imposing church was molded by Father Encarnación with his spirit and it has existed forever. There is the plaza where history, absurd and playful, plays in the mouths of talkative old men. These old chatterboxes dress it up like a clown, like a village girl, like a beggar. She gladly allows this, tired of tinsel and false finery that others use to turn her into an aristocratic lady. Another part of Santa María de las Piedras consists of the hills stretched out in the shape of a half-moon with jagged peaks at each end, facing the esplanadelike prominence where the dead rest. The Spaniards decided to call these hills the Cathedral, but the Indians had already named them the Twin Tits. Although Santa María de las Piedras is like any other town, it is also unique, not to be found in any other epoch. You might well ask why Santa María de las Piedras is located in the middle of sand dunes and scraggly plants, with only sahuaros as sentinels, in an oasis of stones. Say a world of stones, although in the middle of this wasteland there is nothing more than a fistful of pebbles and sand. In these parts everything is true, no matter how much it seems to be a lie. Everything seems funny to these people. For if the water runs deep, the bitterness comes from above. Time in Santa María de las Piedras moves backward because it knows this is a town condemned to oblivion, living only on the memories of memories made into dreams. Only one man from Santa María de las Piedras happened by chance to enter the future. Madness freed him from this petrified dream and led him to tread solid ground while navigating forbidden spaces that open onto profound mysteries. Crossing the United States of America, he stumbled onto God's tracks and devoted himself to seeking Him everywhere until he found Him. . . . Some might say that Santa María de las Piedras is just a myth: they would dare to deny its existence, looking for it on the maps but not finding it. Yet Santa María de las Piedras is recorded on no chart, except here on this pile of rocks surrounded by dunes that challenge the gaze of strangers. People who do get close are often lost in the dust storms when the wind blows. The dust usually covers the sun, and it covers the town even more. There are some who have even failed to see Santa María de las Piedras because of the light that falls in torrents from the sky, bounces off the stones, blinds the area around it, turning all this into a lagoon of magic. Thus the pilgrims turn away from the luminous outlines of Santa María de las Piedras, believing them to be magical mirrors put up by the fevered atmosphere. Anyone wishing to know this town of Santa María de las Piedras should walk along the ridge of the desert, should get to know death, should ignore the scorching heat, should let blisters form on the soles of his feet, should drink the hot earth, and should walk and walk until he arrives. This way he'll be able to tell his grandchildren someday that he discovered a town walled in by soaring flames called Santa María de las Piedras. Can you hear me, Teófilo? How could you hear me? You're sleeping like one of your great-grandchildren. Since the ones who keep you amused are not seated now on the benches of the plaza, beneath these burnt shadows, you can dream and snore. What I have to say doesn't interest you, I know that. But, what about what Don Nacho has to say? Ah, you fight with him and become sly and witty! How you like to swing your cane at Güero Paparruchas when he makes us laugh with his stories! They'll be back tomorrow, along with others, if we're lucky. Sleep, old man, sleep and dream while I dream with my eyes open. I hear you, Abelardo, I hear you. You know I'm sleeping and listening at the same time. You've already forgotten about the gold rush years? That was when thousands of adventurers came to Santa María de las Piedras. You forget that now our young people are leaving for the United States, fleeing from hunger to face so many dangers, with only faith as their friend and the whole world as their enemy. How can you say, Lalo, that nobody enters or leaves this town? Pay no attention to me, Teófilo, they're just the ideas of an old man. The only reality I behold are these burning sand dunes, these smoking piles of stones, these peak-filled hills and this dead river violated by the summer floods, for they remain while we last only an instant. At times I don't even believe we are here. Ah, Lalo, how we need Güero Paparruchas and Don Nacho now! With them around there is no reason to cry with nostalgia. They're good for a lot of horsing around and lots of talking. Those doddering old men will come. They'll come and we'll once again recall everything that has happened in Santa María de las Piedras. Here, seated on these benches, beneath these trees, in the middle of this plaza. We'll repaint the memories dimmed by time.

Just look at how pretty spring is—families going to mass, children laughing in a single fluttering of bodies, everything turning green again. Except for you, Nacho, you're drier than the sun. That's what you think, but I can still shake a leg. Sure, even with this damn rheumatism both of mine still move. You old goat, you still keep going. Here comes Güero Paparruchas, laughing over his little lies. What's up, Güero? Nothing's up—it's all stuck down. Here comes Lalo being led by the hand by one of his great-grandchildren. Hurry up, man, we're waiting for you; Güero here is anxious to talk his nonsense. Good day, gentlemen, you can see no matter how many telegrams I tap out with it this cane won't let me down. The four of them add up to more than three centuries. The church bells draw the parishoners in with one peal after another. Father Hilario is full of congratulations. All of Santa María de las Piedras needs a mass. The trees are full of birds brought together from all over the plaza chattering in disagreement with each other. While everybody else is taken up with sermons and prayers, the old men begin their day with "Do you remember?" "I just remembered," "What happened to that guy?" Until a story comes along that sweeps them along together, they gossip among themselves, talk to themselves, or joke together. You look a little serious, Don Teófilo. Oh, I feel a little messed up. My kidneys are on vacation, and I hope they don't give out because they're mad at me. You just like to suffer, you crabby old man. I told you to eat the foot of a cooked grasshopper, and you'll even pee out your ears. You and your damn remedies, Nacho, your feet belong to a grasshopper. In that case I'll prescribe swallows for you. I'm fed up with boiled this and that. I'm referring to the swallows the musicians play in the cemetery. You old goat. You talk, Güero. These guys are picking their teeth. Come on, what are you thinking about? Give us one of your stories. I was remembering that season when I was working in Sonoíta planting beans. I'd get bitten every day by rattlesnakes. I would kill them, cut their heads off and eat them fried with chopped chiles. I never got anything except for a real bad rash in the groin. What a line you're giving us, Paparruchas. Maybe it'd be better for Abelardo to tell us about when the hallelujah man came to Santa María de las Piedras. Where can that damn Trini Brown be now? He always seemed like a weird type to me. Don Lalo, you've studied people a lot. What's your opinion about that gringo who almost took Father Hilario's people away from him? For a few days it looked like this whole place was a revival camp; at least during the whole time trucks were rolling up with the clothing and food that Brother Trini Brown passed out with both hands. By the end of the week he was gone, and he never came back. According to him, he'd planted the seed. What he didn't know is that seeds from the outside almost always dry up here. It's pure luck if they grow into anything. But there were a few hallelujah men left around here to get together to sing and shout from one night to the next. They're peaceful people and don't offend anyone. And you should see how they had the sins all counted out on their side. What Father Hilario couldn't do by promising them eternal glory, Brother Trini Brown

6

could by frightening them with hell. That's where they'll cure your kidneys, Teófilo, with fire enemas. They'll warm your piles, Nacho, with burning oil to straighten your asshole out. Be quiet, fellows. Hey, Güero! Didn't the Brother baptize you? Not me, but they got Don Nachito here. You're lying through your teeth, Güero. I was only poking about to see what weird things Brother Trini Brown was up to. Nacho, go tell that to a chile pepper. It hasn't got any eyes. I saw you acting the apostle. You were helping the hallelujah man pull the women from the water, blind and soaking like rats. That's only because he was paying me and in dollars, so there. Let's keep things straight. Maybe, but what you can't deny is that the hallelujah man got to all the old folks who'd been sitting around in the shadows so long. Just listen to what I've got to say to you straight. Don't interrupt me, because I won't answer you. Go on, man, between all of us we'll make Brother Trini Brown's ears ring. You also ran after him, Abelardo. I remember him very well; the heat of Santa María de las Piedras had already gotten to him. They carried him off to Tucson all dehydrated. I understand they revived him there. The rains that fell over in El Claro brought a lot of water down the river for something like a week. The preacher man arrived here with his tongue going full speed yakking about eternal damnation for hours and hours, night and day, until he ran out of steam. By that time, and excuse the comparison, he was panting like a dog and gesturing with his hands because he couldn't get the words out anymore. He was a tall, stocky sort with a potbelly already, sure enough, and his face was a collection of different races: black and Indian, with blond curls and very green eyes pulled back like a Chinaman's. The brother had full cheeks, a big nose, with nostrils like a turtle's, stronger than a track burro. The devil only knows how he got here. With the flood or a dust storm or riding a dune. In any case, he stood up in the middle of the plaza, the Bible in his hand, facing Father Hilario's church. Then he started lashing out against the Pope of Rome himself. One thing and another about the Romans, friends of money, allies of the devil, hardened sinners. His voice was like a bull's and his fists were clenched. He was constantly going on about the threat of fire and how those who were unrepentant and hard of heart would fry. Brother Trini Brown's deep voice left no one unmoved. People lay in their beds in the secrecy of their houses and clasped pillows to their ears. But the voice of that strange man would always get through. The men who scratch the hills looking for gold among

7

the scrabble came running down to the plaza to see what strange thing was happening. Farmers abandoned their work with their ears sticking up like hares, and they fell over each other to see what was going on. The hallelujah man spoke clearly, with a gringo accent but with a good Castilian style. He would meow when he was really excited. Blood would flush his skin. He would swell up, his face all contorted, while he was speaking. The whole thing even looked like a dance. Generation of vipers, I sought to take you under my wing like the chicken protects her chicks, but the slobber of concupiscence was stronger. I am the way. I am the light. He who follows me will have eternal life. Oh, vile sinner, you will have no rest! When you burn among the coals the demons will come to flay you. They will grind their nails into you, they will tear your flesh, and with their forks they will disembowel you. Your eternal resting place will be there among the weeping and the gnashing of teeth. My kingdom is not of this world. Woman, stop adoring earthen images. Free yourself from false redeemers. I am the one who gives life. They brought before the Lord a man possessed of the devil, and He said: Get ye out of that body, demons, and behold the spirits of Satan entered into the bodies of some pigs on their way to slaughter and the pigs ran away squealing and threw themselves into the river. I have come to pray so that you may cast forth the demons that inhabit you. Spying from the belltower, Father Hilario followed all of the unusual events. He had never seen all of his parish together, and now that damn frothy chocolate monkey had performed a miracle. He felt angry and jealous and wished fervently that his flock would ignore the intruder, cast him from the town, shout to him their faith of centuries in the Catholic religion, cover their ears, leave the gringo standing and seek him, the true shepard, Father Hilario, the only true guide. But no, there they stand rooted, fascinated by the intruder. Brother Trini Brown is no more than thirty years old, and his athletic body indicates he has eaten well and abundantly since birth. He seemed so tall and so robust, vibrant with fullness, alongside the people of Santa María de las Piedras, who were skinny, bony, and hungry all their lives, kept alive by miserable diets, hardened by constant poor nutrition like the leathery roots of the bushes that bore themselves into the hard and dry earth and cling to it in order to go on enduring the torture of their thirst. Night came and the hallelujah man continued his Biblical arguments, his voice hoarse and powerful. Like a swollen river, he carried along the spirits of the people, stunned by the onslaught that, rather than decreasing, grew. Father Hilario sent for the police chief, Don Rumboso Noragua. You're the authority here. That fried gringo is creating a public scandal. What are you waiting for to apply the law? Run him out into the desert this very minute. I grabbed him right away, Father Hilario, and I ordered him to get going back to his own country whether he wanted to or not. But he showed me documents signed and sealed by government bigwigs, the freedom of religion bit. He has a letter requesting he be given full assistance and ordering us not to interfere with him, signed by the governor, Father Hilario. Damn heretic. He's doing that just to ruin us. That's his dream. He humiliates us, but he bends over backward for the gringos. He persecuted us like dogs and he still does. He never comes here because there's nothing to steal, and now he sends us that foreigner to rob us of the only thing we have left. Forget him, Father; the heat will take care of him. Listen to me, Father. His eyes were very green when he got here, and the sun which knows how to feed on outsiders is bleaching them out. He no longer shouts hallelujah! quite so often. Leave him be, Father; give him enough rope to hang himself with. That was when Moses led his people through the desert. Plagued by hunger, the children of Israel bemoaned their plight. Pray and have faith, said the holy man, and He will feed you. And thus it was that on the next day the Almighty rewarded their faith: manna fell from the heavens— bread! Bread, my brothers!—to cure hunger. Brothers and sisters of Santa María de las Piedras, fall to your knees and pray, and if you pray with faith I promise you that tomorrow manna will fall from the heavens. All Santa María de las Piedras falls to its knees. Brother Trini Brown prays at the top of his voice like a circus hawker, everybody else deadly quiet. Father Hilario sees and hears him, sprawled like a lizard on the floor of the belltower. He clenches his fists and pounds the wood. A fraud is what you are, a liar, a clown. Manna my . . . As for you, you stupid fools, how can you be so simple-minded and such asses? His flock prays to the sound of Brother Trini Brown's yelping. I can't stand how mad it makes me. How bitter, my sheep stolen by this damn hallelujah man. Forgive me, Lord, you who died in order for us to learn to love, but I just can't stand this overwhelming desire to stomp the shit out of that hateful charlatan who claims to be your messenger. So, tomorrow manna will fall on Santa María de las Piedras. . . . The young and the old returned to their houses. With sidelong looks halfway between

9

frightened and timid at the saints (the earthen idols that Brother Trini Brown preached against). It hurt them to face the Virgin of Guadalupe more than the other saints. That night all of Father Hilario's sheep slept with their eyes wide open.

The next day, more out of fear for the eternal pit or because of the powerful pull the words and gestures of the Brother held over them, the inhabitants of the town approached the plaza animated by an enormous curiosity. They wished to witness the supposed rain of bread. Besides, most of them began to be pricked by that legion of devils that inspire silly behavior and on more than one occasion serious misbehavior on the part of the people of God. From his outpost among the bells, Father Hilario looked without seeing, gripped by an intense melancholy. All care and feeling had abandoned him. As many tears as stars had touched his eyes. Those of you who would receive the grace of the Lord, follow me to the river. I will do unto you like the Baptist: I will baptize you in the name of the Lord so that you may be saved. Know that this will be the true baptism and not the one that you received as ignorant children. Then you were unknowing, but now you see that you are to follow in His luminous steps. I am a true shepherd, not a false one like those puppets directed by Rome. Your whore of a mother was a puppet, abortion of Lucifer, snout of an anteater. May the devils confound you in your evil; you will pay for your maliciousness, shepherd of a whore, jackass. Verily I say unto you that before the sun sets manna will fall on Santa María de las Piedras. Listen, Cirilo, aren't you going to go get a basket to carry the bread home? No problem, this guy is crazier than a hoot owl. But when the day had worn on with its burning sun and the afternoon began to turn into shadows, a truck pulled up between the plaza and the church, a battered old wreck like the castoffs of the gringo army. The doors of the truck carried this inscription for identification: "Brothers of the True Faith in the Lord," followed by "Lord, give manna to your servants." The back of the truck is full to the top with packages and stuff. A crewcut gringo was driving it, a tall guy who talked and laughed out loud. There was a blonde lady next to the thin man, wearing a tight pair of pants and a green blouse. According to the he-men, the woman was quite a piece, or, as others said, real hot. She greeted Brother Trini Brown with a long kiss and embrace. The Lord's minister cried with warm emotion, Oh my beloved! My companion in the work of the Lord! A world of words lay submerged beneath the many looks and smiles people exchanged with each other. Formed by Catholic precepts, the believers of Santa María de las Piedras truly believed that every leader of the faith must necessarily be celibate. Helped by various onlookers, the gringos began to distribute the contents of the truck: canned food, pants, women's dresses, shoes, etc. The miracle of manna turned into a jubilant confusion; children and old people whirled around, grabbing first a can and then an article of clothing. Follow me, follow me to the river and I will make you into true Christians. The procession turned streets, crossed the boundaries of the town, and reached the river. The water there by chance, daughter of the rains that fell in Magdalena and Santa Ana, still flowed with a certain force, not enough to drown anyone but just enough to provide a bath. Trini Brown, assisted by his fellow citizens, readied himself to proceed. He looked like he belonged in a movie on John the Baptist.

Only a single soul was left behind in the town of Santa María de las Piedras: Father Hilario. The friar poured out the tears of his disillusionment. Once let loose, the tears flowed in torrents. I came to this town a young man, full of spirit, with all the power of youth. I could have fled this infernal heat by seeking comfort in other places. I paid no heed to wealth. I disdained the love demanded loudly by my blood, because these unfortunate people required my compassion, my priesthood, as something that would save their lives. I pretended to be deaf in order not to hear all the stupidity with which the masses damn their priest. First it was the communion wine, and then my abuse of the women. The only truth has been this hell made of fire and routine. For what purpose? Who stood up for me when that foreigner slung mud at me? No one, no one remembered me. Now he buys them off with a bangle and leads them off to the river, a leper who recites the Bible. How many times did I whip my spirit pursued by temptation and how many times did I defeat the devil by imploring God at the top of my voice? Consumed by the desire of the flesh. Those who now deny me are bored to death and give themselves over to mounting women or wasting away on booze. They speak the vilest of words to get rid of their anger, while I on the other hand have had to swallow my thoughts or to say them to myself, to give a model of humanity. Look at them now with that Martian jackass! Let him make fools out of them, motherfuckers. I'll stay here alone in this church of the ages. I'll stay here alone with my broken shoes, my patched cassock and these bones and these guts that have shrieked and ground with hunger for so long. Let all of you shout hallelujah, you pile of slugs. Play into the hands of that heretic governor who has no mother because he was born of Aunt Cunt. Hallelujah jackass, toady to Yankee imperialism. Yell all you want, Father Hilario. Pull your hair, spit, shit in your pants, cry like an old lady, kick the bells, excommunicate all the atheist bastards who call themselves governors. It's all over for you, Nacho, you stuck your ear in. Don't you know that the storyteller should stand on the outside? I don't give a damn about all these rules. If I want to I stick my ears and my nose in, and if you don't like it, Teófilo, you tell the story. Okay, okay, go on, Nachito. Don't get mad. Bring that old lady over here, my brothers. I'm waiting for you. I'll bathe her in light for her eternal salvation. They hold on to her tight, and the current comes up to her knees. There's a ceremonial air about the place. The people gather around. Some are soaked with water. A mischievous tone begins to prevail. With each baptism there is smirking and joking that is not at all religious. Doña Ascensión approaches the minister now. He's shouting and the old woman is trembling because she's afraid of the water. This is surely a miracle, Doña Ascensión saved, the queen of blasphemy, she of the terrible mouth, sticky fingers, contentious by profession, viper's tongue. Do not be afraid, sister. Peace be with you. Brother Trini Brown is shoving her now. Doña Ascensión slips, sinks into the sand. They grab her and set her on her feet. She waves her hands in the air and shouts like an enraged devil, falls again. The Brother picks her up, and she grabs onto his hair, scratches his face. The two fall in the water. You're drowning me, hallelujah man, stupid motherfucker, abusive shit, pervert, taking advantage of women. Go shove your salvation up your ass. Demons be gone from the body of this woman! In the name of my Lord, abandon her temple! Apparently some demons leave the old woman and install themselves in some of the others present. Those who just the day before listened with horror to the infernal pronouncements and seemed to be attentive and contrite begin now to joke. I have always gone where they called me. Even when I was sick I never missed mass. No matter whether it was someone dying or a newborn, there was Father Hilario, anytime, anyplace. Now that I feel old and tired they turn their backs on me, when what they should do is thank me for so much sacrifice. The little girl was already pregnant when they put her under my care, and the child is the son of a mule driver. They defame me systematically, heretics like that thieving governor weeping in public for the poverty of the poor while fleecing them without mercy.

It's night now. The eyes of all Santa María de las Piedras are on the strangers. People are walking around the plaza, spying on the camp of the Brothers of the True Faith of the Lord. The old men form groups and tell each other jokes. The young toughs keep vigil from a perch in the trees. They look the minister's wife over. She is pretty. Because her body is wet you can see all its outlines. Her breasts thrust upwards. Look at those legs. The vertical incision of her pubis shows through. Her pubic hair must be blond. The thin man is snoring on a mattress. Brother Trini Brown is going crazy with desire. As soon as the intruders leave the bare camp he will mount his beloved. Meanwhile they kiss and grab at each other and breathe hard, they're so hot. Finally everybody falls asleep. It's past midnight, and the moon has come out. Let the man enjoy his wife's breasts. The blonde and Brother Trini Brown strip. The hour of love has struck. Of the three brats, Chicho Sandoval was the one who held the slingshot, pulled it back as far as it would go, and sent the rock slamming into the naked backside of the preacher. He jumped like a monkey, flinging himself naked after the criminal. It was a useless chase, because he melted away. They were pestered all night with people running back and forth, shouting obscenities, bombarding them with outbursts of laughter. The next day the word spread among the people and everybody shouted the news: Brother Trini Brown and the pretty girl were fucking. For a lot of people he wasn't Brother Trini Brown anymore. He was Brother Fucker. The enraged hallelujah man continues his furious preaching, clenching his fists and clamoring against sin, evil and the Satanic spirits that engulf the people of Santa María de las Piedras. On the fourth day the wandering pastor has a real shock, breathing heavily. The brother collapses in a puddle of water, shriveled up with fever, hoarse from shouting in a voice that thunders over the hills to fade away in the immensity of the desert. Come . . . come, come and hear the word of God. Verily I say to you that I will go unto all the corners of the world and that there will be no place where they do not know of Him. Before the day of fire all mankind will know His name. Brother Trini Brown falls down sick, consumed by the fever and the fire that rains in soaring flames from the sky. The sun in Santa María de las Piedras knows no mercy. The skinny brother-in-law of the preacher brother snivels disconsolately for his sister's husband. She is praying in pain for the health of her beloved. The people have returned to the fold of Father Hilario. The mass is for the recovery of the shepherd of the Brothers of the True Faith of the Lord. Pray, my children, for this man who in his own way goes about the world preaching the word of the Lord. His intention is good. He abhors sin and seeks the salvation of souls in the name of the Redeemer. Now they are making Brother Trini Brown comfortable in the truck, and the people are offering him gourds containing water and provisions. They will take him off to Tucson. He is dehydrated, and they will treat him there. Forgive me for my pride, Lord. Forgive Brother Trini Brown for his pride, and forgive the people of Santa María de las Piedras for their pride. In the face of so much bestiality we love you, Lord. You are our only hope. Little Virgin of Guadalupe, purest mother, save our brother Trini Brown. Save him, Lord, save him.

The Brother never returned, right, Teófilo? At least not as far as I know. Well, no, Güero Paparruchas, he wouldn't come back for anything. They must have cured him in Tucson. The American doctors can cure anything. They can even cure old age. Well, then, we'll just have to get you up there to those little doctors, Nacho. The worms have already got their eye on you. Hell, Teófilo, if my nose isn't playing tricks on me you're the one already dead. You and Don Cucufato are the ones dead as lead. What are you thinking about, Lalo? About everything that has happened in this town which doesn't appear on a single map.

The Noraguas were different from the majority of the inhabitants of Santa María de las Piedras for a very special reason. Numerous generations had inherited the fame stemming from an endless string of anecdotes with the Noraguas as protagonists. Everyone knew these stories, and they grew in number over the years. In every family with a Noragua, if there were several brothers, at least two would be mad. Those who did not go mad, nevertheless, begat madmen. The Noragua defect, like a blemish of damnation, had been marking them since time immemorial. Not even they could remember which remote ancestors had planted the tragic seed of this homegrown dementia. Despite their Opata Indian name, their mestizo roots were obvious. It was apparent in those born with clear eyes, a few blonds, and those with broad chins. Spanish lace could be seen in the features of many of them. They were to be found now in both camps, in a mixture so balanced that the Spanish and the Indian could be perceived in equal parts, although there were a large number of Noraguas that looked like Indians. Whenever a Noragua was born, he would be examined anxiously to see which side prevailed in his genes. But people were even more anxious to see if there was any sign of the cursed stain. The Noraguas with Indian features would say when they were older that their madness came from a Spaniard forebear who had gone crazy in Mexico. Those with Hispanic features would affirm, to the contrary, that their problem had begun with an Indian witch who could raise the dead with potions, was wise in the use of herbs, and who was involved in all sorts of witchery. There was a solitary room set aside for those born with vacant eyes and slobbery lips. Madness manifested itself in the Noraguas in all degrees. There were those incapable of any sign of intelligence and, by contrast, there were superbright geniuses, bright shining lights. Alongside the passive and the violent, there were also the melancholic and the pensive. It was not unusual to find among the Noraguas the chronically insane. These were the more balanced ones, suddenly beset upon by a passing storm, only to return to normality. They would travel to distant towns in search of a spouse, somewhere where nobody knew them or had heard the whisperings about how their madness had its origins in a long series of marriages between blood relatives. Living in an isolated town, bereft of communications, and with the constant danger of Indian

15

attacks, there would always be romances between first cousins who were almost brothers and sisters. It was said that some of the girls resulting from such marriages cursed by genealogical proximity often turned out gorgeous, except that they were born with overly sensitive eyes and were unable to withstand the light of day for long stretches. Over the years some of the Noraguas who went forth in search of other horizons became famous as intellectuals, politicians, financiers, and other important men. These changed their name. There are today many distinguished people who have Noragua blood in their veins. It is not an impossibility that among those mentioned, there may have been more than one governor and in all probability at least one president. As for mayors, they must be a legion. Rumboso Noragua was born after the turn of the century, the seventh of some ten brothers who sprang from the trunk of Don Hilario Noragua and Doña Felícitas del Rincón. Of the ten, Tiburcio often had to be tied up, and Rosendo wanted to marry every girl he set eyes on. There was nothing special about the others, except maybe for an occasional wandering glance or a scandalous outburst of laughter for no reason at all. Rumboso married Marcolfa Pérez in the twenties. They in turn had five daughters and three sons. Timoteo was the fifth of these children, born in 1930, to be exact. Of the girls María Josefa was the one born with a complete lack of intelligence. She never knew why she had been born and lived forever lost in a colorless vacuum. The other four, Tina, Chona, Clara and Mónica, were a bouquet of laughter, always happy and chattering. They all had a rare aptitude for art. Tina imitated birds, chirping in the morning with such grace and force that old Rumboso would holler at her to go move in with the damn birds. Chona made flour tortillas in the form of stars. Clara composed poetry for Christmas and birthdays, and Mónica was crazy about painting sunsets. Chano, who discovered gold, had an industrious character and preferred to work in the fields. He was always in motion and spoke the same way, with references to his daily work and his plans for future tasks. He was always the reason the chicken coops the old man financed were a success and why they produced more eggs than Santa María de las Piedras could ever remember. The case of Bartolo, the oldest son, was exceptional. He was very bright, and his teachers were surprised to learn that he knew algebra without studying it. As for dates, he could make them to stick in his mind more easily than any famous intellectual. It is more than likely that he had a profound knowledge of astronomy because his intuitiveness was so sharp; he would spend the entire night scrutinizing the stars and doing calculations. He would rebaptize stars and constellations. The Big Dipper was renamed Mother Bitch, and the Little Dipper Baby Bitch. He called Cygnus the Duck. He took charge of the books for the egg business, and he guarded them so jealously that no customer was ever sharp enough to get the better of him. Eggs are eggs, he used to say. If you want eggs you have to pay for them. Curiously, one day when he was nine he called his father with a hint of timidity in his voice. What do you want, my son? Papa . . . I . . . need a woman. I want to get married. Don Rumboso looked him over carefully, not knowing whether to laugh or be worried. Do you have a sweetheart, son? No, Papa, you get me one. Now Don Rumboso did smile. Everything in its due time, son. People would be startled by Bartolo's luminous mind. They would speculate about his enormous possibilities as an oarsman in a sea of numbers. With one eye he would count the eggs and take care of the nanny goats, while studying a book with his other one. What a bright talent that kid's got, everyone would say. But when he reached puberty his tastes and his interests changed, and he had no other activity or object in life except to play with his masculinity and, quicker than quick, to set his mind to rubbing tits and riding vaginas. Bartolo, really just the favorite child for his prestige as a whiz and for his cheerful and noble disposition, ran away from his father's home one Thursday afternoon, precisely at that moment in which the minute hand marked the passing seconds of seven p.m. one fiery month of July. He had left the nanny goats to wander home to their pen, while he stayed behind to tend to a fulsome wench and protect her from the wild beasts of the night. These concerns caused him to lose all notion of time and place and to fail to notice the presence behind him of his progenitor. Rumboso surprised him inserted in the aforementioned lass with a sharp face and a languid look. Bartolo could have avoided the swift kick that smashed his tailbone. But the fact is that he spied his father out of the corner of his eye just as the very moment of pleasure's spasm. The terrified young man started to run, dodging chollas and prickly pears, although no more terrified than the old man who ran after him in order to stop him and save him from the rigors of the desert. Bartolo put more and more distance between him and his pursuer without hearing what the latter was shouting at him desperately. Don't run away! I forgive you! I'll find you a woman for your health!

17

Come back! It'd be a secret between the two of them. He wasn't the only one, and others did it with burros and even made chickens and pigs their lovers. It would be impossible never to have heard about such diversions. The boy had no idea he was being pardoned, and he lost himself forever, crying out of shame, fear and despair. With the same sense of pain, the old man turned back, sobbing with defeat. There were rumors, after many springs had become winter since Bartolo's departure to the great metropolis, that he changed his name there and became a noted politician who turned demagoguery into millions and who had at his command a flock of beautiful lovers who bleated in harmony with his sensual whims.

Everyone thought Timoteo was mute until he started talking like a professor at the age of eleven. As a child he was the model of serenity, apparently detached from everything going on around him, solitary by nature, always standing apart from the rest. He never cried for food or water, even though his lips were white and dry. Doña Marcolfa even forgot about Timoteo for three days, constantly occupied with the chickens. There were times when the child slept on the back patio with a dog for a pillow and two others to keep him company. Nevertheless, when his parents recognized his existence, they were solicitous toward him. Timoteo smiled at them calmly. As a consequence, people called him "innocent." Since he was innocent and didn't talk, he was spared domestic tasks. On day in February when he had just turned eleven, Timoteo was sitting as usual under a mesquite tree, playing with some speckled eggs, when Don Rumboso came out to the corral with a whip in his left hand and his right hand holding onto Chano. You're going to get it now, you disobedient child. Let's see if you can learn your lesson. He was going to whip Chano because the chickens were dying and he thought Chano was not taking care of them. Chano balled himself up like a fetus, protecting himself with his hands, and the old man hit him so hard with the whip that the sparrows flew up from their nests in fright. Timoteo got to his feet and went over to his father and spoke for the first time. It's not right for you to use violence like that. Chano is noble and you're going to make him go bad. The old man and Chano looked at him startled with a blank stare. Then they yelled for Marcolfa. The revelation caused a scandal. Timoteo was speaking perfectly well, and moreover with a larger vocabulary than his brothers.

The Noragua house was situated just as you enter Santa María de las Piedras, on the edge of the world of cactuses. The cactuses stretch out toward the enormous sand wastes of the Sonoran Desert. The travelers came in that direction from Carborca, Trincheras, Sonoíta, Altar, Santa Ana and other towns in Sonora. The Noragua house was made of adobe, with very thick walls. The beams were long, thick mesquite branches, and the roof was a reed base covered with a sort of mud pie. There was a corral made from very green and thriving ocotillos, and a ramada made of thick leaves. The floor was dirt pounded solid. You entered via a wide corridor, with three rooms on each side and the kitchen at the end. The secret room was hidden away from the rest of the house to one side, and there was only one door. Right in the middle there was an iron post driven into the ground reaching up to the roof. This isolated room was always to be found in every Noragua home just in case it became necessary to tie someone up at the least expected moment. The possibility was so real that no room like this ever went unused. Later, when Chano discovered gold, he would construct the chicken coops under the supervision of an expert in the subject. After his discovery, the old man refused to allow any member of the family to continue in the quest for gold, believing that greed woud kill the goose that laid the golden egg. He increased his chicken business so much as a consequence of the investment of Chano's gold, that the barn built for that purpose was not large enough, and the chickens ended up laying their eggs in the surrounding area, in addition to taking over the house. Every day the Noraguas would fill pillowcases with the eggs. They would find them under the ocotillo bushes, the prickly pears, the chollas, the creeping bushes and in the open fields. Inside the house, they gathered eggs under and on top of the beds and in the corners. There were eggs all over the place—dozens, hundreds of eggs. They would step on them with their feet; they would sit on them. The floors grew thick with albumen, and their clothes were sticky with yolks. There was a riot of eggs everywhere. As a result, the work was a rough, gelatinous, sticky routine. They started watching the roosters closely, and the ones who appeared to be uninterested or queers ended up in the pot.

Old man Rumboso smiled, his dream of invading Santa María de las Piedras on a tide of eggs complete.

He had placed a sign at the entrance of his house: "Eggs for sale." He had enough eggs to give to his neighbors, who showed up with baskets or carried them off in knapsacks. He also had enough to truck them away to eateries and food stalls. Don Rumboso liked personally to provide the community with eggs. Don Rumboso had become in a certain sense the benefactor of children, for the fathers of Santa María de las Piedras never had enough eggs to feed them well. The Noragua eggs reached every home. The old codger felt an intimate pride in knowing himself to be the egg king. Old Rumboso was respected for his fairness and loved for his generosity. How many times had poor women come up to him to ask for a dozen eggs and he, smiling, had given them two dozen. The Noraguas never went after the grimy and crafty children who hung around the chicken coops and stole eggs to their hearts' content. The Noraguas only pretended to scare them off with Apache yells, waving stones and sticks in the air. The old man would brandish the skeleton of a shotgun that even made the hens laugh. I'll show you damn kids! I'll cut your balls off! We'll beat you to death like rabbits! Go steal your godmother's eggs! The startled brats would run off, thinking it was all great fun. Five egg-stealing kids became more than ten when they realized there was no real danger. They no longer stole to eat, but as a game, as a form of real fun. The last straw came when the Noraguas went out to scare off the ragamuffins, chasing after them as usual with a lot of shouting and yelling. But they were met by urchins armed with eggcups and in combat formation. They were so aggressive and accurate with their ovicular artillery that they coated the chicken raisers from head to foot. The four little girls laughed their heads off to see themselves soaked and spotted with bits of eggshells. Doña Marcolfa wiped the yellowy snot from her face and shook her hands, heaving all the time with nausea. Chano chased the little thieves, assuring them he was going to beat the shit out of them. Timoteo was gasping from the thick layers of slimy eggs. The old man, in addition to being coated with egg, took one smack in his right eye. Needless to say, the urchins did more damage than the coyotes and foxes, and old man Rumboso was able to bring them somewhat under control by taking them prisoner with the idea of personally handing them over to their parents and demanding authoritarianly that they receive an exemplary punishment.

In those days Rumboso Noragua was a thin fifty, scrawny, tall, and sharp. He strode around in his best long-legged fashion, twirling his arms like a windmill and thrusting out his long neck crowned by a small melon-shaped head. He had a big nose, a small, round mouth like a coin and dancing eyes. He adhered to the typical ideas of a medieval Spanish gentleman. As a consequence, he imposed a spit and polish routine on his children. Marcolfa, with all the centuries-old knowledge possessed by women, accorded him the constancy of a wife and the attention of a page, in addition to arduous and meticulous service, never flagging in her dedication to providing meals at precise hours and keeping the home in shape. Marcolfa had gotten fat, and she was a four-cornered sphere. She combed her hair back in the form of a ball of wool. Her round face revealed tenderness, a certain air of nostalgia, and always considerable fatigue.

No thirsty and hungry traveler ever passed in front of the Noragua home without sharing a meal with that strange family. They never charged for their spontaneous hospitality by telling bad jokes or asking stupid questions. Every day strangers would show up to replenish their exhausted energies, thanks to the generosity of the chicken farmers. They always felt a nagging frustration on any day they did not provide aid to someone who was hungry. They felt content when they spied them navigating through the fiery atmosphere across the barren plain dotted with cactuses. At first the kids fought for the right to run out and guide the adventurer toward fresh water and a supply of eggs. Later they took turns, inventing a game in which the best Samaritan was the one who brought in the hungriest and thirstiest wanderer. Details were of utmost importance in this game, like wounds caused by thorns or a collapse. Anyone who brought a traveler under the protection of the roof, his feet doubled under him but still breathing and alert, earned a few points. What really counted as a major deed consisted of dragging them in, oblivious to where they were, gasping their last and babbling indistinguishably. Marcolfa would serve them fried eggs and corn tortillas until they begged not to have to eat anymore. The old man would watch them eat with an attentive and merciful expression on his face. He would fill them up with coffee and fresh water, and he would see them off with a bag filled with hard-boiled eggs for the road, despite the fact that they had already made it to Santa María de las Piedras. One day, somewhere between two and three in the afternoon, Chano came home all excited, shouting for help. He was carrying a dehydrated, exhausted gringo on his shoulders. They put him in the shade, gave him hot coffee to counteract the effects of sunstroke, along with soft-boiled eggs. When he could speak, it was in English. Whenever he spoke his language, the Noraguas would break up, adults and children alike. How can these people under-stand each other, they said, holding onto their sides hilariously. Chano was all excited, like someone who has just won a fishing contest by catching the most exotic one of all. They took the resuscitated gringo in under their roof for a few days. When he felt revived, he took his leave emotionally from his saviors.

Even though they communicated with gestures, they could un-derstand each other well. They all had taken special pains to take care of him. When this gringo later became wealthy thanks to the gold he discovered, it was his turn to play good Samaritan and save the Noraguas from total ruin. It is also true that someone gave the gringo a nickname afterwards, when he was scratching away for the coveted metal along with the others among the lumps of hard earth. Being blond with big green eyes that turned red from the sun as the day advanced, they began to call him Traffic Light. To round the nickname off he became Mr. Traffic Light. Although Mr. Traffic Light was about thirty years old, he was a serious and industrious man, careful about the norms and concepts to be found in a foreign country. He rented a modest room. After shaking the gold loose, washing and panning it, he would devote time to his goldsmithing hobby. Legend says that during the year he spent in Santa María de las Piedras he amassed a fabulous fortune. The Noraguas, on the other hand, experienced the inevitable: ruin, failure, hunger. The chickens began to die by the dozens, and the eggs stopped coming. Now their work consisted of digging ditches to avoid the stench of rot that filled their nostrils. Hundreds of chickens died in just a few days. They wrung the necks of the ones that survived so as not to have to see them with fallen wings, open beaks and turned up feet. When they had finished their feverish activity as gravediggers, the Noraguas sat down to rest beneath the ramada, covered with feath-ers and with their expressions devoid of words and gestures. They were still sitting there by morning, without exchanging a word. The one talking to himself in a torrent of stumbling words was Timoteo. During the last days, Don Rumboso had brought Timoteo back when he was about to lose himself in the desert. Timoteo promised the old man that he would not leave if he bought him a burro. When the old man swore he would, Timoteo, a young man on the edge of puberty, told him half begging and half as a secret, that he needed a woman, asking him to help him find someone to marry. The old man trembled with the recollection of Bartolo. I'll get you a wife, even if it's an Indian woman, the poorest and the ugliest. Four years later when Timoteo was just about to turn sixteen, the old man came through on his word. Days passed, and the misery of the Noraguas grew. The poor among their friends helped with modest gifts of food to keep them alive. Of the legion of hungry explorers that they had helped out in former times, not one came forth. Of these, rescued from starvation, there were several who were able to return home rich. Triumphant in their return, they passed by in front of the Noragua house, ignoring their misfortune, and glancing at them coldly. More than one smiled disdainfully. The old man himself and his sons, their ruin weighing on their shoulders, would run into them in the streets of Santa María de las Piedras. The ingrates either looked the other way or pretended they did not know them. You cannot give charity a price or charge interest, Don Rumboso Noragua declared to his sons. One afternoon, as the sun was dying, it began to rain heavily, like a joke being played on them by teasing old men spitting down on them from Cloudland. By morning the roosters were crowing their hearts out, bloodying the dawn. Tina began chirping like a chorus of canaries with so much force that the Noraguas had soon gathered around her. Tomorrow our luck will change. How do you know that, my daughter? You know full well, papa, that we can see things others can't understand. By the time the sun was up, they had cleaned the house of chicken shit and feathers, and they had cleared the area around the house of all signs of filth. The film of squashed eggs disappeared from the furniture, utensils, clothes and hair. By midday the Noraguas were shining like stars. By three in the afternoon, each one looked like a statue— standing still, petrified, with a distant look on his face. Tears streamed down Tina's face. Just as the sun and the Noraguas' hope began to set, an automobile stopped in front of the house. It's Mr. Traffic Light! It's Mr. Traffic Light! A man dressed like a Texan came in smiling. Then they all smiled. Mr. Traffic Light had acquired a funny kind of Spanish. Don Rumboso whispered something to Doña Marcolfa, and she motioned to her daughters to follow her into the kitchen. There she gave each one a dish and told them to go ask for food from the neighbors. Only in this way could they receive their guest properly. They felt terrible that they could not give full rein to their hospitality as they usually did. How you business do, Mr. Rumboso? Everything is just fine, Mr. Traffic Light, everything is just fine. How do business with chickens? Fine, fine,

fine, fine . . . Mr. Traffic Light admired in silence Don Rumboso's integrity. Everyone ate with enthusiasm and good humor. A few minutes later Mr. Traffic Light got to his feet and walked over to the door. You could see the sadness shining through the Noraguas as though they were transparent glass. I travel for time home. I want tell you many thanks. I always remember you saved my life, big favor you did me. It was nothing, Mr. Traffic Light, just doing our duty. Good-bye, everyone, good-bye. Good-bye, Mr. Traffic Light. God go with you. No sooner had Mr. Traffic Light stepped outside than he came right back in. Oh, I forget something! He took a package out of his pocket and gave it to Don Rumboso. The expectant faces were glued to the movements of the trembling old man. He unwrapped the object. It was a gold egg!

Timoteo Noragua's bones continued to grow. In the forties he left childhood behind. Taciturn since birth, he would spend days in complete silence, a wayward pilgrim lost in a world of dreams in which he explored his own universe. With a distracted air, he would wander the streets, stroll through the plaza, go into the church. People would look at him sympathetically and with a measure of pity. His madness was not offensive, even if it was a little strange. Despite his passivity, it was not long before he was the butt of jokes and tricks. That sort of thing stemmed naturally from the idleness and routine that weighed heavily on the souls of people alien to those spectacles that make up for the lack of bread. First they were innocent jokes. They would push him over on top of someone down on all fours behind him, and it was a good joke for everybody to see him fall. Once they tied a cow's tail to the back loop of his pants, causing him shame but bringing hilarity to those who saw it. Things got out of hand on more than one occasion. Despite his tender years, he was the town madman, the moderator of bitter feelings. One Monday afternoon, they stoned him pitilessly. Timoteo stood there self-absorbed, with blood flowing from his head and streaking his face. He stood there for two hours until someone told Marcolfa and she led him home by the hand. His own people always looked on him with superstitious respect, since he looked more like a reincarnated grandfather than a kid, to judge by the tone and nature of his words. He was excused from all chores, and in order to keep him out of trouble in the street they surrounded him with dozens of moth-eaten books, books of the sort townspeople own without knowing how or why destiny put them in their hands. Rumboso and Marcolfa, what with their brood, couldn't help but laugh to see Timoteo glued to his books, moving his lips and sounding out unintelligible words, looking exactly like someone who really knew how to read. If the truth were told, Timoteo had in fact attended grade school for the space of a year, first grade, when he was seven. But the teachers themselves advised against his going on. They never heard him utter a word, nor did they ever see him paying attention to his lessons, always absorbed in a supposedly empty inner world. Nevertheless, there was a big surprise in store for the Noraguas: Timoteo read just fine and, moreover, he thought about what he read. Papa, he said to Rumboso one day, I understand this book perfectly. Its contents are so pretty, worthy of a genius. But I'm certain its author, Octavio Paz, couldn't understand it any more after he finished writing it. Doña Marcolfa was stunned to see that, in fact, the author of that book was the famous poet. Then he went on to read them what he called a page of oceanic beauty, from top to bottom, without missing a single comma and emphasizing the italics. While everyone wondered in silence, startled and worried, they saw out of the corner of their eyes Timoteo's quizzical smile, while at the same time he commented mentally on the literary work. At the same time that respect and compassion for Timoteo grew in the opinion of the family, malevolence grew among strangers to the point of ignominy. Timoteo's vivacity was followed by long intervals in which he put a padlock on his mouth, refusing to utter a single word. The profound journey through the spaces of his own inner realm brought him by chance to discover the mystery that his intuition had refused to reveal. . . .

With the frenzy the gold provoked, Santa María de las Piedras became the eye of a hurricane. The course of life became frantic. Father Hilario wasted away, his cheeks and jaws growing more pronounced, while at the same time his eyes sank into pits. The shadows of their sockets grew in circumference. From the time that Santa María de las Piedras succumbed to the demonic whirlwind of grasping after the corrupting gold, Father Hilario did not sleep a wink. Sleeplessness held him firmly in its clutch. Sleeplessness in his case meant the unleashing of persons both known and unknown. God's orders were barriers that his former flock, devout and dignified, chose now to trample down. Of course there were exceptions: persons who, despite their faith in the ecclesiastic rites, in one way or another benefited indirectly from sin. Commerce flourished, money-making activities multiplied, and the town government filled its coffers to the sound of the bellies of its public officials. Father Hilario didn't miss the fact that shopowners and their employees were doing great, and if they went to mass and to confession every week, they also were responsible for the clothes worn by both the brothel whores and the streetwalkers. Restaurants arose, frequented by drug smugglers and political bosses, the corrupt representatives of utopian laws. In short, there flourished a whole cast of characters disguised as decent and devout citizens who would cause the good seed he and his religious forebears in Santa María de las Piedras had sown to go straight to hell. Worst of all was that, among so many outsiders, he lost track of his local people, and he no longer knew who was who among so many faces. Purveyors, dealers, loafers, shysters, whores, panderers, thieves, and honest men all lived together in a shaky and constant flux. Father Hilario was so stunned that he looked his parishoners over at mass to see if he could remember a few names. He no longer knew who were local people and who were outsiders. He raked his face with both hands, rubbing his eyes with the knuckles of his index fingers and pulled away more and more cobwebs. But the devil would not leave him in peace! The worst of it was that naked lust lurked everywhere, drooling all over the place like a pack of bitches in heat. The young people of Santa María de las Piedras who formerly would enter marriage in a state of purity and who used to show their tenderness toward each other by holding hands, who before would scarcely brush each others' lips in a furtive kiss while Grandma dozed at their side, now got together at all hours and sought out hideaways cloaked in the shadows of night. What is more, they paraded their lack of modesty in the plaza, publically. They nibbled each other's lips and ears, smothered each other with kisses, and plunged their tongues into each other's mouths. They were learned in the most secret folds of their anatomies, with concave hands holding convex breasts like caged doves. Their hands wandered down between each other's legs, fingers tracing the vertical incision despite the forest of Venus. The girls, lacking in all modesty, squeezed pricks nonchalantly as though they were squeezing cucumbers. Urgent moanings, spasms, languishing yelps, damp hands, silence. My God! The same hands they used to cross themselves. Father Hilario took note of all the evidence and peered into the recesses of their souls as though he were looking at skeletons in a Santa María de las Piedras x-ray machine. The ladies of the league of decency commented infuriatedly on the situation.

But he couldn't help but notice that they dressed with greater elegance, showing up each week wearing new shoes, suits, hats, necklaces, and watches. It looked more as if they were going to church in order to compete with each other's fashions. And then there were the little old ladies, the eternally pious women. They were indignant in their commentaries on how the whole neighborhood had exchanged sensibleness for vulgarity. Nevertheless, it was obvious that they ate better and some wore newly made petticoats, if not new shawls. The husbands brought the gold fever of Santa María de las Piedras home. Rarely did they appear in the house of God, and it would be the women who would save their souls by dint of their prayers. Father Hilario was dying to sleep soundly just one night, serene in spirit as in the past. He drank tea made from malabar, from orange blossoms, from quince leaves and warm milk like the elderly take to make them fall gently into slumber. But it was all in vain. He had already rid his face of cobwebs, and he continued to beat his chest and pull his hair, attempting to disembowel the blind rats that his imagination let run loose through the corridors of his tortured subconscious. Ever since the sudden arrival of wealth in Santa María de las Piedras, the parishioners had made decidedly splendid contributions to charity. The more they sinned, the greater the amount donated to the temple of the Lord. If they were cured of some illness, they brought as an offering little golden ears, noses, eyes, or whatever the injured part was, as a token of gratitude for the intercession of some saint. Zenona, the most prosperous of the town's madams, was a devout follower of the Virgin of Guadalupe. She weekly sent a bag of gold coins to the Virgin via him, a humble shepherd. The same could be said of the merchants who provided liquor to the alcoholics but donated money in quantity. What alms! He knew who they were. He would see them down on their knees with their eyes rolled back, ecstatic, some giving thanks for a fortune that had come their way, others begging help to find it. Nobles and common folk alike had given truckloads of money to the church that I, Father Hilario, represent. I have played the fool's part, looking the other way, so as not to yell at them that God and the saints cannot be bought with money. Yes, support the church so it will survive. But it is not an institution where you can save your soul by paying a bribe. I have remained silent. I am an accomplice. I absolve them; I smile at them; and the money keeps on coming. I will restore the church. It will be a jewel. My superiors will receive their share; I will open an asylum for the elderly, a hospital for the needy, learning centers. Damn Rémulo! Cursed be the devil that disguised him as a sacristan and sent him to me. I took him in out of pity because he has the face of a martyred saint with that pious little voice and because he seemed to bear his poverty with faith. Thanks, I don't drink, dear Father Hilario. Liar! Now he's a sponge, drinking my communion wine and dipping his hand in the collection plate. With his eyes filled with malice and his crafty little ways, he says, "You keep the money, dear Father Hilario. I know where you stash it. I will be happy with the leftovers, just anything at all." The little sneak spends money drinking like a drunken sailor. It's public knowledge that he's mixed up with one of the black women over at the Golden Hive. Adulterous, indecent, he has a woman and a pack of kids and the alms flow through his hands to the prostitutes. If I get rid of him, scold him, tell him to shape up, he'll go tell everybody that I hide my holy Church's money. My superiors will come and I'll be left with my former misery, hungry and without shoes. No, for many years I was the model of poor little Assis. It's a sin to turn your back on good fortune. Father Hilario falls fitfully to sleep at dawn. He tosses in his sleep, thrashes his legs about, clenches his fists, murmuring that lust impregnates the air of Santa María de las Piedras. In dreams he sees Susana, the young girl who sweeps the sacristy and helps out in the kitchen. Her parents brought her home when she ran off with a mule driver. In dreams he watches Susana bathe and sees her naked. Susana's breasts are two apples; her nipples are two peaches. Between Susana's legs there is a door to an abode grilled off by the fine artwork of spiders. Susana's lips form a parenthesis of sensuality that beckons. Father Hilario dozes, harried by the preoccupations that beleaguer the inhabitants of Santa María de las Piedras. The flesh is weak and lust roams wild. Lord, give my people strength of spirit. Help them. Saint Michael, vanquisher of the devil. Cast down the evildoer, nail him to the ground with your trident, humiliate him, send him to his filthy abode and may he never return.

The gold of pleasure discovered in Santa María de las Piedras has let loose all the demons to wander the streets. The blasts of the trumpets, the beating of relentless drums, the squeal of the violins, the noise of the guitars, the penetrating and tuneless voice of the singers, together with the savage shouting of the drunks are all too much for Father Hilario. Damn fucking sons of bitches! In the back, beneath the din of the abandoned fun of alcohol and knifings, you can hear the moans of forty youths dying of sores and gonorrhea. The old women boil herbs, wash their sick privates, and weep. Their fathers sprinkle their cocks with gunpower, setting them on fire to see if the ensuing flashes will burn their cocks off. The youths weep and cry, awash in pus. The whores are not sleeping well. They have a lot to do and they are not allowed to rest. There are hundreds of laborers fighting for a turn to jump them. They had never mounted a woman before, either because they were poor sons of bitches or because they were afraid of an avenging brother or father. Hop to it, fierce fuckers of mares and dogs! Zenona brought her first-class whores for just that. Among the women there are blacks, gringos, French, Mexicans, and even some from China, all squealing in terror. They try to escape. Money no longer matters. All they want to do is save their skins, but Zenona keeps her eye on them. The police do, too. Go to sleep now, Father Hilario, it's only the dogs barking and the roosters shattering the dawn with their crowing. Sleep, little father, the musicians and the drunks have dozed off from weariness, and the forty boys dying of sores and gonorrhea have passed out.

One autumn day, around noon the four old kibbitzers were dozing, seated facing each other on the benches in the plaza that, by right of custom, belonged to them. October's gold crowned the trees. The wind sweeps the dead, fallen leaves together before carrying them off in a gust. It is a washed-out red graveyard. It's just passing through, in a hurry to move on to remote unknown places. The old men have opened their eyes, but their mouths remain shut. Their thoughts travel like October's wind. The peal of a bell, a child crying, a bird, the isolated voices of neighbors, and the eternal murmur that arises from the cemeteries break the calm and spur conversation.

I bet you won't believe I fell asleep. Why not? You could tell from your snoring. Damn Nachito. You don't snore, you grind your teeth like a burro in love. You and Machado are just two old men. Come on, fellows, come on, neither the day or the time is right for arguing. So then tell us a story, Abelardo, even if it makes us cry. One day Death was seated on a stool. She let down her guard, and the devil came along and stuck it to her. Be quiet! Paparruchas, you're a dirty old man, a blasphemer, a heretic. One day Death was seated on a stubby stick, using spongy scissors to give herself a lick. You're going to get it, Güero Paparruchas, you're going to get it for being so dirty, leprous, vulgar, and lacking in respect. Respect, Teófilo. I'm just a poor old blind man from San Fernando, begging for alms and dragging my tail behind me. I'll respect anything I can get my hands on, Abelardo. If you hit me with your cane, you old goat, I'll let you have it where it'll really hurt. Don't let the devil deceive you, then. Order, gentlemen, order. Sit down, Güero, and behave yourself. Good, let's talk about something else. For example, there's a rumor that we are rich, very rich, immensely rich. Who'd let out something like that? Nacho, you tell me. How in hell would I know? Don't worry about it, Teófilo, what counts is that people are talking. That's for sure; you don't hear anything else. You'd think this place was nothing but a jet stream of petroleum, with Mexicans up to their butts in oil. The problem is to get ahold of enough barrels to hold it all and to make enough baskets to hold the money from its sale. Damn it, Güero, do you have to make a joke out of everything? Keep the faith, man, it won't be long before you'll shine like a well-dressed and well-fed dandy, and that's just the beginning; not even a flute serenade will wake the dead. Look who's talking, Nachito, since you can't hack it, you think no one else can. Go to hell. For your information, last night . . . Say something, Abelardo, before these old rakes get going. What can I say? It's nice to think these towns are going to be recognized on the government maps. Everything will go down in price, and people'll have enough money to buy stuff. I can already see this pale desert with stripes of paved, tree-lined roadways, with enough water to drink any time of the day and even to take a bath in. I'm happy for my grandchildren and for all the young people condemned to misery. At last, at long last. May God hear you, Abelardo. You know, it makes me want to remember the past when we were dying of hunger. This very minute I'm remembering the teacher Cloromiro del Huerto. Sure, that teacher who showed up in Santa María de las Piedras with his wife and four kids, a young boy, two just starting to walk, and one still in diapers. They were a real mess when they got here, all skin and bones from not eating. What a difference between what we can expect now and the past when nobody had enough to eat. Cloromiro was certainly patriotic, honest, proud and honorable. Well, just count all the young people who come to us: one, two, three, two big ones, nine all together. Now we've found something to talk about, go on, Nachito. I'll tell the story if you help me out when I get lost. Let the others hear the story, because we all know it by heart.

Pay attention, then. First of all, Cloromiro arrived in a bus owned by one Rabbit Ortiz and who of course . . . Leave that damn Rabbit out of it, Nachito, and stick to the story. Don't be a pain in the ass, Teófilo. Anyway, they got the furniture down, a ton of stuff, all of it a sight. The kids were yelling for something to eat and eight arms would not have been enough for that poor suffering woman to take care of everybody. Cloromiro looked at the townspeople for the first time and gave them a slight nod, muttering a greeting under his breath at the same time he touched his pale and grimy switchman's cap. He wasn't old and couldn't have been more than twenty-eight, somewhere around there. The man smiled sadly and as though he were very exhausted. His tie was constantly whipping about. He never loosened it, but kept it tight around his neck, so that it looked like the tongue hanging out of a panting dog. So, Cloromiro and his family were newcomers to Santa María de las Piedras. The neighbors discussed their presence endlessly. For hour after hour they would talk about the new director of the local school. The man intrigued them because he exuded dignity from every pore, while at the same time the furniture and clothes of the Del Huerto family were clearly of the sort that would belong to a beggar. This was in 1940, in September. In those days, rural schoolteachers would often go months at a time without getting paid. Often they could barely stand up from not eating, but their heads were full of ideas for saving mankind. Well, Monday came, and the other three teachers assembled the student body: seventy-three kids. Cloromiro del Huerto stood up in front of them. Every single one of them showed him the same face: the face of acute undernourishment. He felt his eyes blur and swim, but he didn't shed a single tear. He spoke to them about their country, about studying, about work, about the economy and about a glorious national future. A few days later, he imposed a quota on them: each child would contribute one peso. With the seventy-three pesos they would start a school cooperative. A community store that Cloromiro would be the director and treasurer of, because those were his orders from the education office. At the end of the school year, the students would get their original investment back plus earnings. The thing went like magic. The kids bought candy and supplies from the cooperative. They learned how to organize, how to keep books, and how to save, and they saw how work and justice could go hand in hand. The money multiplied and the grumblings stopped. Cloromiro del Huerto was a learned, industrious and well-intentioned man. The children adored him and the older people called him a wise man. He fed himself on books and spoke like an apostle. Like a miracle, the tender minds learned their lessons. But hunger haunted them. The faces of Cloromiro del Huerto's children hardened, their eyes got big, their lips cracked, and where there should have been shoulders there was nothing but bones. For months he bought food on credit. The shopowners no longer smiled at him, no longer told him take whatever you want, we're here to serve you. They pretended not to see him. He continued to ask for some beans to stay alive and other modest things. They ate prickly pears and greens until winter deprived them of these wild foods. The government's money, the teacher Cloromiro del Huerto's salary, failed to appear, failed to appear, failed to appear . . . during the entire school year.

Days turned into weeks, and weeks into months. Cloromiro's wife, Tencha, was dying from worry, heartbreak, and despair bordering on hysteria. They had married twelve years earlier, joined by a love as grand as the illusions of youth. Now she was a wreck with her nerves in tatters. She accused Cloromiro from time to time. Why had he yanked her out of her village and taken her away from her family to let her die of hunger? Why had they had children? Ah, for the same reason, to starve them to death, with no money to take care of them when they were sick! Cloromiro listened and stared vacantly, saying nothing. After a while, Tencha would hug him, crying and asking forgiveness. Cloromiro crossed the plaza, wandered the streets, carried books, greeted his neighbors and smiled sadly. Not even heaven could be fooled by his shoes, and his clothes had more patches than a homemade quilt. The little one was in a fit because Tencha's breasts could not provide enough milk. He would bite her breasts, leaving them black and blue. Listen, Nacho, excuse me for interrupting to criticize your style of storytelling, but it seems to me like you are invading Cloromiro's and his wife's privacy. Why you are interrupting me, Teófilo, to say something so stupid, I'd like to know. Because you said that the child used to bite Tencha's breasts, and as far as I know, you never saw the breasts of that woman, bitten or otherwise. Jerk and double jerk is what you are, Teófilo. It's just a way of saying that mother and child had nothing to eat. I'd like to know how you would say it. You might say that Tencha's boobs were squeezed dry. Ah, that means you saw the woman's boobs! Now you got me, Nacho, just go on. Don't you go butting in again while I'm telling a story. And, for your information, it's nicer to say breasts than boobs. Boobs or breasts, just go on, Don Nacho. The story's interesting and even more so the way you tell it. That's right, fellow, thanks. As long as it's not the ass. Shut up, Güero, you're gross. Gentlemen, we are getting out of line. Excuse us, Nacho, please continue. Out of respect for Cloromiro we will respect your story, right, men?

With June came the last day of classes, and summer vacation. The children of the school "Effective Suffrage without Reelection" of Santa María de las Piedras have assembled on the patio. All that is left is for the teacher Cloromiro del Huerto to dismiss them with profound and pretty words and distribute to them the money each has coming as investors in the school cooperative, nothing more, nothing less. They've been waiting for an hour, but they remain stoic and firm, despite the sun and its sadistic rays. One of Cloromiro's younger children starts to cry. They all go to the small room that serves as the principal's office. It's closed. Mr. Principal! Are you there? He's been shut up in there for hours; he's doing the accounts. Cloromiro, open up! Nothing, no answer. That's really strange. Force the door open, quick, something is wrong with the principal. Use a crowbar and push a little harder, come on. My God! What a sight! There is the teacher Cloromiro del Huerto, his head lying on the desk, the account book filled with numbers before him. Only numbers and no money. His left arm hangs loose, looking like an empty shirt sleeve. All of the rivers have converged on his wrist, flowing from there to trace other channels on the floor. He had slit his wrists with a razor! Can you imagine? Because he did not have the hundred and some pesos for a strict accounting of what was owed to each of his beloved students, he decided to take his life. All Santa María de las Piedras bemoaned the tragedy of the honorable man who preferred death to suspicion. He was not a thief, but a good man, honorable and full of pride for his country. Poverty had cornered him and he had no recourse, which is why he took the money. I'm certain that he never intended to steal it. He believed that he would return it in time when he received his salary from the government. We all know that, Nachito, everybody knew what bothered him. The teacher's wife, Tencha, received a money order in July for more than two thousand pesos owed to Cloromiro. She paid what they owed and left with her children for God knows where. They floated away on their own tears, carried off by the winds of sadness. But Cloromiro stayed behind here in Santa María de las Piedras, buried in the cemetery. His tomb is a living monument to what is meant by shame. I hope future generations, blessed by fortune and wealth, will not forget the Cloromiros and learn to be honest, Abelardo, and that they will not be thieves and steal from their own grandchildren. Any public employee who steals should be hung by his balls in the middle of the public plaza on Sunday, the bastard, and even if that means we have no government left. You know what, Güero Paparruchas? I bet you'd do the same thing. I might be a liar, but I'm not a thief, and if I exaggerate it's only to entertain you guys, so just dry it up, Teófilo. Just make me, you old windbag. Shut up, you old jackass. Let go, Abelardo, let go, you heard what he called me. Calm down, fellows, calm down, night's coming; let's go home and count the stars; we'll see each other tomorrow, God willing.

The old men shuffle off toward their homes. They bury their feelings in October's wind. The wind puffs and whistles just like the trains used to when they passed through, burdened down with nostalgia. It is a wind like the dead leaves it sweeps along, a wind that will not return. Instead, spring will bring back the brightness and green of new foliage. The air will once again be purified and renewed, tender and friendly. The old kibbitzers cut their way through the afternoon and the wind. To make itself seen, the wind has become dusty. The horizon turns yellow, then red, violet and purple, like a golden and luminous bed, so the sun may die and the stars, too numerous to be counted, be born in all their celestial glory.

Go ahead and make a joke out of it! Make fun of this man, just because he is an innocent unable to vanquish your ill will. Jobless vagrants, fat asses, fools, retards, outcasts, uncouth and worthless cowards. I hope you have a crazy son some day like this poor unfortunate and that other bastards like you will treat him like an idiot, like a circus puppet, like a poor clown to be spit upon. Then maybe you'll learn to be human beings! Then maybe you'll know what shame is!

Timoteo entered the streets of Santa María de las Piedras riding on Salomón's shoulders, looking like a stick. Giddy-up, giddy-up. Whoa, burro, whoa. It was a June afternoon; the sun was reeling free like a monster of light. It soaked up everything damp or fresh. The people awoke from the lethargy of their siestas protected by roofs and thick walls. The earth was burning with thirst. Not only were the dogs nothing but skeletons covered with scrofulous hides and that begging look of poets or apostles, but their tongues were hanging way out of their mouths, aching for water. The avid flies darted about, avoiding the tongues and hands that slapped at them every time they landed on eyes, mouths, noses. You could see flickers of dead hail in the yellow eyes of the hens. With their beaks open and their lost gazes, they looked like the shadow of human idiocy. Timoteo's face and eyes told you that he was made to contemplate hills, barren wastelands, birds' nests, and vast empty spaces lacking in water and vegetation in which the horizon loses itself. His ears held the rustle of the sands that flow through washes and passes when the wind gallops through the dried channels. The Indian spurs the flanks of the burro. Come on, Salomón, let's go. He did the same as always, taking his hat off as he passed in front of the church and crossing himself. Then he took the street in front of the plaza. The street counted out the measured steps of the four hooves of the burro. It was that time of the afternoon when the whole world is silent, when eternity plays with things as though they were dolls and statues. As was to be expected, there were old men seated on the benches, dreams galloping after the rescue of some memory. They smiled with their eyes closed, reinvented their childhood, saw themselves as spright as colts. They are the old men who daily review the lives and miracles of those who have lived in Santa María de las Piedras. They are terrified by forgetfulness, and they reject any death but that of the body. They do not want Santa María de las Piedras to die for history. They want the dead and their deeds, grandiose or vile, to cling to the earth like roots resisting the threat of time. How is it possible that Santa María de las Piedras has seen the terrible things that these old men relate . . . Come on, little burro, come on, don't be afraid. Ah! Here's Timoteo Noragua coming down the cross street. He's going to fall into the clutches of the townspeople. The earth and the walls pour forth evildoers who chase him, shouting fiercely. Crazy old man! Jab the burro in the behind so he'll start! Scarecrow! Where did you come from, you ugly Indian! There are about twenty urchins. They hurl stones at the Indian and throw dirt in his face. They pull the burro by the tail, making Salomón stumble and go around in circles, almost falling on his behind. They enjoy tormenting the Indian and burst with their laughter. Faces appear at the windows and doors open. The spectacle breaks the boredom that traps space like an iron deadweight. Timoteo smiles meekly when it looks like he is really about to burst into tears. The people go wild when they see the grimaces of suffering on the face of the Indian, and they dance around wildly. Whoa! Now beast and rider are rolling on the ground. Timoteo gets up, arranging his shirt and trousers. Two rivulets of blood flow from his nose. If it weren't for old lady Lugarda, the one they call Churrunga, they would eat him alive. Even though she's a pitiful old woman, the mother of a hoard of bastards, abandoned over and over again by her men, she stands up to all of them. With one hand she flings the tangle of hair from her face, grimaces, squints her eyes, twists her mouth. With her left hand on her hip and her right hand clenched into a fist, she screams her head off at them. Wretches! Isn't that nice, making fun of this poor fool who isn't bothering anyone. Bastards, you're completely gutless. Shits! Why don't you pick on the ones sucking you dry. No! You kiss their hands. Cowards, you're scared to death. Get out of my way! As for you, you little fool, it'd be a good idea if you learned to defend yourself so these s.o.b.s wouldn't always be picking on you. Now get out of here, all of you, and go bother the bitch that bore you. Timoteo climbed back on his burro and continued down the street on some errands. Let's go on home, Salomón, come on, little burro, come on. Timoteo trots off toward the mountains facing the pink melancholy of dusk. Once he was out of sight, people clamped their mouths shut. Silence once again fell suddenly, like a metallic air. Men and children stood in an ecstatic daze, their arms hanging by their sides. Their hands opened to let stones and clumps of dirt fall to the ground. They included the scrawny kids aching with hunger for a woman, the pensive, the squalid, those with features eroded by the rigors of hunger, children with angelic faces covered with grime and stinking of shit, and one or two pimple-faced adolescents. Thus night fell on them, sensing their humiliation beneath their hats. Then night swallowed them up as though it were a cosmic wheel with stars for teeth.

Seeing him in that condition, no one would have thought that the innocent man, scorned by the townspeople, would be led in mysterious ways to fulfill the most fantastic of destinies.

Timoteo Noragua was not like the majority of people. Most considered him an "innocent." The simpleness of his character made him appear to be immensely happy. Timoteo lived in his own world in harmony with his own spirit. Common things acquired a noble image in his mind. His best defense against bitterness and adversity lay in his passivity. At bottom, everyone felt sorry for Timoteo, but they derived a perverse pleasure out of playing tricks on him and making fun of his appearance. His hat always seemed to be unraveling and, as it lacked a crown, his head of tangled hair served as a nest for birds. He wore a shirt and pants made of coarse cotton, and he wore huaraches for shoes.

The spirit of the inhabitants of Santa María de las Piedras was rough like that of the region. A hostile nature produced in its midst an astute and coarse population. The tremendous heat fried people's brains and made the sea of the frustrations and hatreds that had overwhelmed them for generations boil. Certainly, they were soft people on the inside, like cactuses, but also like cactuses they were thorny on the outside. From time to time strong men and politicians would break the monotony in their own way, and then the stones of Santa María de las Piedras, scorched and thirsty, would become sated with fresh blood.

People who live in Santa María de las Piedras also have mortal enemies among nature. Snakes who live camouflaged on the ground hear footsteps, pivot around in a semispiral in the dirt, throw their heads forward in a straight line like a bullet, open their mouths, and by sinking their teeth in, inject a yellowish-green liquid that looks like liquified avocado. All this in a second, to the accompanying of the gangrenous laughter of their rattlers. There are also rabid, ferocious dogs, taciturn and grim wanderers, who bite the unwary who happen to cross their paths. One might say that there are a million silk worms in their snouts that weave incessantly, with feverish dedication, the frothy threads that spring from the mouths of the diseased beasts. And it is not only the pests on the ground that threaten the citizens of Santa María de las Piedras. Death may also come from the sky. The sun kills children and causes women to miscarry. The strong and robust caught by the sun out in the open, with no shade or water, are reduced to their knees, their prayers scorned, enveloped by a death of fire. Santa María de las Piedras stands in the desert with its back to the rocky hills, facing an immense desert of sand. It will never cease to be a mystery how and why people live in Santa María de las Piedras, where the ground is rocky and stingy and where tragedy dwells like just another neighbor.

Timoteo Noragua came down to town from time to time to buy provisions while his wife and five children waited for him in their hut. Timoteo Noragua had a hut in an untamed spot near Santa María de las Piedras at the foot of forbidding-looking hills. Vegetation was sparse and consisted of cactuses and stubby, almost naked bushes, with the exception of the proud sahuaros that stood out imposingly. From a distance it looked like a strange forest, although from close up they turned out to be rather spread out. The whole area was covered by a creeping, thin grass that gave the impression of hair scattered among a pile of stones. There were so many stones of so many shapes and sizes that one could have used them to build fortresses, cathedrals, houses, jails, schools, brothels and enormous walls to surround the town. And even then there would be enough stones left over to satisfy the hunger of a whole legion of catapults.

A figure could be discerned in the distance, something that could be mistaken for a viznaga or a young sahuaro. But, no, the object was advancing. It's not a coyote, either, growing larger as it approaches. The children peek out from behind the green giants. It's Timoteo, and as soon as the dogs sense his presence and the children make him out, they come barking and shouting. The uproar is so intense that the silence, by nature taut, becomes wrinkled. Chabela greets him, a quizzical look on her face, half opening her lips in a smile half reproachful and half compassionate. They all pitched in to relieve the burro of the packages that hung from the saddle tree. Salomón, closing his eyes, allowed himself to be shoved around.

Look, Mommy, here's the sugar. Here're the beans. Timoteo,

one of the nanny goats didn't come back from pasture. Daddy, where's the wheat? Ah! Here it is. Timoteo, the water level is dropping in the well. Look at what Dad brought! Candy! Candy! There's a piece for each of you. Give your brothers some. José Candelario, don't run, damn it. Timoteo, María del Refugio picked up some cholla thorns. She's got one stuck in her and she's been crying and crying and she wants you to get it out. Daddy, José Gabriel hit me with a stick. You hit him back for me. What little food you brought, my God. They must've paid you very little for the cheese. Make tortillas, Mommy. Okay?

For Timoteo Noragua, the day away from home seemed endless and he was all worn out. He took in his family and his home, filling his soul with the sight of them as you might fill your lungs with clean air. He always smiled with eyes that had never shown anger. He regulated his heartbeat with a deep affection. He performed his tasks distractedly, although at times his eyes and lips cooperated to look down with a timid smile that might be confused with a great, hidden sadness.

From the very bowels of the horizon the light of the sun emerges in a red riot of intense shades. The hills take on human profiles and the desert plains yield their surface pallor to the appearance of emptiness that the shadows provide. His wife and children look at Timoteo curiously. Muttering and half smiling with evident concern, he seems more distracted than ever. Come in and eat, Timoteo. Night's coming, Papa. A snake might bite you. Let your father alone to think whatever he's thinking. Go on in. While his wife and children enter the hut, Timoteo Noragua sits on a large stone without seeing. The tuneless chirpings of the cicada can still be heard, and the serenading crickets can be heard for miles around. Night amplifies the rustle of the rabbits' feet and the whistling of the air around the sahuaros and squalid paloverdes. While coyotes and owls howl at each other and squawk their frightful mysteries, Timoteo Noragua contemplates the distance with an obsessive curiosity.

That day, after coming on the townspeople who mocked him, Timoteo had headed for the general store where he usually made his purchases. There at National Dry Goods he dismounted and went in to take care of his purchases. He noticed that a group of people were gathered around a tall, fat Indian with a placid expression who was speaking ecstatically of his experiences in a foreign country. Now his memory carried Timoteo back to that scene with a backdrop of irreality, like the reflection of a trick mirror that gives back twisted images of absurd thoughts. In his imagination he saw how the man told his story and made faces while gesturing broadly. People listened to these portentous marvels with a foolish look on their faces. The face of the speaker grew large, emphasized by his wonder. His eyes jumped about, popping out halfway as though in their joy they were going to jump out of their sockets.

No, in reality no, you can't even imagine what that world is like, a marvel! The United States is a magical country, a glory. You can't believe it without first seeing it. Look, my friends, the palefaces are like gods; not only do they have bridges over their rivers, but also across the seas—long, long and very wide. They hop into huge, very fancy cars, and they travel with very pretty and well-fed cats and dogs over the bridges to Europe itself. The gringos are so tremendously wealthy, they don't know where to store all the money they've got. They wear pretty-colored shirts. Young and old alike wear cameras hanging around their necks and take each other's pictures constantly. They've got gigantic airplanes, and thousands and thousands of people can fit in one of them and whisk off anywhere. You get aboard and, whoosh, in a flash you're there. Now, if you want to talk about boats, they don't bother with boats at all. Instead, they manufacture floating islands, right, with streets, cathedrals, cantinas, the whole thing, anything you want. Ah! You wouldn't believe it, the only thing those gringos don't know is how to talk like us. Pay attention and listen to what I'm about to tell you, because I saw it with these very eyes that are growing dim. In Los Angeles I saw a place where the trains fly on wheels. You can see the people in the windows waving their arms and laughing, all very happy. I also saw baskets that climb up to the clouds, full of shouting kids flying like they were eagles. Every minute rockets filled with people leave for heaven. In the United States all you have to do is have a good time. Let me tell you, fellows, Gringoland is glory itself. And that's not all, there's more. The Americans have very powerful armies. All the president has to do is lift a finger, and all the soldiers are off running wherever he says. Just so the enemy can get an idea of who's who, they level a mountain or two with their cannons, and all of a sudden no one wants to mess with them. Just let the devil try something. But don't think that the Americans are alone with their power, no sir, it's not that way. They are doing the holy will of God, our Lord. God himself assigned them the task of establishing order

41

and of helping out any country in a jam with a lot of food and money. So, if there's a dictator in any country who's messing up the poor, the United States goes and knocks him off his feet but good. The Americans can't stand to see poor people exploited. Hot damn! When I got to New York I couldn't get the crick out of my neck. You can't even see the tips of the buildings, and if you could climb to the top of one of them you could slap the moon herself in the face. Americans don't walk on their feet like dogs, no sir. They have lots full of cars of all shapes and colors. The highways are really wide, and sometimes they are even three or four stories high, full to the top with cars whizzing by. What a beautiful sight, the cars shining like little suns! And food? You want to know if they have food! There's enough to play ball with. I bet you guys don't even know what a hot dog is; how could you? Now there's a delicacy worth dying for. See, it's a long piece of bread like a person's arm, slit like this down the middle, and they stuff it with a piece of meat that looks like a banana, along with onions, other stuff, and a yellow gunk that doesn't look very good at first, but is real tasty. Ummmmm . . . Dee-lish-us, pure glory! They have some sort of black-colored cold drink that leaves you licking your mouth for more. No one suffers from hunger there, no ma'am! No matter who you are, everybody is making a big bag of money. If someone runs out of food, then he can get more from the government. And if you get sick, they'll get you right back on your feet. Just thinking about the hot dogs makes my stomach want to get up and dance. Hold on tight, guys, because no matter where you turn you can find those gorgeous American chicks! You can go crosseyed just looking at them, and if you aren't careful you'll end up with a crooked mouth. The gringo women are real cute, and they wear see-through clothes so you can see their legs and everything. What breasts, fellows! Now if they like you . . . hell!

The face of the yakker disappeared and other images came to the entranced Indian. Timoteo's sight now focuses on a multitude of thousands of individuals marching in waves, laughing like they were thrilled at just the idea of so much happiness being possible some place in the world. Men and women of all ages were running toward the United States, the Mecca of happiness, land of abundance, paradise. The old people were not even held back by their age, nor the children by their tender years. They were running alongside the youths, the adults, the skinny, the fat, the dying and the living. The lame and the halt were running along, working their crutches with prodigious skill. The pain of their sick members was replaced by a crazy happiness, for they were on their way to the United States, the pearl of democracy, refuge for the hungry and the handicapped. Abandoned women with their packs of ragged children, malnourished and dirty, were shouting as they ran along, crying with the profound emotion of being freed from an uncertain life under the scourge of suffering and fear. He could also see the indigent elderly. The deep sadness and defeat that stamped their faces was now replaced by the glow of light sparked by hope. And it was that multitude dreamed by the Indian with his eyes open, an amalgam of faces of all the races that people the planet, as though all of the forgotten had met to journey to the only place where hope has not perished. All humanity scarred by bitterness showed a face illuminated by the sublime joy of replacing suffering by happiness.

Timoteo's face was lined with wrinkles, like the sinuous stretches of sand dunes. He half closed his eyelids. Once again his imagination was peopled by many, many men, women, and children who were crossing a desert licked by fire, a fire that wounded the skin and obliged one to close his eyes because it hurt. He saw them stacked up against the fence that lines the border like cattle watching the fields while pushing against the wire fence. No! There was no fence, no river, no desert to hold them back. They swept everything before their headlong rush. They raised their arms in triumph, and laughter was even more pronounced in their skeleton faces. Help yourselves to the presents! Food and justice! Peace and freedom! They entered the United States at a mad gallop, exuding hopefulness.

For a few seconds Timoteo's eyes grew wide and his breathing heavy, the intense emotions making him see images of what he had heard in the streets. Bunches of skeletal humans fell from boats overflowing with Asians who reached the shore in search of refuge. Old people and children dragged themselves along shouting, ready to burst from joy, their tears and laughter blending in a single rush of sound. Standing on the shore their blond brethren received them with open arms, blessings, and food. Now he could see abused and starving blacks who came in growing swells, flung by the waves against the American coasts. They were at last reaching the promised land, crazed with joy because they would no longer suffer the abuse of bestial work, scorn, and all kinds of injustice. The whole multitude intoned hallelujahs, free from tragedy!

Smiling children who rode in flying baskets? Trains that flew? Animals that spoke? Food and freedom for an entire hungry humanity? I want to go and see this promised land with my own eyes. Timoteo smiled foolishly. The image of the joyful multitude stretched up to the sky and disappeared among the stars, leaving behind a soft murmur of strange music like the mystery of something very beautiful that one could feel.

He saw once again in his mind the Indian who was gesturing in the National Dry Goods store, but without the jumble of laughter and voices. Curiously, the same man who enumerated so many marvels was contemplating him from a philosophic pose, seated without moving on a large stone facing a vast plain of sand wrinkled up into dunes and streaked like a labyrinth. He spoke to himself with the serious expression of someone deeply troubled. "I truthfully don't know how the gringos have been able to do such wonders. I have the suspicion that not everything I saw is the work of Christians. Perhaps a god or something like that makes the things for them . . . Or God our Lord does it himself. Otherwise how could you believe something like that? No, I'm dying to go back. The United States is glory on earth. But to get there you've got to cross the desert. . . ."

Timoteo emerged from his daydreaming. The ocotillos, sahuaros, viznagas, chollas, and stones were all sleeping, but the shadows remained awake like a watchful presence. He saw the stars alive like the steps of God advancing in the construction of worlds just by feeling the spaces, materials, and fire with which He molds things.

The days passed with Timoteo and his family going about their daily routine of struggling with the modest livelihood that came from tending the five goats they owned, three of which had babies. The children ran about playing, laughing, and shouting. The goats bleated out their stuttering song. His wife attempted to add her voice to this concert with shrill screams that were swallowed by the echoes, along with the stupid chattering of the chickens and the barking of three hounds and a bitch called Estrella.

The Indian woman and her kids suffered to see Timoteo so pensive and to hear him speaking over and over again about a strange world. They could not understand why the man neither smiled nor burst into laughter as he used to do continually, or why he would fall into a rapture seeing within his inner universe a world populated by strange things that he could not describe but that he knew were beautiful and splendid.

The sun came out that morning in all its power, trapping the dawn and invading the dark. The blue of the sky overhead sparkled on the ochre color of the land and the sharp green of the sahuaros. The outline of the short range and the vast desert reflected oblique torrents of light.

Timoteo Noragua was equipping his mount. After putting the saddle and reins on, he attached with a belt half a dozen gourds filled with fresh water, a sack of pinole, and a saddlebag half filled with dry meat and topped off with corn tortillas. Where are you off to, Timoteo? Why are you taking all that? Papa, Papa, don't leave! They formed a questioning chorus around the Indian. The goats, roosters, and dogs had their questions to ask. Timoteo Noragua answered with a gesture of melancholy from deep within himself. I'm going to a land called the United States. They say that it's the prettiest place in the world and that it has things so beautiful that you have to see them to believe such marvels. Besides, you can find happiness there if you look for it. I will seek it until I can find it for all of us. His wife and children began to wail. Don't be a fool, Timoteo. The gringos will throw you in jail or they'll work you to death like a common slave. I'll be fine, I'll bring back lovely things for you and the children. We'll have good land and water to irrigate it and the corn will grow. I'll also see things . . . Can't you understand, man, that the gringos will tie you up like an animal, they'll drag you through the thorns, they'll brand you with burning irons, they'll slice you with razors, and they'll spit on you because they hate us, Timoteo. My God! We're happy together here with you. Papa, don't leave, don't leave, don't leave . . . A smile crossed Timoteo Noragua's face while he contemplated the distance. The Indian blessed each member of his family with a sign of the cross. He splayed his legs over the burro's back and whipped at it until it started to trot. Waving his hat in his right hand, he called good-bye to them. His wife and children were sobbing dreadfully. Now he's really gone crazy on us. He's lost his mind completely. Take care of him, sweet God, take care of him! Dawn fell on Timoteo as he crossed the Sonoran Desert. Seen from above he and Salomón are a black ant dragging a line across the dunes. Along the surface, the two of them, the man and the burro, look like the dark vision caused in the eye by strong light. Seen up close, they are two stoic beings determined to survive. The man looks ahead with his eyes half closed, while the beast stares at the ground he is treading. He knows that once he has conquered the immensity of sand he will find the country of his dreams. But now he has to prevail against a vastness stripped of all vegetation, lacking in shade or any hope for water, with only sand and a glaring sun that produces fire in the air, on the ground, and in the very innards of the land. If the sky is a zealous eye, surely it can see how those who cross through the fire are legion, that Timoteo is not the only one to have the guts to violate the gnarled land of this inhospitable, barren waste. Other men, many, thousands of them, also march triumphantly across the dunes. They seem like Christs who can walk across the waters of a sea roiling with waves and malign spirits. Some make the crossing at the side of a friend. There are those who travel in groups of three or more companions the length and breadth of a vastness whose mounds of sand streak the distances. Timoteo is traveling on foot, leaning against Salomón's back. It is already night. They have freed themselves from the presence of the sun but not from its embers. Their flesh aches and the shadows embrace them. The air is a fever that stirs up the sand like tiny blind meteorites that shatter without being consumed in their eternal swirling. Just to make the trial more painful, the devil now appears in the shape of a storm to pursue them. How his filthy toothless snout pants, spitting burning sand. The sterile beds of the wasteland spring up like the wrathful dead in a diabolical conspiracy. The points of light go out and everything becomes shadows. It is a cursed travesty of a genesis inspired by evil. The men who violate the domains of the monster of fire no longer struggle to make their way, but rather to free themselves from the grave that descends on them from the heavens. Calm returned with the dawn. The desert revealed new dunes, identical to the ones it had pulverized. The devil, exhausted from his hideous deeds, climbed up to the sun and lost himself in its caverns to take a nap shrouded in flames. No one could say how many pilgrims had been buried. Those who escaped did so as half-buried insects. They moved their members like antennas, their arms freeing their trunks, then their shaky legs, to continue on with the same determination to reach the destination they had set for themselves. Timoteo Noragua emerged from the depths of a dune. He and his burro Salomón had brought back and haunches together against the bombardment of sand, thus giving shape to a mound covering them. With the darkness and the storm gone, the Indian emerged from that womb, as though born this time from the earth itself. Digging with the care of a mole, he uncovered his burro. It looked like he was sculpting in sand a placid statue. Timoteo grabbed one of the gourds and drank deeply. Timoteo Noragua saw in Salomón's eyes his own suffering, and he embraced him like a brother while two large tears rolled down the dusty mask of his face. Along with the other adventurers scattered about that hell, they set out for the great country to the north, climbing and descending the streaked crests, ready to reach a country that Timoteo dreamed was a world inhabited by miracle-working magicians. The fence is high and woven like a net. It runs along the border and blocks access to the marvelous country. The monotony is relieved. Now dunes can be seen, along with sand and a metal fence. Nevertheless, the tracks stretch out. Timoteo stops alongside the burro, squinting in the distance, seeing beyond the expanses of sand. His eyes radiate the phosphorescence given off by dreams, and he smiles to himself. Now he is ready to cross with strength and confidence. Timoteo Noragua pushes the burro from behind. The animal balks. Come on, Salomón, don't be afraid. The Indian gathers strength and pushes with all his might against the burro. He makes him take a few steps; the animal makes it through the entrance gate, followed by his master. They now stand on United States territory. There before them stands the country of marvels. Let's go, Salomón, let's go and see.

There is nothing written about Santa María de las Piedras. Its history flows through the toothless mouths of old men in the plaza, mixed in the weather forecasts, absurd fantasies, a parade of ailments, silly reminiscences and a vast repertory of home-made remedies. Sometimes on the corners, other times in the plaza, the old men get together with their tales.

The aforesaid town exists in the middle of a barren waste, surrounded in part by craggy hills at the very edge of the Sonoran Desert. Santa María de las Piedras has no sky, but rather a convex lens that lets through rays of sun that strike the ground and are transformed into demons of fire. Pity anything damp they strike! Whether water, sap, or blood, because they will suck it up and leave it cleaner than a skeleton.

After years and years of hunger and thirst, Santa María de las Piedras suddenly found abundance. It was during the thirties; yes, sir, when Santa María de las Piedras saw a change, for better or worse, who knows. It was only a flash in the pan, because ten years later everything was just as it had been before, or worse, due to the bad ways brought by the foreigners. Did you look for gold, too, Don Teófilo? No, sir, I don't run about looking for what I haven't lost. But I can tell you the whole story, because I haven't budged from here, nor will I, unless others move me to you know where. Who was it that discovered gold scattered around Santa María de las Piedras, Don Teófilo? Look, my friend, if you really want me to tell you, make yourself comfortable on that bench. Have you had breakfast? Because it's a long story. Don't get excited if the birds crap on you. I don't like to end up talking to myself. Talking's not a joke to me, like it is for Nacho Sereno. He'll be along any minute. Damned old loafer, saying that I can't accept what he has to say, as though he were such a great storyteller. In any case, friend, if you can't understand me or you don't like what I have to say, just keep your mouth shut. The others will be along. If Don Lalo feels all right, you'll see him here, and perhaps even Don Pablo and Güero Paparruchas will show up, too.

The one who discovered gold was in reality Chano Noragua, one of the sane Noraguas, when he was tracking down a nanny goat who'd been missing from the flock for two days. What happened was that Chano had taken to eating prickly pears so much that he was up

48

to here with them, and he couldn't eat another one, that's a fact. So, out of ignorance he also started to eat a lot of cheese wrapped up in corn tortillas, with the result that he ended up as constipated as if he'd been glued up. And so he hadn't been able to do his business for about two weeks. Chano went to see Chiriquiqui, the medicine woman, and she prescribed mezquite peelings as a cathartic in a dose big enough for a horse, to judge by the effect it had on the patient. Old Rumboso, his father, had told him that if he didn't come back with the goats he was going to tan his hide with the whip. Well, what happened was that out there among the chollas, between the purgative and the fear of his father, he finally felt the urge. Days later, Chano excitedly told how, after unburdening himself, he looked around for something pointy to clean himself with, and, not finding anything, he hopped around squatting like a rabbit, until he saw the tips of some stones sticking out of the ground, and, after putting the first one to good use, he wanted to take a look at it, as often happens, and that's when he noticed something strange. Like a thunderbolt he realized it couldn't be anything else but gold. Chano reached this very plaza where we're sitting shouting his head off: I found gold! I found gold!

Well, look who's here. Hi, you old devil. What did you do, fall asleep in the plaza? What do you care, you old buzzard? I bet you think I lie around between the sheets all day. Is that what they call the bedroll these days? If Don Lalo weren't just walking up, I'd really give it to you. Come on, Don Lalo, come on, we're recalling things that have happened here in Santa María de las Piedras and, in the process, filling in this boy. So what's left, friend, tell me. Is there anything left except talking about things that have happened? Otherwise, we'd be just like these eucalyptuses, pines and ash trees around us here. Go on, Teófilo. I was saying that Chano come along yelling like a parrot, I found gold! I found gold! Chano had several nuggets of pure gold in his pack, but he was so excited the only one he could show us was the one coated with his own shit. Well, the whole world was off in a flash. They lost no time in reaching the leveled area and starting in to dig like moles with shovels, picks, their fingernails, or anything else at hand. Every so often you could hear the jubilant cry of a lucky old lady, the joyful yelp of some guy, or the cackling laughter of some kid. People who could barely afford to eat quelites, prickly pears, beans if they were lucky or a skimpy hare, were filling their hands with gold like nothing. Of course it's

49

true that the lottery is cruel. Some win while others lose, and the ground bloodied the hands of the unlucky ones, who had to return home silent and crestfallen. The news didn't take long in spreading everywhere like wildfire. Like the thundering of thirsty cattle who smell a waterhole, people started to arrive day and night from all over. Santa María de las Piedras saw the arrival of big palefaces from Chihuahua, small-time prospectors from over in Jalisco, fat asses from Sinaloa, even people from Mexico City. It was quite a sight, because everybody wants to be an artist or a politician in the capital. People came from Chiapas, Michoacán, and God knows where. It was a mess of people like you wouldn't believe. The poor are always on pilgrimage and the rich always have them up short, not to mention the politicians. Since they are so dark they can't feel their hunger like they can feel the bloodsuckers. Fine, but don't get sidetracked, Teófilo, and go on with your story. That's it, that's all I needed, Nacho Sereno, are we going to start? I'll just let you do the talking, but keep your beak shut until I tell you to. You are my witness, Don Lalo, if I smash the gums in this old mummy. Just go ahead and try to, phlegm face, you're just my errand boy. Come on, fellows, cut the crap. I also like to recall the old days. Don Teófilo, tell this young fellow about the gringos who came to excavate. How did the gringos know there was placer gold here? Ah! My boy, because even when they're asleep they know how to find it. But of course the thing didn't stop there. Even the foreigners came running to scrape for Santa María de las Piedras's gold. There were Europeans whose nationality nobody knew, and they spoke incredibly strange languages so that they had to take care of themselves with grunts and gestures. By that time there were thousands of golddiggers, more outsiders than townspeople. They slept wherever they could, in the streets, here in the plaza, even in the open fields just like animals. A lot of them made makeshift dwellings, using bushes, stubby mesquites, garambullos, ironwood for the roof. There were even those who took shelter in the shade of the chollas. A lot of them spent day and night digging in the holes they made. Once they found gold they became distrustful and wouldn't come out for anything, with the result that some died from thirst and hunger in their diggings. But their packs were jammed with gold. Later it became clear that some came looking for gold, while the goal of others was to take it from them, some by whatever means they could and some by selling sky-high even the air and evil looks. The storekeepers had their day selling food at outrageous prices. For a miserable plate of beans, a skimpy corn tortilla, not to mention a cup of toasted bean water in place of coffee, they demanded the Virgin's pearls. Meat was a luxury for millionaires, and any old piece of tough skin almost cost an arm and a leg. The poor people who could find no gold ended up a bag of bones, like a cheap marimba. Everybody wanted to get rich in Santa María de las Piedras. The most voracious improvised cantinas where mezcal and beer were worth their weight in gold, which didn't stop the drunks, who filled the places as soon as it started to turn dark to drink until dawn. You can't believe the things that went on there. There was a sudden explosion in transportation. Teams of burros, horses, and mules couldn't keep up with the demand to haul merchandise. Whiskey, champagne, and a series of European wines arrived in boxes. Others brought in foodstuffs. Sardines packed in tomatoes were popular. Cereals and vegetables in large containers weighted down the backs of the animals. Enormous bales of the dried meat of the burros that had been killed in Trincheras arrived by burro. There was also a rage of fashion clothes, and high prices were synonymous with elegance. The shop owners were dying with laughter. Pretty soon buses and passenger coaches took the place of the mule drivers just as soon as there were passable roads. When things reached the fever pitch, Zenona and her troop appeared on the scene, with Silvestre as her righthand man. With the arrival of the whores—and what whores!—it was gangbusters in Santa María de las Piedras!

That Zenona was born to be a madam. Ten years earlier she had run a sleazy bordello in the middle of nowhere, out by the river away from the houses. But in those days she hardly made enough to eat. The townsmen, really bad off at a time when hunger was a real scourge and got to everyone alike, never had money to spend on the services of whores. The result was that, depending on how the tart struck them, the fornicators paid with ears of corn, pumpkins, beans, or peas. When times were good, the girls got chickens, maybe a pig, even an occasional goat. Zenona left Santa María de las Piedras in a hurry around 1925 when the generals were divvying up what remained of the revolution and the landowners were leaving like drowning rats. Zenona left town because of the funeral, the saddest one ever, according to the town gossip. The bosses cried like babies on each other's shoulders and pulled their hair out with grief. But those were bygone times, Nacho Sereno. We're talking right

51

now about 1934 when the gold flowed like water, so you'd best keep quiet. I know my own story, you old goat. I've got to fill in the details before getting to the point; you can't just start in the middle like some drivelers I know who don't know how to tell a story. Go talk to the driveling prickly pears if you don't want to believe me. Okay, fellows, okay. We've got enough of an audience. Go on, Don Nacho. No kids around? This story is for grownups. I don't want anyone to say I'm corrupting minors. Only kids from the last century, Don Nacho, and these last two to join us, but they're of age, so get on with it.

Zenona arrived well armed. By dint of persuasion and the eloquence of bank notes she rented the place where don Garcí Fernández de la Barrera had had his general store, with the understanding that he would get a cut of the new business. I don't have to tell you that Zenona's enterprise became a magnet that brought in iron as well as gold. Iron in the form of knives, razors, daggers, awls and machetes that were all involved in shady dealings. You didn't have to do much more than look at someone sidewise and there'd be a fight, not to mention minor skirmishes involving cuts and bruises. That's how that taco vendor called Maifren lost his nose, the same guy that became a hallelujah man in the days when Brother Trini Brown was getting everyone into the water with his story about hell. Another time it was Romualdo Bringas who got his guts spilled out by that bad guy known as Tombocha. Wasn't Tombocha, don Nacho, the one who used to eat paper? Just to show you're right, in school we had to tie our notebooks up with a strap because he would gobble them like they were cheese if he found them lying around. Zenona arrived in Santa María de las Piedras with the gang of hand-picked whores, all young and tender. The ripest was Lucrecia, twenty-three years old, and the youngest was Teté, who was sixteen and from France. Three of the young ladies of dubious reputation were Mexicans, supposedly from Chiapas, although they spoke with a Sinaloan accent. Their names were flowers: Violet, Lily, and Daliah, all very pretty and naughty, and they worked day and night. Three other pleasure workers were black, and they were deluged with clients. Siboney was the most successful of the three. There was also a little gringo in the cast, a former contortionist in a circus, she said. She caused a real sensation, and the men would leave her cubicle tripping over everything with their eyes spinning in circles. Who knows what mystery of nature made Teté the one who drove anyone who saw her crazy. She was blond like a waterfall, with eyes that sparkled with the color of whatever dress she put on. Sometimes they were green, sometimes blue, and occasionally a very clear brown. Her body was perfectly cut, so to speak, with nothing added or missing. Her greatest asset, nevertheless, was more subtle: her placid gestures, the way she moved her fleshy lips, the spreading of her nostrils when she got excited, and a certain indifferent manner. By contrast, the men who came to Santa María de las Piedras from all over the place were ugly at best, the majority of them uneducated and mean; adventurers and lowlifes, with the exception of one or two real gentlemen among the lot. From the south there were squat Indians with big noses, darker than bad luck, covered with liver spots. The north sent big-belly types, hellraisers, bullies as noisy as chatterboxes. Many of these men had never been with a real woman, although real is a manner of speaking, since some queens and princesses have horrible big mouths and big feet and are sluttier even than Zenona's girls. Zenona's pleasure troupe made such a hit that when several of the miners found gold they lost no time in cashing it in for caresses. Some who already had the valuable metal in large quantities saw it slip through the hands and legs of the beautiful courtesans. Often the women went to bed exhausted, to be awakened by Silvestre banging on the tambourine because someone was showing his gold and demanding a woman in exchange. Either because they were lacking in training or lacking in water, the men never bothered to bathe, and they would show up sweaty and with their clothes a mess, smelling like dead goats. The women, compelled by Silvestre's shouts, threats, blows, and curses, prepared themselves to invoke Eros with their cunts still raw, covered with scratch marks, their nipples bitten, completely strung out. The prostitutes stayed only because they were afraid of being caught out in the desert by a pack of rapists. Despite the barbarous exploitation they were subjected to, some of the gold stuck under their fingernails. The army of scum dying for sex became a nightmare for available young women. All they had to do was see men and their reproductive system would start to burn. The only ones who were safe were the French and the gringo girls who, because they were blondes, white-skinned, and exotic, went for a very high price.

Musical groups wandered the streets like stray dogs: guitar players, mariachis, bands from Sinaloa, even marimba players showed up all over the place with their instruments. Zenona had her own orchestra at the Golden Hive, the Green Club, according to Don Luis Quijada del Toro; the Pitolocos—Wild Pricks, as they were commonly called. Curiously, these were the musicians who cried the loudest at the saddest funeral ever held in Santa María de las Piedras.

There was quite a crowd the night of the first dance when the madam announced the price of each one of her nymphs. All the troublemakers and rowdies were out in full force: the Botellos brothers, Saúl and Evaristo, Chencho González, the infamous Romerazo, others who were legion, above all that squat hellraiser who was just a hair bigger than a dwarf, Misérrimo García, a brawler and hired killer like we'd never seen around here before. Misérrimo García was from Las Coyoteras.

Zenona presented her girls at the top of her voice, setting the price of the mestizos at 75 pesos. The peso was worth quite a bit in the thirties, although it's not worth a hill of beans now in the eighties. You know, no cash, no bash, nothing about I'll pay you later, forget it and we'll catch you next time around. I'm asking 125 for these black beauties, and that's a bargain when you think about the memories they'll give you. Just look at how great they are. They look like they've been carved from pitch. Taylor goes for 150, because she's supple and pretty and she's blond like a fairy. Once with this girl is like doing it with a whole troupe. For the French girl she established the price of 200 pesos, claiming that she was almost a virgin because she always tried to get away at the moment of action, and besides she was so young. No woman could equal her in tenderness, not to mention the fire that burned in her underwear.

The veteran Pitolocos, who had played ten years before at the saddest funeral ever held in Santa María de las Piedras, struck up a heavy dance beat and the Golden Hive was turned into a den of whooping and swaying. Misérrimo García danced with a very pretty young blonde, and they looked just like a gnome and a fairy dancing together. Misérrimo García shouted his feelings at the top of his voice. This is a real woman and not the stick of wood I've got at home, hot damn! Romerazo showed up after the orchestra had played its set. He was built like an animal, dark with curly hair, his face square and his hands like baseball gloves. He wore overalls with suspenders. Romerazo sidled up to Teté like a dinosaur, paying no attention to the presence of the dwarflike Misérrimo. The French girl shrunk back out of a sense of self-preservation while at the same time fixing her gaze on the large man. She noted that his fingers were very thick and long and she began to turn as red as a pomegranate about to shed its seeds. Romerazo took out a money pouch whose contents exceeded the fixed price and threw it in Zenona's face. He grabbed the fragile Teté by the arm and demanded she show him the way. The small room held a narrow bed, just enough space for a small table, a mirror and a basin of water. The man smelled of goat, and she smelled like rancid fish in spite of her perfume. Seeing her naked was like opening the cage of a starving beast. The girl opened her eyes wide and jumped back, and he approached her like he was about to pick a flower. Teté withstood the impact by curving herself like a bow. The bones of her pelvis and hips made sounds like sprung piano keys. A half hour later the vertebrae of her spine were still making chattering noises. With her eyes wide and tearful, Teté snuggled up to Romerazo's chest, asking him to take her away wherever he wanted. He wouldn't have to pay a single grain of gold for her. The little girl hung onto the prick of that stud with her whole hand. Romerazo and the French girl spent four days holed up together. On the morning of the first day, Silvestre kicked the door and threatened to chase them out with a club. The lover came out and smashed him in the face and kicked his ass, and they weren't bothered again. On the second day the rumor went about that they were stuck together and that it would be necessary to separate them to keep them from dying. The popular belief is that when that happens, there's a loss of will to go on living, and if they're not separated they die. No sooner had they come out into the living room than Romerazo started pounding the bannister and demanding something to eat and drink. They brought him all sorts of canned seafood. He downed sardines in tomato sauce and various cans of oysters. He ate roast beef, a stack of flour tortillas, and drank a liter of rooster water, which is a concoction of water with ground garlic and chile peppers. The French girl ate shrimp delicately with two fingers. Her eyes now looked very clear, like distilled water. Her mouth looked like a recently opened and flowering rosebud. She walked like she had ridden bareback on a horse for a long ways for the first time. I want you to get the mariachis for me, right now. I have the money to pay whatever they ask. I'll buy drinks for everyone. I don't want to see anybody sitting around on his ass. What the hell, let's have the Ballad of Cananea, that's what I want, along with other songs. He downed food and liquor nonstop until the evening clients began to show up. He still had three bags half full of gold. He had himself served like a king, to Zenona's joy. The spongers hanging around him would laugh at anything he said, no matter how dumb. He took pleasure in ordering Silvestre around. Hey, bring me some beers. I said tortillas, stupid. Are you deaf? What the hell happened to my chitlins? Are you deaf or isn't your name Silvestre? A little before nightfall, with Romerazo surrounded by a half dozen pals with Teté seated on his legs, everybody drinking and the music playing away, two tattered young men showed up in the Golden Hive, one four-teen and the other twelve. They were wearing rough homemade tehuas, and their shirts and pants were falling off, they were so old and full of holes and tears. Their dirty faces still showed signs of a starving childhood and a world of weariness. Romerazo saw them so suddenly he didn't have time to say anything because of the surprise and anger that overtook him. The older one brought himself to say humbly, on the edge of tears, that his mother had sent him because there wasn't even a grain of flour left in their shack, not a single bean, that his little brothers had collapsed from hunger. Romerazo stood up in a rage. The kid was barely able to say, "I'm sorry to bother you, Daddy." The man took a handful of coins out of his pants pocket and threw them in his face. Tell him to get the hell out of there and not come back. The boys left in tears, losing themselves in the crowd that hung around the streets of Santa María de las Piedras. They cast sidelong glances at the eateries, sniffing and crestfallen.

When the Botello brothers and Misérrimo García showed up at the Golden Hive arm in arm, they began to make fun of everybody. It was obvious that they were fighting drunk. Romerazo could smell blood, and he preferred to slip out with the blond girl. How much do you want for this one? he demanded of the madam straight-out. Well, she's not for sale, really. I'm going to take her anyway, so let's see who's got balls enough to stop me. In reality no one would have been able to stop the man in heat, much less argue with him over the woman. But what did happen was that, while he went toward the door, Misérrimo García dropped his hand down between the young woman's legs. She covered her triangle instinctively and at the same time she pulled away, muttering a protest. The giant turned violent, roared at Misérrimo, raking his ratlike figure with his glance. Listen here, you dog fetus, what are you doing grabbing my woman's cunt? God damn! You know something? I didn't try to grab your woman's snatch. I only tried to smooth her corset with my hand. And so what? The most normal thing would have been for Romerazo to wipe Misérrimo from the world of the living with a single slap. But the sharp little shit pulled out a small pistol not much bigger than a thimble and shot the lover right between the eyes. Later, thanks to the autopsy performed by Caballo the nurse, it was learned that the projectile had gone through the socket of his right eye. The bullet lodged in his encephalic matter. There were those who were to say later that God's punishment was swift and accurate, for the hatred that the deceased had awakened in his helpless hangers-on. The guardians of order wasted little time in descending on the place, two policemen sleepy from two nights on duty and commander Rumboso. The latter asked who the assassin had been, and all eyes turned to Misérrimo, who was still waving his little pistol about. Rumboso tried to detain him when he came toward him. Hold on, colonel, because I'll shoot. You're the one doing the shooting, so let's go now. Colonel Rumboso took Misérrimo by the shoulders with his left hand and with his right hand on his holster, he lifted him up to the level of his own head and threw him like a ball against the wall. Shut this piece of crap up in a cell for me. Choloy, one of the policemen, tucked the murderer under his arm. Stop squirming, you bastard. Even if you are unconscious, from now on you're going to live just like a bird.

It's night and, mounted on his donkey, Timoteo Noragua is about to enter the capital of Aztlán. Something's different that night. Order and logic reveal a crooked symmetry, as though the moon had gotten the idea to come out square with the face of a coyote instead of the usual man in the moon, or as though the stars were to appear lined up in parallel lines stretching off into circular distances lost in eternal space. The nighttime people stop to watch and whisper to each other, fascinated, the anthill of curiosity turned inside out. Then they turn around to stare back. Between the sky-scrapers the streets appear to be narrow, despite the fact that they are wide. Astonished drivers slow down. From in front they look like the flow of a river of silvery fire, and from behind like a river of scarlet flames. An enormous clock crucified on the thirty-third floor denounces old Cronos crossing ten at night in a bound. The old devil laughs out of the side of his mouth. The daily comings and goings send on their way home millions of nervous systems convert-ed into harps, with some strings loose and others on the point of snapping. It is the time of day when alcohol paints faces with stupidity, dousing the dancers with lust. Weapons deliver the dead and many women suffer in despair in their houses, devoured by seconds swelling like festering wounds. It is the hour when the dying flee through the dawn, when champagne goblets copulate in toasts wild with pleasure and laughter and in the intimacy of bedrooms the miracle of the fish is called forth by naked bodies that writhe togeth-er, tumbling like phosphorescent fish that have just been pulled from the ocean. At the time of day that either falls or rises, just after ten o'clock, a burro pounds his four paws on the sidewalk, a Mexican Indian on his back. The two of them contemplate the city: Los Angeles. The man and his beast are astonished by the explosion of lights that flow and the sparkling fixed points of light around them. They stare overwhelmed at the city's naturstructure made up of glass, cement, iron, chemical products, and gasoline, like it was blood. From among the beehive of voices that float like a cloud in the atmosphere, the hysterical horns, the whine of wounded sirens, and the screams of the murdered aborted by television sets, the voice of Timoteo Noragua emerges: he asks who the maker is of all those extraordinary things. A deaf old man with smog-filled eyes and a humped nose adjusts a listening horn in his ear and shouts back in answer, What'd you say? Timoteo Noragua smiles stupidly, his mind trying to understand. What a man! Was Huachusey responsible for these marvels? He must be a genius, good grief!

A jubilant multitude crowds in front of the doors of a gigantic stadium. There, at the entrance, there is a name traced out in the form of a rainbow-colored arch: "Cosmicland." The door of the enormous place looks like a dizzy whirlpool that swallows up the thick procession of vacationers coming from all over the world. They are people of all ages, those who use a cane and those who are still nursing, everybody laughing happily. They exchange words in many languages, very excited and happy. Right before you go in under the arch, there's an antique scrolled message. "Pilgrim, your past has been left behind and you now abandon the present in order to tread the future. Take delight in the world of tomorrow with the spirit of a child."

When they were all right, there was no one in Santa María de las Piedras who exceeded the Noraguas in dignity and nobility. But if one of them was on the crazy side, red lights would flash and then look out, neighbor! One day, just when spring was turning into summer, the wizened old fellow came out just as the sun was lifting the semicircles of its luminous eyelashes. There were birds, still confident that the flames and flares of summer were not yet ready to fry their wings. Nevertheless, these feathered creatures failed to take note of the presence of the gang of kids skilled in the use of the slingshot or in the simple casting of a stone through the action of hand and arm. No sooner would the stone be thrown, than there the bird would be, rolling its eyes and opening its beak, or the lizard, quivering its legs for the last time. There was never a lack of stones in Santa María de las Piedras for the purpose of killing animals and birds and beaning someone on the head. All you had to do was scratch the ground and any sadist would be armed and ready to bash the ribs of drowsy cows and overly confident burros. Don Rumboso Noragua heads toward the river with longer strides than usual. Nevertheless, his figure is bent. He meets Elías, called Pig Hands, and he growls out to him: look, friend, when you want to walk a long way without stopping for anything, walk bent over and take long strides, because if you try to stop you'll fall on your face, god-damn son-of-a-bitch. Now we're in for it; Don Rumboso Noragua has stripped a gear. I've just come from the den of thieves, filled with a pack of bastards. Look who's coming, it's Don Rumboso Noragua, and it looks more like he's carrying a beam than a cane. Flaco Carrasco, Chapo López, Gangoso Gómez, and Espaldón Félix are standing around in a circle chatting. The scrawny old man stops in front of them smiling with the beatitude of an apostle. They examine him with affection and respect and continue, engrossed in their conversation. The lanky old fellow looks them over. Suddenly, with greater speed than a cat in love, he raises his stick and brings it down on the back of Espaldón Félix. It makes a noise like a circus drum. The crazy man continues on his way, and the others surround Espaldón, who is writhing in pain. God-damn madman, he almost killed me. Women and children enter their houses. A band of husky types is out looking for the madman. They find him asleep in a patch of prickly pears. They lead him home. They put him in the solitary room. They tie him by a leg to the iron post in the middle of the room. They fasten the chain and exit, leaving him tied up. The Noragua family cries silently. Chano wanders about, and Timoteo, in a trance, reads the adventures of the gentleman with the sad countenance. The girls are lost in thought, their faces very sad. Doña Marcolfa is sobbing. Late at night they can hear loud voices coming from the sick man's room, and they go up to the door. He is speaking in strange languages. What language is your father speaking, Timoteo? English. I'm going to talk to my father. Father and son strike up an animated conversation punctuated by outbursts of laughter until the old man falls silent, but not before announcing that he's going to dream in English. He proceeds to emit a strange snoring that sounds like the meowing of a cat, turning into hiccups, murmurings, and the cackle of a crafty laughter. What did you and father talk about, Timoteo? Nothing, just sounds we made up, maybe two or three words that everybody knows. For example, *maifrén* means my friend, *gudbay* goodbye, *sanabagán* son of a gun and *sanababichi* son of a bitch. Be quiet, for the love of God! On the next morning they went to the windowless room, shadowy by day. Come here, Chano shouted, father isn't here. They went in, and in fact the chained man had disappeared. They stood around in a circle, examining the metal post. From on top of it they heard the terrible roar of an infuriated tiger. Don Rumboso slips from the roof to the ground. Everybody's heart sinks. Two long months of suffering without letup pass for the Noragua family. No one bothers to eat, no one sleeps. One day in June Tina wakes up chirping at the top of her voice, singing like one hundred birds at the same time. My father is well! My father's come out of it! How do you know, Tina? Leave questions like that for strangers. You know full well that we move in deep waters. They shine a lantern on the crazy man's face. He's crying like Mary Magdalene. Mother and children are overjoyed and laugh happily. At last! He's crying now, he's crying now. Don Rumboso hugs and kisses them as though returning from a long voyage.

The entrance to Cosmicland has one unusual feature: the souls of the adults return to their childhood. No sooner do they enter into the marvels of fantasy and invention, than everything is laughter, healthy madness, and crazy happiness. Look! Look, a man riding a burro! Who is it, Mama? Someone acting silly. He must be an artist, a newspaper man, someone who likes to dress up. It's a Mexican Indian, only in disguise. He's probably advertising for some business. Look at how white his outfit is! The pants and the shirt are rough cotton. Look at his huaraches and his straw hat. Look how the burro bucks; even he has gotten into the spirit and looks like a kid. Despite all the marvels to be seen, the presence of the ass provokes a sensation among the people. As they walk about, despite being strangers to each other, people hug and wish each other good luck in a very friendly manner. The street is wide, and there are tall buildings on each side of the street that are replicas of older ones. The avenue is dotted with lawns and beautiful fountains in the shape of ballerinas, and there are exotic flowers to be seen everywhere. Suddenly the street turns into the world of tomorrow. Overhead, the basket carrying children of all ages whistles on its way through the sky and trains that fly go by! In the back there are boats that navigate among islands populated by trees that, in addition to being leafy and green, offer the wanderer exotic fruits in abundance. Many birds inhabit the islands, with plumages and a variety of colors so beautiful that you could almost say a rainbow had burst to enhance life, animated by the grace of song and music. Noise and songs are heard against a background of laughter.

Right in the middle of Cosmicland there is a white mountain crowned by a tuft of clouds, with caverns in its center and a road that spirals up from the bottom to the very top. It's unbelievable! A train filled to the brim with souls in search of thrills wends its way up the spiral climb. It goes up and then comes down! Its movement is so fast that you can't see it. There's just the extended wake of screams and laughter.

In Cosmicland there are elegant buildings where mystery and curiosity lure one to living fiction and fantasy. Come see the incredible. Hear and feel what has never been seen or heard before. Come see the forms take shape that imagination creates, forms really to be found in that part of the mind that preserves the childlike with the friendly feelings of poetry.

In a large circular space people from all races of the world dance and sing. They wear the typical outfits of their countries of origin. They whirl and whirl, singing: it's a small world, it's a small world . . . In their midst, Timoteo, astride his mount, shares the back of the beast with an elderly lady dressed like a fairy, an Eskimo boy and a second boy from Asia. Suddenly thousands of faces lift to the sky. The shouts of happiness and the music become intertwined in a rising swirl of joy. From up there, from the depths of space, a bright shaft bursts forth. Various marvelous heroes land on a sort of platform, wearing tights and a cape: Superman and Batman have brought to Earth, directly to Cosmicland, a piece of the satellite Kryptonion that crashed to Earth with a tremendous impact. Now they are being honored by a young naked woman who places luminous sashes about their chests. Her private parts are covered by tiny grape leaves. She's none other than Superwoman, the terror of bank robbers and the villains who harm women.

These superheroes carry the space rock to the top of the mountain that rises in the middle of Cosmicland and place it like a crown amidst the jubilation of the crowd. Naturally, they fly up to the top with it, and the crowd is overjoyed to see them play with it briefly like a ball. Then they are assisted by a green monster like a troglodyte with signs of madness in his face and by a powerful young woman named Superprettywoman. Some allege that the fragment of the Kryptonion satellite is green, others that it is blue, while some swear that it is brown and others black, until they realize that such a rock has the rare property of taking on the color of the eyes of the beholder. The superheroes rise up to acknowledge the thunderous applause with gracious bows, doing a few acrobatic turns to please their fans, and then they fade away into the distance with blinding speed.

The joyful tumult continued to mill around, here and there, among the mechanical rides and the exhibits where mystery and magical events captivate incredulous spectators. The tourists are astounded by each extraordinary thing they find along the way. Off to the side at various points there were beautiful women offering the tastiest of food. They wore short skirts, and their smiles were friendly and inviting. Ice cream, pastries, sweets, soft drinks, hamburgers, tacos, and other delicacies highlighted the pleasure of such happy moments. Groups of musicians dressed like clowns danced randomly among the people crowding by. Timoteo Noragua and his burro Salomón shared in the jubilation that marked the setting. Wandering about, carried along by the curious, they suddenly found themselves before a beach pounded by a rough sea. Large submarines emerged one after the other from the water, taking on people in one group after another. A hole opened up in the belly of the monsters, and a naval officer emerged to serve as guide. Wait a minute, Salomón. I'm going to ask the man coming out of that whale what this is all about. Between the pushing and shoving of the crowd, Timoteo enters the boat carried along by the tide. It was a trip full of excitement and untold horrors for him. Once the vessel went down, walls of colored coral rose up around it. They were on the verge of perishing in a storm that shook the ocean like a rattle. God, His mother, and all the saints were invoked by the chorus of screams and shouts. Calm and beautiful vistas followed: exotic meadows, hillocks, forests, patches of fish traveling in shoals like bands of animals roaming about. My God! A gigantic octopus watches over a ship he has destroyed, devouring men trapped in his tentacles. Timoteo covers his face. His hair stands on end and his teeth chatter a serenade of fear. They come to a stop some distance before a submerged city that the ancients called Atlantis. When they arrive back at the starting point, they disembark from the submarine stunned, despite a flowering of smiles. Timoteo thought to himself, "The things Huachusey does. How great is his talent."

Timoteo was again carried along by the tide of the gawkers, looking from side to side and sobbing because his friend Salomón is nowhere to be seen. Finally in front of an ancient mansion of somber colors with a black door, he found his burro eating the grass growing between the tombstones decorating the main entranceway. People were going in whispering among themselves and casting sidelong distrustful looks. Others buzzed as they exited, their eyes rolling, pursued by a catlike cry that vibrated with a violent shaking. They would rush headlong out into the crowd of passers-by who enjoyed seeing spectacles free of horrible emotions. Since the truth is that curiosity is greater than fear, Timoteo and his mount heeded the call of other marvelous adventures offered by Cosmicland. As they entered, black forms crossed by in front of them and disappeared into the ground without leaving a trace. At every step of the intruders, moans and cries came from the depths, as though their feet were treading on the suffering souls of the dead. Other horrible cries seemed to come from victims being put to the knife or whose skin was being ripped from their bodies. Reduced to terror in their hearts, their ears were assaulted by the screams. In their haste to escape they quickly found themselves in the middle of a cemetery. Various bodies of the dead, shaking the dirt from themselves, emerged from the graves and approached the visitors. Timoteo could make out among the group of skeletons the engineer Maximino Ruelas, ex-chief of the Rural Bank in this town. Ruelas was opening and closing his jaw as though something hurt him. Timoteo was paralyzed with terror. Suddenly he began to run, followed by Salomón. The skull of his mother-in-law had shown her teeth at him. He recognized her because she was wearing the fuzzy shawl she had used for years.

Once again the people were drunk with happiness: the music, the songs, the laughter, Cosmicland and its marvels: madness. Timoteo Noragua contemplated the crowds, their arms in the air. At the height of the outpouring of joy, there appears a fancy procession of floats decorated with thousands of light bulbs. The whole setting is flooded with a melody so gay that it sets even the heaviest feet to dancing. Some couples take each other in their arms and dance; others dance and dance with only their shadows. In the lead, perched on an enormous float in the shape of a ship, is Admiral Walt Movieland, all elegance, greetings and smiles. With both hands he throws kisses that turn into multicolored butterflies. When the people try to grab them, the butterflies explode like soap bubbles in a rain of ethereal confetti that evaporates in the air. It is he, the discoverer of the famous island of Doughland, famous because, as everybody knows, it is inhabited by talking animals. Alongside Admiral Walt Movieland, jumping up and down, there are dogs, elephants, cats, mice, chickens, and monkeys; in sum, a whole talking zoo.

Not only did Admiral Walt Movieland get rich with such an extraordinary discovery, but the entrepreneurs devoted to the exploitation of stage animals multiplied. They booked the talking animals in theaters and auditoriums of all kinds, including churches and enormous stadiums. They performed before audiences made up of thousands and thousands of keyed-up, delirious spectators. The animals in turn have amply demonstrated their grace and probing intelligence, to such an extent as to influence the behavior and philosophy of the common man. Seeing and hearing burros discuss politics, dogs recount military accomplishments, and goats, chickens, and other animals debate eloquently and convincingly liberty, economics, justice and so many other topics that would seem dull if they weren't being dealt with by talking animals is nothing to sneeze at. These animals from the island of Doughland discovered by the explorer Walt Movieland speak English with such charm and fluency that Shakespeare himself would be envious to hear them express themselves so well and with so much intelligence. What is more, they have traveled the world over and they have all come back multilingual.

The chanting crowd buzzes like a swarm of wasps, now trouping behind the procession led by Walt Movieland. The shouts and the music are reduced in volume to the sound of a swollen river rushing in the distance. Timoteo allows himself to be carried along, drunk with joy, ecstatic. Overtaken by the thrill, he happens to go up to a young girl with large blue eyes, all blond grace and beauty. Miss, who has made all this world? To whom does all this beauty that I see belong? What'd you say? A'h! So Huachusey did make all this of which he is the lord and master. What a man. Good God, what a man. Timoteo rides his burro, looking back wide-eyed at all his eyes can take in. There are no longer any glowing lights, only a soft light fading into dull tones. Voices and music can now be heard far off like the rustle of crickets and the ticking of clocks. The crowds have disappeared. Lost in the enchanted jumble of dreams, the result of his recent experience and other reminiscences that come to mind, Timoteo the Indian wanders into a forest. He is thinking about Huachusey and smiling because he has established his name. To judge by the deeds attributed to him, he must be more than a human being. . . . The burro has come to a stop; the silence is suddenly disturbed; there is a rush of strange voices that emanate from the tops of the trees, from the jutting branches and the trunks with which they form an angle. Where are you going, Timoteo? Hah, hah, hah. Salomón the fool, the burro, the long-eared. Hah, hah, hah. He can make nothing out, aside from the fronds that extend their greenery into the dark. Perhaps the trees in Cosmicland talk? Crazy old man, scarecrow. Hah, hah, hah. All of the trees around him pronounce his name in jeering tones. Timoteo, ugly old man. Ugly Indian Timoteo. Timoteo, ugly, ugly. Hah, hah, hah, hah. Swift shadows race before the startled pair, laughing uproariously. In a matter of seconds they surround the Indian, chattering ceaselessly. It is a school of parrots. They cover Salomón's back and head and the Indian's shoulders and hat. Stay and live with us, Timoteo. We will teach you to fly, hah, hah, hah. It is true that Salomón has a college degree? Hah, hah, hah. Salomón, Timoteo on his back, takes a few steps forward. Timoteo is laughing joyfully as he never laughed in his childhood, as he will never laugh again. No, little parrots, my burro is a Spanish professor at the University of Arizona, hah, hah, hah. Timoteo, ugly old man, what a great man is Huachusey. Hah, hah, hah. Do you know him? Yes, Timoteo, he is a two-legged animal like you, hah, hah, hah. Crafty parrots, crafty parrots. Hah, hah, hah. Timoteo, ugly old man. Hah, hah, hah, hah. The flock of parrots flew off home, shedding their feathers from laughter. The man on his mount laughed along with them. Goodbye, Salomón the venerable. Goodbye Timotwerp. Hah, hah, hah, hah. Goodbye my perky parrot friends.

Timoteo did not know how he had lost his way, with the darkness and the trees guiding him. The more he tried to return to the crowded party, the deeper and deeper he found himself in the wilds. He could hear the roar of savage beasts who communicate their intentions to each other over great distances. Reverberating echoes thundered like cannon shots and sounded like a phantom battle between ships waged day and night by mysterious pirates off the coast of Cosmicland. Suddenly he could hear nothing in the midst of a dead silence. It was as though Timoteo had fallen into an abyss of time where in an instance he was going back millenia after millenia to reach the bottom, where he would behold the fateful days of eruptions and catastrophic earthquakes and the broad swamps filled with enormous amphibians and giant-sized winged insects. They continue forward, sensing a different atmosphere; the trees are different, the ground they tread is different, everything around them is strange. The Indian grasps his situation when he hears the squeal of the burro. Salomón's ears are standing up straight, nerves and muscles ripple on his back, and his eyes take on the fire of the warrior advancing to the sound of battle. They go toward a strange thicket of gigantic plants with coarse and tangled leaves. The silence of his inquisitive and startled mind weighs heavily. My God! A horrendous noise can be heard from below ground, rumbling with a wrenching power. Man and ass are filled with terror. Columns of fire burst forth from crevices in the ground on all sides.

Timoteo and Salomón avoid the terrible cracks by jumping over them and running around them until they reach a short promotory surrounded by swamps and covered by enormous flowering plants whose colors are so intense, outlandish and intoxicating that they are almost violent. The earthquake suddenly stops. It is one of the tremors that frequently shake the unstable crust of the earth, seeking internal stability. The water from the marshes looks just like the grease used to lubricate cars. Timoteo does not take long to realize that the sky around them is also inhabited.

Insects with large transparent wings and bodies the size of sheep fly over them. They are inoffensive and do not attack. They have eyes the size of baseballs and a foolish look about them. They feed on the buds of the treetops in enormous quantities, but they are victims of other monsters the size of small aircraft that behave like large bats. These zoom off at great speed, and just when it looks like they are going to crash into a tree, the surface of the marsh, another object, or into each other, they veer off with such unheard-of speed that it's hard to believe their tremendous strength. Their feet end in curved claws that grab on and won't let go. They have a trunk that is about five feet long and widens at the tip like a horn. With this cornucopia horn they suck up their victims while at the same time digging around in their innards with a long and toothlike tongue. When this happens, the big-bellied insects emit a strange cry, a combination ambulance siren and human wail. The vibration of the cry of the stupid sheeplike insects is sharp, and at its highest pitch the leaves of the plants tremble and some of the pale-colored flowers half close. These sheeplike insects hatch from nests of eggs that they incubate in their own ears. The monstrous suckers and bombers are born every nine months in pairs. In their mating techniques they resemble homo sapiens, but without the same uproar and scratching. The male dies torn to bits by the females when they become impotent. They end up finished by age and their sexual drive.

The desperate appeal of one who is contemplating a tragic end to his existence appears in the eyes of Timoteo and those of his beast. My God! A bloodsucker has seen Salomón and is zeroing straight in to nail him. Timoteo rummages around in his saddlebag, brings out a handful of pinole and throws it right into the eyes of the monster, who crashes to the ground, where the burro stomps it in the groin and incapacitates it. In its death throes, the bloodsucker expels through its beak a thick liquid between red and purple. Timoteo prays at the top of his voice, while the burro brays for help in its own fashion. What will happen now? An island seems to emerge from the marsh, rising up, swelling, thrusting out a muddy head from whose snout a cylindrical tongue extends which whirls and whirls like a whip. It bellows louder than a locomotive roaring down a canyon grade. It's all over. In a matter of seconds they will be lodged in the stomach of the marsh beast. When the latter exhales his stinking breath, he splashes upward a spray of swampy water from the pool. When he breathes in with a rasping noise, he inhales by the dozens a species of birds that are nothing other than turtles and winged serpents. Salomón and his master buck and curl themselves up. If they flee they will fall into crevices. The beast will decapitate them with a single blow from his tongue. Suddenly various winged creatures appear, flapping their wings: an old fairy carrying a wand like a baton from which stars flash, a pink elephant that vibrates its wings like a hummingbird, a tiny little boy called Peter Choochoo-chooy who flies like a fly, and a man with large wings of a thousand colors, famous for his zeal in defense of the law. It's Superbutterfly. They try to lift the threatened man and his burrow up, but the latter slip, and the effort is in vain. Timoteo closes his eyes in order not to face his death. A ship descends at this very moment with elegance and precision, shooting bolts of thunder at the beast, which retreats and falls on its back to reveal thousands of paws moving like antennas stripped of all solid support. An elegantly dressed captain and an equally attractive young woman step down a ramp. With a gracious gesture they invite Timoteo to step right on up along with his asslike mount. The Indian looks at the pair, confused. He asks: Who has made such a, such an unbelievable machine? What'd you say? Huachusey made this ship? What an intelligent man! I can hardly believe it . . . Huachusey.

The ship lifts off with an exploding array of lights and colors. such a fireworks display turns the sky into a living, fleeting, and incandescent glory. What terrible beauty of moonless nights, when the dense gloom is splashed with luminous and iridescent microinsects who glow ephemerally in the atmosphere the moment they are born, only to die seconds later in the very same place they mate. Engaged in reproducing, they disintegrate in clusters of eggs that in turn burst with newborn insects and flare in a variety of luminous and vivid colors. Thus they follow one another in a constant rhythm wherein they are born, copulate, and die in the air, such that both the living and the dead are travelers on the wind in a period of time as small as an atom. These insects appear mysteriously during the summer, showing up at about 9:30 at night, and for the space of fifteen minutes they provide this extraordinary spectacle. And don't believe that they cover everything. Not at all. They appear like clouds that the wind whips along hurriedly. Suddenly, they expand in a flash of light, in myriads of multicolored sparks. There's no spectacle like Cosmicland.

That's the way love is, I tell you, friend. It shows up when you least expect it and in such strange ways. Moño Flores, with his sugary voice, ran off with Tina Noragua on horseback during the Saturday night dance. He took her to a hut he had put together out of ocotillo branches on the other side of the river. His action was all planned out. Don Rumboso would not agree to him as a son-in-law because he had no hair on his chest and his voice and manners were those of a young lady. What is strange about the whole affair is that the old man didn't find out until three days later. All of a sudden, in the middle of mysterious comments and secretive tears, he noticed she was gone. He wasted no time in becoming alarmed. With a desperate tone in his voice he asked Clara, the one who composes poetry, Where's my little girl? She's in her little home. I'm talking about my daughter who sings like a bird. She's with her little boy. What do you mean? Only that the she-burro has a runny nose. Brat! What are you saying? Scratch your nose. Where is Tina? Damn it, tell me! Ay, father, Moño stole her! Marcolfa, is it true what this kid is saying? Yes, it's true. Doña Marcolfa is weeping with fear. I told you not to let them even talk to each other. They wrote to each other, and he would leave notes for her in the nanny goats' ears, and she would leave him return mail. I didn't think there was any danger, since you said that Moño Flores was a queer. Old man Rumboso grabbed his carbine and strode off double-time toward the river. By chance during the last days of June, as happens every year on the 24th, right on Saint John's day, the Saint says: You are no longer the Asunción River. You are the River Jordan. I will open the floodgates and you will become a torrent. The curious observe with fascination the flow of time and space in the current. They see Don Rumboso and they know what's happening. The man's noble blood has surfaced, and he's on his way to beat the shit out of the man who stole his honor. No one attempts to stop him. He jumps into the river, which swallows him up, carries him along and then spits him out like a flying fish. He brandishes his carbine, sinks back in, floats on the surface again, struggles mightily, is lost from view. The river is in a hurry, and the Sea of Cortés drinks it down in large gulps. Dogs, cows, humans, horses, trees, and anything else that is loose are swallowed up by the Gulf of Cortés. All manner of things enter its belly, tumbling head over heels. It is a river that goes mad a few days out of the year. Don Rumboso lodges himself in a tree floating along like the skeleton of a ship, and inside of an hour he reaches the other side. He reaches his destination exhausted, fueled only by the energy of his rage. He enters without knocking. What a sight! The lovers are sleeping like children. Their happiness can be seen between a parenthesis and a smile. The old man yanks Moño up by his hair. The lover rolls his eyes and cries out in fright. Don Rumboso kicks him in the ass. Tina begs forgiveness on her knees and pleads for the life of her doll. Now he is shoving them along in front of him with the end of his 30-30. They reach the edge of the river bathed in sweat. Moño whines for help. He is afraid to cross. Hold on to my neck, the old man orders his daughter. He slaps the boy. Get going, asshole. If you were able to jump my daughter, you can also jump the river. Saint John must surely have felt sorry for the trio. After considerable effort with some ropes the onlookers cast out to them, they are rescued. The lovers and the old man, raging like a lion, reach the house of the priest, followed by dozens of witnesses. Father Hilario was taking his nap. He gets up in a bad mood, but he holds his tongue when he sees what's going on. Marry these two for me, and right away, Father Hilario, and give them a harsh penance for having dirtied the sacraments. Don Rumboso Noragua did not sleep that night. He spent the night in front of his house watching over his carbine like a noble knight keeping watch over his arms. His wife and children accompany him in his vigil from the window.

Bed how can so many strange things happen in a town without anyone knowing about them? Because there are many stories: those that historians polish in something like a literary work with only one window, alongside what passes from mouth to mouth on the street corners and in the plaza as a legend that is forged. Yes, Don Abelardo, but the two are opposed to each other and fail to agree on one and the same incident. Which is the truer? Look, fellows, the only thing that counts around here is our own. You inherit it, live it, observe it, and dream it. Some of you will become old men and will continue to tell what you hear now and what you will live, observe, and dream tomorrow. If someone on the outside so much as records the name of this town in history, that will be something. What you have to say is sadder than it is funny. Is it something that ought to be known? The ball rolls whether it's convenient or not, and nobody orders these stories to be told or pays for them, much less because they might make us famous. Stories are told here for the pure pleasure of it, or the pain if you will, even more so, gentlemen, just because we want to. From the point of view of a storyteller in the plaza, no neighbor is too important to talk about nor is there any government censorship, much less scruples about styles and forms. He uses language freely with or without the approval of the academics. We're the only chatterboxes here that matter. No question, it's here that the secret history of Santa María de las Piedras comes out, because that's our main interest. If episodes and individuals happen to get mixed up, let the listener straighten things out; what's most important is the essence. Maybe there are some myths and fantasies, but they're the ones the people make up to give flavor to the stories of life just like you add salt and pepper to soup. We're curious, Don Lalo, about what you said about the saddest funeral in this town. Isn't that a bunch of baloney? Baloney, my foot! Don't tell me you're fresh from the egg and the bitter truth about things hurts your ears. I want you to understand the storyteller's not immoral. He only describes life, and it's life and those that make it dirty who deserve the fury of those who are scandalized. Calm down, Don Nacho, the young fellow was just expressing an opinion. Yes, yes, Don Abelardo, but it makes me mad as hell. Anyway, I'm not going to tell you about the funeral. Let Don Teófilo do it. He's an old gossip who makes things up. Now, that's a fine thing to say. Old windbag! Okay, that's enough of that. I'll do the telling. But listen to me good and clear, because I'll knock anybody in the head with this iron cane who tries to interrupt me.

It was somewhere in the mid-twenties, more or less, when the saddest funeral Santa María de las Piedras has ever seen took place. Although maybe there's been another one I haven't heard about. According to the man who was mayor at the time, Colonel Rumboso Noragua, even the tombstones shed tears. For a long time afterward the echoes of that day have reverberated when the musicians hugged their instruments, crying loudly like professional keeners. It happened during the days of the great hunger when the revolution had swept through and was still mowing down everything in its path, no matter whether it was food, money, or women. Not to mention that anyone who tried to get in the way would get it in the neck. That's the way things were, with no one having a thing, and Zenona was the madam in charge of a rundown brothel, the Sleeping Dove, with eight whores in service for the needs of local clients and surrounding areas. The prices were a matter of "pay what you can," more to keep prices down than anything else. The tragedy took place in December. The victims were Pelona, Cuataneta, and Rafaila. They held the wake for them in the same room that served as the "parlor" for the clients. Right where they danced, drank to laughter, shouting, and the happy notes of the Pitolocos' orchestra. Some of the witnesses are still alive, and one is the mayor Colonel Rumboso Noragua. Every time he tells the story he doesn't leave out a single detail. In fact, in a moment of carelessness he might even add an extra one. Whenever he talks about it he shakes his head and affirms that Santa María de las Piedras, in the days when hunger gnawed at everyone, never saw a funeral like that one, not even during the wars. The parlor was dark, with patches of light from petroleum lamps that couldn't do any better. The five remaining whores knelt praying before the bodies, the madam among them, and each held a rosary in her hands. Their fingers told the beads one at a time to the accompaniment of the murmurings of the supplicants. Standing in the background were all eight pimps, including the three widowers, along with the regular customers of the Sleeping Dove. There were five solemn and tense policemen on watch, on such an occasion more out of respect than duty. And, finally, the mayor and former subaltern of Pancho Villa. When the whores struck the end and the beginning of the rosary, there was a profound,

explosive silence, like the crash of a painful echo exploding into a
scream. The whisperings ended, and time pretended that it, too,
was dead. Old Chronos struck ten hurriedly, casting a sidelong smirk
at the little whores whose clocks no longer ran. Later when the
whole town commented on the event, they did not talk about it as
the whores' funeral. The abstract monsters regained their reality as
young ladies through the miracle of death. Several hours after the
burial, people of all ages and conditions began to show up at the
cemetery. They arrived in groups with real and artificial flowers. The
three graves were small mountains of roses, nochebuenas, forget-me-
nots, and other equally beautiful flowers. The crosses themselves
were buried beneath the garden of flowers. Shared grief showed on
the rough faces of men, the tender faces of children and the tired
faces of crying women. Poor little girls, innocent creatures. May
God take them into heaven. How cruel life was to the poor little
girls. These words and others like them served as greetings and as
the topics of conversation. Not a single conscience was at peace that
twenty-fifth of December. Even Father Hilario was heard to say
"poor little girls," despite having refused to offer a mass for them
because they had been responsible for their own fiery deaths.

The night of the wake, the whores' parlor was made into a
funeral chapel. The whores dressed in black, and no one could
recognize them because, strangely, they wore no makeup on their
faces and combed their hair out straight. One of them broke into
deep, piteous sobs, and the others followed suit. More softly, the
pimps began to cry. The tears fell in large drops from the faces of
both the policemen and the regulars. Don Rumboso wipes his eyes
with the back of his hand, just like nothing. The musicians in their
usual place seem lost in deep thought, silent and absorbed. Silence
once again falls. Then Zenona takes out a piece of paper from
between her breasts and says in broken syllables: the girls left this
note requesting music at their wake. Maestro Don Luis, one of the
lines of this message says: Dear Pitolocos, we want you to send us off
with 'I'm All Fagged Out' and 'The Swallow.'" Then the heavy-
hearted musicians, who had already been informed of the last request, strike up the chords. Halfway through the set, Romualdo
stops playing and grips his violin, convulsed by sobs. Old Luis drops
his saxophone and cries like a hysterical old woman. Huilo Larios
doesn't know where to set his horn down in order to cover his face
because he doesn't want anyone to see him crying. Cachetitos stops

pounding the drum, rakes his hair with his fingers with the sharp squealing of a child. The young kid on the guitar makes faces like you've never seen on even the funniest clown. He sobs out: how terrible, how terrible. They all seem to be crazy with grief, the five whores yelling and wailing, while the madam bawls hoarsely. The pimps are overcome by grief. The customers and the policemen forget they are men and embrace each other with the uncontrolled grief of little girls. Colonel Rumboso Noragua finds an excuse to leave the room and goes outside to cry under the open stars. The dead girls are buried at dawn.

Against the backdrop of dawn, the funeral procession wends its way to the cemetery. The two-wheeled wagon carries the three humble caskets containing the charred remains of the whores. With no regard for hierarchy, the musicians, pimps, authorities, whores, and a couple of all-night clients follow behind.

Little by little the news gets around, the details passed in whispers from one mouth to another. Santa María de las Piedras is beset by grief over the sacrifice of a few unhappy whores.

They had committed suicide for various reasons. First, because their bodies had become the laboratory for an endless string of venereal diseases. They were eaten up by gonorrhea, they were already syphilitic, a mass of sores, infected, smiling like dead dogs. What was worse, in addition to these secret diseases, they were filled with crabs that fell from their eyebrows like sesame seeds.

They were no longer women, but rather heads of hair floating in a sea of tears. When they showed their faces they were the very image of suffering horses.

The can contained several gallons of gasoline. The three of them got so drunk they could hardly stand up and then doused themselves with the gasoline. Good and soaked, they embraced each other with a single cry. Here goes! . . . then the explosion. They lighted the match there on the patio, a little bit away from the Sleeping Dove in order not to endanger their colleagues.

Father Hilario's sentence was solemn: we cannot say a public mass for these children because they took their own lives, and that is a right that belongs only to the Eternal Father. I'm sorry, but you and I will have to pray for them in silence.

Churrunga tells her husband, Morrongo, between her sobs, they are not gone yet. They are still here among us. Like the spirits of all the recently dead, they take up to a week to depart. They are wearing white dresses and they look as pretty as movie stars. They are looking upon us now. Ah, they are laughing so hard their eyes are closed! They are thankful and happy. This is the prettiest day of their lives.

Father Hilario during the mass that afternoon asked people to pray for them. He spoke of Mary Magdalene in his sermon and explained to his flock how she had made an effort out of her love for our Lord and how she had redeemed herself although she was a pros . . . po . . . poor woman of pleasure. But he quickly caught himself, because it's a euphemism to say a woman of pleasure, since in reality they are women whose lives are very sad. Father Hilario made a big hit with his sermon. The Pitolocos never mentioned the matter. On Christmas they no longer play with the joy they used to, according to what people say. The one who does talk about it is Colonel Rumboso Noragua, who shakes his head and says: I have never in my life seen a funeral like that one. According to him, the whores were peasant girls of Indian descent, very, very poor, who had been tricked into prostitution. What news, Choloy Pérez announced when he was drunk. With no law or anyone to protect them, what else could they expect? The flames consumed them just like garbage, my friend.

Damn weepy people, the survivors went right on being whores. The fathers of the whores got blisters on their feet going from one place to another trying to pull strings to get them released, but what the hell. What can you expect, who's going to stick up for the poor; who's going to help them? Just tell me who's to see justice done, who'll say I will. It's all talk. Give me another drink, Zenona, because it hurts real bad right here in my heart.

One morning in December, the Noraguas got an unpleasant surprise. The first roosters to announce the dawn could be heard one by one, to join their efforts until their song could be heard like a waterfall. It was the very hour in which Doña Marcolfa usually got up to get the kitchen going. First she would place pieces of mesquite wood in the stove on a bed of paper. Each sound that her hands and feet made sounded clearly in the close darkness. Even her breathing could be heard by the others, despite their sleepiness. She would light the papers and then blow to quicken the flames until they sounded like the galloping of hundreds of horses approaching from a distance. The pots and pans became percussion instruments that clanked noisily together: the hot water kettle, the skillet, and the cooking pans. She would go out for more wood, and you could hear her coughing. By the time the sun was saying good morning to Santa María de las Piedras, Doña Marcolfa had the table set. Her tenderness and amiable industry floated in the air along with the aroma of the food. The freshly brewed coffee tasted like an elixir of the gods to Don Rumboso. This was the pleasant manner in which the Noraguas got going. But that December morning, everything was different. Doña Marcolfa was dead that morning. Perhaps while she was dreaming a pleasant dream, death had found her and taken her away kindly. Misfortune usually comes in pairs. Along with the death of the mistress of the house came Chano Noragua's madness. Both at the wake and at the funeral, Chano took to dancing, humming tunes and laughing over silly things. In the middle of the mourning and the pain that scarred the faces of the mourners, Chano provoked laughter among the Noraguas' acquaintances who showed up to keep them company during such a sad occasion. He would stick his tongue out at them, making faces and obscene gestures. The last straw was when he started to grab at the old women and, with greater gusto, at the young girls. Old Rumboso dragged him off toward the door of the dark room reserved for that purpose and left him there filled with grief. Not now, my son, not now. Wait until morning if you want, because otherwise I will chain you up right now, by God. Chano, with his eyes glassy and red, stared off into the distance, sat down without a word and did not budge for a long time. The next day while the funeral procession was climbing the hill to the cemetery, Chano followed at a safe distance. He hid behind some boulders until the mourners had started back. Several youngsters came running to Don Rumboso's house, interrupting each other and all talking at the same time. Chano's digging Doña Marcolfa up! The old man strides off, climbing the short hill that leads to the cemetery. What is a stride for him is a race for the boys. Chano has already uncovered Doña Marcolfa's casket by the time they get there. What are you doing, son? Why are you unburying your dead mother? She is not dead, papa. That's just a story. I have discovered that death is nothing but a fantasy. If they didn't put people in coffins and bury them, Papa, I assure you they would wake up. There is no such thing as death, Papa, that's a superstition, the beliefs of the ignorant. There is no death for the soul, my son, and your mother's soul is in heaven, but the body is dead, it is rotting and turning into dust. Ah, how they have deceived you! Death is a priest's lie, something the Church has made up. Can't you see if there's no death, there's no religion. Death is a lie to take what little they have from the people. Father Hilario must have all those so-called dead people hidden somewhere. Look, Chano, I have seen the sick die and people murdered. Their breath flows out of them, and their blood, and then they swell up, rot and smell. There is nothing left to do but bury them. You don't give them time to get better, Papa. If there is a cut, it takes time to heal, and even longer for knife wounds and bullet holes. Don't you understand, Papa, there's a grave in my soul as deep as this one. It hurts me so much, and I need for my mother to wake up. You are old and know how to suffer. Come on, my son, let's go home. We must bury that body that was your mother. Don't come close, father, because I'll kill you with this spade. I'm serious. If you don't stop I'll bash your neck in good and leave you for dead, so you'll never get up again. Aha! Didn't you just say that death does not exist? And now you want to kill me. Chano fell silent for a few seconds, wrinkling his brow. Then he started to laugh so hard the kids observing him followed suit. Then they all headed home, the sorrowful old man holding Chano by the arm, with Chano and the kids laughing their heads off. Just to be on the safe side, they shut him up in the dark room. They put the chains on him and tied him up to the metal post. Once again, suffering silenced the Noraguas. They looked at each other with great sadness on their faces. They would not sleep again until Chano got over his spell. That is, with the exception of Timoteo, who lived in another strange dimension.

Illusion, a force that impels the spirit and is the fuel and fire of all dynamic forces, ignoring the barriers of the impossible and attacking and overcoming all obstacles, bore him along through arid desert plains. He crossed valleys of vivifying green and hostile ranges, and he was obliged to ford more than one river in his march. From high atop mountainous peaks he could feel his insignificance. On the ground he looked like an insect, and from a distance his eight extremities seemed strange, with his own joined to those of his mount. Nevertheless, a whole universe fit within his miniscule world. Unlike other explorers who sought power and gold during their day, he went in search of an inner claim on the fantastic beauty masked by the veils of mystery.

He stumbled on yet another marvel, and his spirit drank in through his eyes the beautiful, the incredible and the miraculous. The misty morning made of the bridge a path that extended over the waters, an endless route that seemed to lead beyond the heavens. Opening his eyes wider, Timoteo had an absorbed look on his face, and he hugged his burro in an attempt to communicate to him the intense emotion that overwhelmed him. His poetic feelings did not spring from fine language, but from seeing with awe the magnitude of the grandiose, something one feels mutely, causing the spirit to tremble and swoon. In the simple faith of a man who has inhabited the most ancient states of time, Timoteo Noragua required no other explanation than that marvel that he gazed upon, stunned, the miracle by virtue and magic of an extraordinary being.

The idea at first was like a light that begins to glow: the pros and cons, then resistance and opposition in the face of a challenging undertaking (the compelling goal of a group of engineers), until the culmination of contrasting ideas is reached and they merge into a unique conception. Later, a symphony of typists assemble prefabricated words on pages that will contain the proposal in its minutest characteristics. The order is to build a bridge across the water. Shouts, orders, the blood of the acrobats of construction and the blood of miners (the former fall from the heights of the scaffolding, the latter are buried under fallen rocks), the torrent of sweat of the laborers, the tears of orphans and of women lost in thought commingle in the crucible. The pounding on the forges of millions of hammer blows and the ricocheting stammer of drills piercing the iron can be heard. The machines that mix the gravel, cement, and water churn with their internal mechanisms in a constant rumble. The foremen shout until their throats are raw and they are nervous and hoarse. The workers make a forceful show of will and muscles with feverish determination, joining life and limb to the hard forms of the work plans. Workers who have collapsed receive their last paycheck, and they depart downcast, swearing. They curse their condition as numbers, as simple objects of industry, the inhuman coldness with which they are fired, the anguish of the uncertain days and the eternal pilgrimage in search of employment, always scarce, always . . . They are replaced by new men with great reserves of sweat and new blood, desperate to provide their own families with food and clothing. Their goal is to free them someday, perhaps, from the humiliation of hunger, ignorance and early death. Iron and cement give birth to struts and planes, to precise measurements and stout pillars. The gravel and cement flow over everything. The idea is a fountain of fire, the bridge is molded to the whim of thought. The army of workers continues to run about urgently, feverishly, like ants in an anthill. Finally a bridge appears like an arc across the water. Its extremities planted on two grounds are ports of communication. It is graceful, tall, and solid, with parallel railings to protect the pedestrians and automobiles. The current begins to flow. Seen from a distance the traffic might look like the continual flight of ships that cross, rise up, come down, land, and continue on their way, their destinations lying in opposite directions.

From the top of the miraculous bridge, Timoteo Noragua contemplates the enormous city. A ship, as big as an island, crosses beneath him, the bellow of its siren vibrating. A flotilla of airplanes roars in streaks across the sky. Suddenly the Indian turns to himself and asks, Who can have made this bridge and to whom does it belong? None could be grander or more beautiful. He saw that there were other people at his side who were looking at him out of curiosity. They were people with very white skin, clear eyes, and blond hair. Timoteo went up to them and demanded: Tell me, please, who built this bridge? The fair-haired people looked at each other and then answered: What'd you say? Huachusey . . . the Indian murmured with emotion. My God, what a great and intelligent man he must be. Huachusey. . . he murmured, smiling with secret pleasure.

So then, Don Teófilo, what happened then with the Sleeping Dove? Well, the death of the whores provided an excuse to seal the doors of the brothel. All of the inhabitants in the town demanded unanimously that the establishment be closed, especially since some young men, and others not so young and even married, had ended up getting their members infected with illnesses. The luckiest of them were spreading crabs all over the place. Do you mean us to understand, Don Teófilo, that those shameful illnesses were transmitted to their families? Yes, my friend, it reached such a point that innocent women were infected. I don't mean the whole population, but certainly a part of it. Don Lalo's right in saying that there are various histories for a town in addition to the one that is not told. So then, Don Lalo, there is nothing glorious in our history. Yes, son, there's a lot that is glorious. What can be more glorious than surviving this desert, with the unending sandpits on one side and on the other that half-moon of hills with its two erect peaks? You can see how the river is always dry unless there's a chance flood. Nevertheless, that's where all the occupants of the communal property that surrounds us live. Our people are good people, religious in their own way, respectful and brotherly when the occasion demands it. They know how to be happy and, all too often, how to be sad. What we retell here are the stories condemned to death, to complete oblivion, because I believe that we are afraid they will disappear. Can't you see we are very old and we would like to survive in people's memories? Besides, we old men who hang out in the plaza are young once again by being rebels. Let us speak nonsense, young fellow. It's all we've got left. Another question occurs to me. Why did Don Rumboso Noragua give up being mayor? Look, old Rumboso was mayor while the town was in bad shape, when taxes didn't amount to a hill of beans. As soon as the gold boom came, the guys on top got rid of him and brought in Captain Rastrillo from Tijuana. Order was less than a secondary consideration for Captain Rastrillo. What mattered to him was collecting taxes, and he got you just for breathing, as well as having fines for everything. Scandal for Captain Rastrillo was fine gold, but as they say around here, "machete blows from a jackass of spades." He got involved with the gringo girl over at the Golden Honeycomb, and his luck left him in the honeycomb. The coyotes on top were the winners. Rastrillo was nothing but a

poor errand boy, as is often the case. As for Colonel Rumboso
Noragua, the poor guy, he was all wrapped up in the affairs of his
family members because of that minor hereditary disease. One of his
sons, the one that was a simpleton and used to get the townspeople
all riled up when he rode down the middle of the street on the back
of his burro, took off and, it was rumored, ended up in the United
States. He was already quite a bit touched in the head when the
disease struck him. Ever since he was a child, he would talk to
himself, then to the burro, whom he baptized in the river and gave
the name Salomón. What was that crazy kid's name? Hell, it was
Timoteo. It's been about five years since he went away, and you've
forgotten already. Another son up and left on Don Rumboso too,
but he wasn't married. That's why he left, because he didn't have a
wife, although he was real young. What happened is that old Noragua caught him making out with a nanny goat. We're in 1987 now,
right? The one who was measuring the goat's tail to make himself a
belt left in 1980, and the other one went off as a wetback in 1982;
that's the way it was. After the job as mayor, Colonel Rumboso put
in a chicken farm with the money from the gold that Chano, his
other son, found. That was in the thirties; don't go getting me all
confused. It didn't go poorly for him, and he flooded Santa María de
las Piedras with eggs. Other foodstuffs were scarce from time to time,
but, on the other hand, there were always a lot of eggs on the
market. When he suffered the setback of all his chickens dying on
him, he sank into the worst sort of poverty. But he was saved by
something truly incredible: a golden egg. I'll tell you about that
later, but I feel tired right now. Then let Güero Paparruchas talk to
us for a while. Come on, Güero, what tale can you tell? These guys
won't let me talk, since they are older than I am. If we let you talk,
you'll never shut up. That's why we call you Humbug. Be quiet, Don
Nacho Sereno, or I'll tell Don Teófilo here to give you a serenade in
the face. Hah! You and who else—I can take care of the two of you
with one hand tied. What a pain you are! I'll go on with the days of
the gold rush. I was there and I saw things that you can't believe,
even if they are true. They call me Paparruchas, Hoaxer, because my
head is full and I have the memory of an elephant. Great, so go on
with the story, then.

The gold continued to flow, along with laughter and optimism;
tragedy did not follow far behind.

Telésforo, Aparicio, and Arnulfo had already spent more than ten days clawing at the hardest patch of ground. Old Murrieta was more of a hindrance than anything else, but he couldn't leave the boys alone after that terrible curse. If they ended up in the money, he'd be the first. Throughout their lives they hadn't known anything else but this poverty of an empty stomach and rags as clothes, of menial jobs more suited to animals, or being at the beck and call of masters. Let's get out of here, boys, I know what I'm saying. Come on, we haven't lost anything here. What are we looking for? Just tell me that, old Murrieta would ask, half naked, his face drawn from exhaustion and covered with dust. What do you mean, what are we looking for, Papa? We're looking for gold, remember? Either we'll find it or they'll bury us here. Since you're an old man, go ahead and get out, Papa, I'm serious. Papa, he's right, get on home. Your place isn't here and Mama must be real worried. They're right, Papa, go on and get some rest. You've already struggled against life long enough. Leave this madness to us. How can I leave you? Either we all leave together or they find us all dead here together. After fifteen days, the Murrietas were out of beans, and they were living on water alone. As for clothes, they only had the barest minimum to cover their shame, and not even enough for that. It had been a very long Wednesday when the Murrietas finally gave up. The old man just sat there, his eyes bleary and red. The white disheveled hair fell on his face. They looked like monkeys, naked, hungry, their bodies beaten with sweat and dust. Aparicio spoke to his father with a hoarse voice full of despair. We can't sacrifice you, Papa. You're worth more than all the gold in the world. We will leave for our hut in the afternoon, okay? Everybody nodded agreement with a bitter smile. Their discovery arrived just in time. They weren't chunks, but rather turtlelike rocks. Don Tano's scale weighed in a total of nine kilograms of gold with hardly any impurities. Suddenly the Murrietas didn't know what to do. They sat there thinking, locked in a world without words or ideas. How to get to the store and buy some clothes? Rather than ask for old man's loincloth, Aparicio and Arnulfo gave up their rags so Telésforo could more or less cover himself. That way he was able to go to the store and buy clothes for the four of them. He paid with a handful of gold. Despite the advantage for Don Tano of a scale that weighed a kilogram as 600 grams, Telésforo came back with more than a thousand pesos, in addition to having bought wheat tortillas, dried meat, sweet rolls, bread and soft drinks. Fortune sprang from the ground for the Murrietas. The old man got himself a small cabin, his life's dream for himself and Doña Chonita. Aparicio bought three wagons and a dozen mules to go into the firewood business, and he still had money left over. Arnulfo bought a herd and some land to till. Telésforo, on the other hand, acting like a jerk, announced that he was going to show the world what life was for: he became a real reprobate. At the Golden Honeycomb he assumed the rights of lord and master over one of the black girls, Nora, the one with long legs and aggressive buttocks. That's what the money is for. Bring me and anybody else who wants some more to drink, and tell the Pitolocos not to fall asleep on me. Play "The Black Woman" for me, and tell love to go to hell as long as I've still got sex! How I love this pig pee, which is why I drink it! Telésforo looked just like a three-ring circus. With music this way and that way, he was followed by a parade of spongers, who made him their king. Telésforo said, now you'll see. He strode into city hall, now all fancy with the large amount of tax money it was raking in. The new mayor, Captain Rastrillo, received him. What brings you here, boy? Have you paid your taxes? Five thousand pesos, Captain, sir, I guess you don't remember. Have you come to pay more? I've come, Captain, sir, to request your permission to flood Santa María de las Piedras's streets with beer. Your head's not screwed on right, boy. Look here, they tell me that you are acting crazy, tossing money all over the place. That's my pleasure, Captain Rastrillo, sir, and it's my money. Well, it's my desire, and get this straight, that if you do something stupid again, I'll toss you in jail. Who the hell ever heard of flooding the streets with beer? Jesus Christ. Telésforo walked out of city hall and went straight to the home of Piti Durán to hire him and his truck. Hey, don't be dumb, Telésforo, who ever heard of watering the streets with beer? You'd be better off giving this money to the poor, you fool. No, Piti, advice like that goes in one ear and out the other. If you don't want to help me, I'll just get Chigüegüenzon's truck, so just go ahead and be a horse's ass of a coward. I'll pay you 500 pesos, all you can drink and whatever you need for a whole night at the Golden Honeycomb. Well, that's different. We'll even use wine if you want. They had dumped about fifteen barrels of sixty liters each around the plaza and neighboring streets when the police arrived. That bit of fun cost the now famous Telésforo a fine of a thousand pesos and ten days in the clink. The aroma of beer filled the air, made its way into the houses, the church, and the school, and everybody had to hold his nose. What do you think it smells like? the old ladies on their way to say the rosary would ask, laughing right out loud. The maids acted happy, the old men in the plaza got their muster up, there were fights in the street, love trysts, and the unexpected noise of roosters crowing at the wrong time. Telésforo Murrieta blew his fortune in something like five months. You could see him wandering the streets in a thirst, desperate for a drink. He wandered around like a starving dog, scorned as a reprobate, and denounced by those for whom sarcasm is a profession. He certainly looked absurd, abandoned by the devil and strung out by his fate. The spongers he had supported now turned their backs on him and pretended not to know who he was, refusing to give him a cent and calling him a dumb-ass wastrel. He was left all alone, scorned by everybody, supporting himself by begging.

As one of the many ambulatory attractions that appeared in Santa María de las Piedras at that time, the Great Macaco arrived in town, preceded by his fame as the glory of Mexican boxing. By then the Great Macaco no longer could hold his own with the very best. His ears were two cauliflowers, and the blows received in that thankless profession had turned his nose into a red chile pepper and his lips were fleshy and loose; his eyes looked like money bags. Nevertheless his instinct as a boxer survived, and he could still hold his own. The news spread that a purse of one thousand pesos was being offered to a volunteer willing to do an exhibition match against the Great Macaco. The event was to take place on Saturday night. The ring was set up in a vacant field where the kids in the town played baseball. The townspeople were overjoyed when they learned the name of Macaco's opponent, none other than Telésforo Murrieta. By prior agreement the fight would only be a sparring match, to protect the health and bones of the challenger. The monster of a thousand tongues surrounded the ring ready to amuse itself with the fight. The incandescent naphthalene lamps placed on posts at each of the corners illuminated the spectacle as though it were midday. Animal hoots accompanied the Great Macaco into the ring. Then Telésforo appeared. There was a group of musicians hanging onto the ropes. Come on, Telésforo told them, play The Bull for me and get the one I'm going to fight all riled up. Just so there wouldn't be any doubt as to his fighting spirit, Telésforo went over to the great Macaco and shouted in his face: I'm going to beat the shit out of you, you damn creep. In reality, Macaco was on the punch-drunk side from so many blows received during his life as a professional boxer. As a result, he reacted like a mad dog. After the first bell that marked the beginning of the fight, Telésforo heard the ringing of a thousand bells, and he would go on hearing them for several days. People still talk about how the Great Macaco kept him on his feet in the middle of the ring just by punching him. He was in a real state for several weeks, dividing his time between binges in the cantinas and the brothels, getting by on this and that. The money from the fight didn't even last him overnight. Spongers and whores descended on him like flies, just to prove the old saying that man is the only animal who falls in the same hole twice. When he learned of the death of old Murrieta, he went right away to cry in his mother's lap. He found her starving to death. The old man had bought some fine cattle in the United States of the kind that eats special stable feed. The first drought wiped his spotted cows out. Telésforo assumed his role as a prudent peasant, and he devoted himself to work the land in a rudimentary fashion and to take care of his sainted mother. Fate has its own sense of humor. Doña Chonita's attacks got worse, and she was on the point of dying. Telésforo couldn't even afford to buy her an aspirin, and all he could give her was mint tea. She died one morning holding his hand, speaking a whole world to him with her face. Despair, sadness and remorse, on top of the blows of life and those he had received from Macaco, led the good-time boy to the worst of decisions: to take his life. Telésforo was unusual even in how he accomplished this task. He placed a stone more or less the size of his head under a very tall mesquite. Then he climbed up high in the tree. Nervous, agile, and clever like a monkey, he prepared himself to throw himself right on top of the rock. Here I go, papa and mama, he exclaimed, his face covered with tears. His aim was good, but all he accomplished was to crack his head. He climbed back up, now covered with blood streaming down his face and neck. This time he climbed higher, and even though he missed the mark, he accomplished what he set out to do. Thus ended the life of the man who watered the streets of Santa María de las Piedras with beer.

Güero, can we really believe what you have just told us? If you can't believe me, just go check the story out with my buddy, the dead Margarito. We were drinking companions while he was alive. Or my dead pal Chico Palito. They won't let me lie. Well, you just go and dig them up so they can back you up. No man, Don Nacho, don't be jealous. You remember the events. Yes, I do, and some of the men here do too, but they're no more than a handful. In fifty years, we're not about to forget Telésforo. Men, I'm the great nephew of Arnulfo Murrieta, and except for what Don Güero added, it's all true. Go ahead and tell me what I added. My uncle did not throw himself out of the mesquite tree twice. He broke his neck the first time. As for my great grandmother, she was not alone and forgotten. It is true that my uncle did a lot of stupid things. I'm not lying, fellows. My nickname is just a way of making fun of me, and I can swear what I'm telling you is true. The same goes for your having seen a cow fly by smiling. That too, and I can swear that my favorite dog, the one I left behind in Jiquilpan, in Michoacán, when I came looking for gold, came looking for me until he found me. I don't know how he knew where I ended up, but the fact is that one day I went into Santa Ana and just out of curiosity I happened to look in the train station at the same time the passenger train was arriving. The first thing I saw in one of the windows of the train was my dog, stretching his neck around looking for me. I leave him in charge of the house when I go out. Damned Güero, if it weren't that there are so few of us to get together and gossip in the plaza, we'd kick you out of the club for being such a liar. Maybe so, Don Teófilo, but your story about the revolutionary attack is just a pipe dream. Tell us, Don Teófilo, about when the federal troops entered Santa María de las Piedras. One thing at a time; we're talking about the thirties, there are still some other stories about the gold madness. Let's take it slow and in order.

On that occasion the river had not flowed once during the entire summer. As for clouds, the atmosphere would suck them up before they could even form. The place was a deathhouse of old women and nursing children. Birds fleeing the sky because of the heat would come to rest on a rock and their feet would fry. During those days, the name of the town was not Saint Mary of the Stones, but St. Mary of the Burning Coals. Snakes sought the shade and the cool of the houses. Some humans and animals ended up getting bitten. They would swell, get black spots all over them, and cry in pain. The rattlers that would come out to the surface by day because the ground was boiling hot whipped themselves against the stones and ended up scorched. Lizards brave enough to show their faces would scurry around a little bit and then would fall on their backs, kicking their legs. The eyes and the ears on the hares would grow big from thirst. The dogs ignored each other and crossed in front of each other, thinking of nothing but water. The wells barely yielded half-filled buckets of water, along with all the drowned toads and rattle snakes. All over the place you could hear the deafening sound of the grinding wheels of the handcarts. It sounded like a strange music and irritated the nerves. One thing was on everybody's mind: it won't rain; what will we do? And then a stranger appeared, dragging himself toward the houses, as black as a frying pan and drier than the dust that blows up from the desert. They gave him hot coffee to drink, and then they dampened him with towels and gave him small sips of water. He said that he had left two companions, still alive, five leagues back. Colonel Rumboso Noragua asked for volunteers to go rescue them, and Father Hilario seconded him. Since no one accepted, Colonel Rumboso Noragua asked if there were no men left in Santa María de las Piedras. An old pockmarked man spoke up in front of the whole group of mutes: the only man with balls around here is you, Colonel, so forget it. Then I'll go for them. I'll go with you, papa. Chano, you stay behind. I'm your son, and you're not going alone. Each with a gourd slung over his shoulder, they strode off in the direction indicated by the sun-struck man. It was somewhere between midday and sundown. It didn't take long for them to turn red, and their boiling blood hurt them as it oozed out of their pores. They continued into the desert without exchanging a word. Blisters appeared on their feet. They unsling their gourds and take a drink to clear their breathing. They make their way through the night and among the dunes. There is no growth, and they are surrounded by an ocean of sand. We're losing our way. Maybe they moved from where they were out of desperation. According to the directions, we've passed the place. Let's go back, Chano, you to the left and I to the right. We'll curve around. First they found the guy about twenty years old. The other, neither young nor old, they found later. They had them drink from the gourds, and they put damp handkerchiefs on their heads. They helped them get halfway to their feet and slung them across their backs. They would go a little way and then take a breather sitting down. Twice they fell asleep. The two sunstroke victims were like loose bags of cotton. When Mr. Chronos had already danced his way beyond ten o'clock the next day, they reached the church in Santa María de las Piedras. The oven was already red hot. The stones began to smoke. The cicadas, like good cicadas, were chirping away with a song so high-pitched that it made the air tremble. The expectant townspeople were stunned by the incredible scene before them. Chano let the young man, still unconscious, down from his shoulders. This one will live, thank God. May He hear you, Father Hilario. My God, how heavy the dead are, Don Rumboso observed, and let his burden drop. He died on me about an hour ago. I knew he had because he started to weigh twice as much. Among the people standing around was Birriondo Arce, who had been in the oven the day before, feeling a little better. Don Rumboso looked him in the eye, then looked toward the desert that was a mirror of shimmering flames. Are you sure there were only two? If not, we'll go back for however many there are. Right, son? Birriondo just smiled and shook his head to say no. The Noraguas reached their home and went over to the well. They smiled as they looked at the water in the bottom. Then they stretched out to sleep under a mesquite tree where the chickens sleep and the little girls' swings are. The girls brought water and took their shoes off. Their feet were bloody and they bandaged them. A few hours later when the sun was completing its daily tightrope performance, they got up to have a drink. When dawn came, they were still drinking. And they looked at each other's faces again under the sun.

Well, speaking of sunstrokes, I gave myself up for dead one day. A whole day walking through the desert with no water, although I did have a saddlebag full of gold. I didn't have a drop of water left in my body. You know what, Güero Paparruchas, you'd be better off not telling the story. All you have to do is look at your eyes to see you're making it up. Let him tell his story, Nacho. If he's lying we can beat him up between all of us. Isn't that true, Lalo? Fine. Well, there I was stumbling along. Ah, sweet mother, I thought, I'm stuck here for good. I collapsed very near my house. I could see my old lady standing outside, and I yelled to her, but all I could get out was a squeak. For a moment I went blind. With the last twitches of my hand, I touched something strange. It feels like a very thick trunk. Damn, but it feels frozen. I felt the end of it, wrapping my fingers around it. What is this? A small tube, a knob. I turn it and the jet comes out and I hang on. Friend, it was a barrel of iced beer. I got my strength back and I got back home happy and singing. What's so strange about it is that my gold vanished like magic. Now tell me, you old liar, who left that barrel of beer there? I'm no detective, Don Nacho, and much less a fortuneteller, so I can't say. The fact that I'm telling you the story should be enough for you to believe it's true. You don't mistrust my word, by any chance? Get out of here, you old cynic, before I beat the shit out of you with my cane. Don Nacho, don't estimate other people any less than you estimate yourself. You'll believe me even less if I tell you that another time when the sun got to me, I sent my dog for water and not only did he bring it to me in a cool bottle, but he also brought tortillas with meat and a box of cigars. Whatever will the devil do with your tongue, Güero? You guys are not going to get into heaven because you refuse to believe. I'm going to leave. I'm real hurt you won't believe anything I say. Besides, I've got to take care of burying some sorrel mares I got messed up with last night. A scare led me directly to where that money was. Get off, Güero, get off! When you come back, tell us you're sorry. See you tomorrow, then. Goodbye. Hoaxer. How skinny that Güero has gotten. Is he sick? He's always been sick. Something's not right with him. Maybe it's his age, although he's not as old as we are. We're about the same with our aches and pains. But that Güero never runs out of stories. He can always think of one more . . . It's getting late, fellows, it's getting late. My great-grandsons are coming for me, so I'll see you tomorrow. Good luck, Lalo. Lalo is also getting shakier and more pensive every day. Well, there's nothing you can do about it. They were born to die, but we were born to marry.

Timoteo continued to examine closely where he was going, more intrigued each day by the existence of a marvelous being capable of everything. Each grandiose thing he saw was always associated with the same name spoken by scattered voices, in whispers, in an open shout, Huachusey! The maker of ships, trains, skyscrapers—Huachusey! A sovereign of iron, of mechanical toys, of canned food, the movies, joy, abundance, lord of all gifts. It was no longer enough to find beauty, the fantastic things that he had intuited in the past, but he had to see the extraordinary man face to face, this god on Earth. Filled with so many and such unusual experiences, he began to meditate. Without realizing it, he lost himself in another quest, in a world even more mysterious than the one trodden by his feet.

Thus, by chance, traversing the Earth with his curiosity, one day he came to a forest of thick, colossal trees. It was surprising how many steps you had to take to walk around those things. There among fountains and lakes, surrounded by green hills, in the company of bears, birds, deer and other strange animals, Timoteo Noragua rested in the company of his thoughts and strange dreams. Meanwhile, the burro enjoyed himself to the fullest in that paradise, with the most savory and abundant of grass available and the clearest and most refreshing of waters. An ideal place to relax.

The rustic mentality of the peasant became lost in thought, soft like the feather of a dove borne along by the dreams that carried him ever higher toward the mystery. An unknown language, the archaic key of his ancestors, began to give shape to multiple constellations from which his ideas sprang forth. A particularly brilliant one, that of God as an hourglass with no narrowing in the middle and flowing from one end to the other. A god transformed into man? A man transformed into a god? Who is this Huachusey who has the power to do whatever he proposes? His innocence, humility, faith and love, in addition to an intimate longing, made him believe in an earthly god, incarnate in a physical presence. Undoubtedly he was to be found residing in a place in the world trodden by Timoteo and his burro. He would seek him in every corner of the Earth, beneath the plants, in every house, in caves, even in cemeteries, if need be. Tireless, diligent, he would speak with him. But, why did he want to see him? What would he ask from him? The gift of immortality?

Power and wealth? Aid for the weak? Justice for the humble and scorned, the downtrodden, the victimized? With the help of Huachusey he could take control of all wealth, while at the same time counting on powerful armies to defend its rightful owners.

He would possess power through Huachusey's miraculous concession and use for the punishment of the prideful who kill with the sword and hunger and through air attacks, out of their desire to dominate. Perhaps he wanted to find him in order to commend his soul to God in the final instant of his life. The clarity of a fountain sparkled, as though disturbed by a small fish, the concentric circles identical to the furrows of his own brow. A tenuous melancholy was swept away by the flowering of a smile. Locked in the depths of his being could be found the story of his race, the throng of his ancestors linked by bloody feuds, the war against plagues, the frustrations provoked by the systematic injustice of the mighty, the threat of nuclear war one could feel in the air, and the fear that travels in the genes for millennia. His glowing eyes betrayed his obsessive determination: to find the God on Earth and to speak with him. Timoteo Noragua wanders among the gigantic trees, his soul oppressed, looking like a hermit ignorant of material things. He seeks his spirit with the powerful intuition that inhabits his body like a caged bird.

Dream on, Timoteo Noragua, dream the dream of the simple at heart. No, you do not know me nor do I believe that you will ever come to know me. I live in the heart of every being. There is nothing I do not know, and I know everything from centuries and centuries of experience. I travel in the blood from one generation to the next, I am a passenger in the genes, I am experience and knowledge. From the depths of my prison, I shout out but rarely am I heard. I appear in the dreams that appear in fleeting moments of your age. No, you would not recognize me, nor do you feel, nor are you likely to know what I am thinking. Bah! What does it matter in the end? But take care, because you wound me. Besides, you in particular have closed all the doors in my face. You do not even allow me to appear in your dreams. Well, sometimes you feel my fleeting presence, but you put me aside. Nevertheless, you will see how I destroy the stones and the chains with which you imprison me. Then you will learn a truth that perhaps you should never know. You want to know who Huachusey is. Right? I pity the day, Timoteo Noragua, when you find out. If you continue at this time with your quest day and night and in every place, you will find him, believe me. There is nothing to be done. You are a fool. Your fool's face suits you fine. You're dreaming away with pure ecstasy. You've entered the realm of stupidity surrounded by a string of dumb ideas; you're thrilled with your idiocy. Now you're dreaming about that fictional being who grows and grows in your absurd mind. Huachusey! Who ever heard of such a crazy idea! Who ever heard of such a monumental fairy tale? Your blind idolatry is so big you can't even imagine a face for him. Only hands in the middle of clouds? Glowing lights? Maybe you're wrapping him in divine light now. Can't you see how ridiculous you look squatting on your burro, waving your hands about? I hear you. You're asking him as though it were nothing to burst the walls of a dam as large as your foolish imagination. According to you, it's filled with milk. I can hardly believe it. You're telling him, you big dope, to make the milk flow like the rivers. I hope you're happy so long as you're dreaming. You ride that horrible animal that's nothing but a scrawny skeleton worth more as a harp or at the very least as a drum. Now you're standing by the shore of the river, hopeful, looking at how the milk fills the riverbed, caressing the edges with its foam. You turn around, cupping your hands. You're calling all the hungry to come and drink their fill. What a picture you're painting for me! They all come rushing on hands and feet as though they were paws. They have hairy faces. Their hair is long, and they look more like beasts than human beings. Ah! Now you're calling all hungry children. Look at them. They come in droves. Their arms are squalid, their bones are rickety, their legs are like skeletons, their stomachs are puffed up. Their faces are wrinkled by their suffering and they look like old, senile, ugly dwarves. You position them to drink, their necks stretched forward. If you had a shred of sense in your crazy head, you'd understand that they would explode from drinking that much. You've put them to sleep. They need so much to rest. Wait, I can hear some pretty background music, angels singing in unison. Come on, man! Is that the music of the heavens, the divine music broadcast by the stars? Look at the faces of those children. They are starting to turn attractive and they look like the children of the rich. I'm beginning to like your imagination. Those strong types must surely be workers. They approach silently, their shoulders weighted down. They walk heavily, their humanity drained on more than one occasion of illusions, sweat, and blood. They smell of tobacco, cheap liquor, clothes rotting with sweat and shit. Listen, these don't look like workers from a developed country. I can already see their faces like tame oxen, tired, always wearing their fatigue like an iron encasement. They struggle day by day against poverty; when they can, they gobble down anything at hand like horses in order to replenish so much lost energy. They get drunk and go mad for hours in the very routine that enslaves them. You make them drink with their cupped hands. Is there anything they don't do with their hands? They are sitting there thinking, thinking about survival, with feverish, absent eyes. There's no way to blame you. They're always thinking about that. Hold on a moment . . . Yes, it's a crowd. They're coming at a gallop. It's a legion of worn-out old women, skinny, dirty, smelly, their hair all over the place. I can see how they're being pursued by that troop of screaming children, fighting over scrawny, distended, empty breasts. Those children look like piranha fish, avid, pulling at the teats, biting them. The women strike them on the mouth; breasts and lips turn red, swell up, but now they've caught up. Am I exaggerating? Those women have sunken eyes, pallid lips, the despair of caged beasts in their faces. And how they shout! They sound like frogs gone crazy. They are workers, slave mothers, marionettes of misery. Now they've gotten here, and they stretch out to drink the milk from your stupid imaginary river. They drink slowly and softly. All hungry mankind drinks and drinks from the nipples of mother nature. The picture changes quickly! No, they are beautiful women you're dreaming about! What poetic expressions! They rock the children, crooning to them. You are making me feel tender. Now you're making me laugh. Along the marshy banks of your river there is a bunch of fruit trees. How jubilant your formerly hungry people are! You have built a paradise in your dream. How beautiful your dream is, Timoteo. You have achieved everything gently, without violence, with your good will and your prayers. There is no room there for ill will, only for nobility. All the people you have redeemed are persons of good will, and therefore they are all happy. I can see in your multitude no one who is either bloodthirsty or demagogic, none of those fierce types who devote themselves to fighting for the downtrodden. You have taken care of everything in your dream. Ah! But your utopia is worth nothing if you cannot find him, find Huachusey. Only he, with the strength of the universe he inhabits, could provide happiness, love, peace. Seek him out, Timoteo Noragua, seek him, I assure you that you will find him, but first let me laugh, hah, hah, hah, hah.

Timoteo Noragua had been awake since dawn. Salomón seemed happy all stretched out, his thirst slaked and his hunger placated. The Indian's dreams, like the backdrop of a secret realm, vanished together with the shadows. The animal, on the other hand, looked like he was sleeping. Both lie beneath the shelter of ancient trees, tall and thick as mountains. The very branches of these giants of sap were like trees. The grew straight out, attached to the vertical growth of the collossal trunks. The dawn dusted the tops with glints of purple; the sun split into luminous sheaves. From the height of the clouds, the forest looked like a riot of gold and emeralds. The song of the birds, the rustling of the air through the branches, and the melodious bubbling of the fountains all combined to proclaim the beauty and vitality of nature. Timoteo's hunting instinct had provided him with food, and he roasted a deer on the coals while Salomón chewed over heavy mouthfuls of green, tasty grass.

Thus, in this way, when the Indian and his mount had left behind the ancient grove, they continued on their way through beautiful regions caressed by a gentle spring breeze. It was neither the fire that burns nor the cold that stabs. All they could see around them in the green of the forests, the mountains, and the plains was a gentle setting with laughter, happy sounds, and the chattering of squirrels and wild animals pampered by the heavens. The surfaces are crisscrossed by the lines of the rivers and dotted by lakes. Would he live in the country? On the edge of a lake, on the top of a mountain, in the heart of the forest, perhaps. His figure would certainly be that of an old bearded patriarch, with flowing hair the color of silver, erect, firm, with a staff in his right hand as the sole symbol of his supreme authority. His tunic white like the smile of the innocents, he would wear sandals. What would his home be like? Beautiful like integrity and justice, whose forces are those of balance and harmony.

Here in Santa María de las Piedras, Salomón, the sun has the doors of the sky wide open and nothing can stop it from coming in. If you look at it straight in the face, it will strike you down and blind you. But if you want you can see it in every one of the stones around us. Do not touch them now because they glow and will burn you. It's been many days since it rained here, and columns of fire even flow down the rivers. Now that day is divided in two and everybody takes a nap to escape an atmosphere of shooting flames, you and I will split Santa María de las Piedras in two. My huaraches on the flagstones silence my footfalls, but your hooves certainly set the stones to ringing. I know they tell you their secrets and that you tell them to be quiet because you're loyal and discreet. The houses have thick, high walls, and the parapets on top look like wings. In the middle there are patios shaded by vines. Look at the walls of the church. They are the same color as the look on the faces of the old men and the breath of the sun as it licks them with its dry breath. Now you and I lose ourselves in the distance of the plain that vibrates with the cicadas begging for water. There are millions of keeners, for nature is thirsty. The distances and the seas are blue. Blue is the color of the water. Come on, Salomón, we are reaching the horizon. Can you see how blue it is, waiting for us?

You know what I'm thinking about, gentlemen. How can we know if you don't tell us, Nacho? We're not mind readers. The burro always goes back to the wheat. You sure like to bug people, Teófilo, and you're not happy unless you're making trouble. Tell us what you're remembering, but if we don't like the story, we'll kick you right out of here for being such a simpleton. Then I'll just wait for you to go to sleep, you old fool. It won't take you long to start snoring. But I still listen, one ear to the ground and the other all over the place. You remember, Don Lalo, that dopey type who never took the pipe from his mouth and used his tie to dig. Yes, yes, Julito de la Flor, the one who came for wool and left naked. Rather than calling himself Julito he should have been named Agapito. Why that, Güero Paparruchas? I'll tell you why after Don Nachito has had a chance to talk. But like they say, if you work too hard the others will hang around your woman. And was Lucía Potosí ever beautiful, friend; what a doll! Let's hear it, Don Nacho.

Jorge Julito de la Flor was one of a lot of pilgrims who came looking for an easy fortune. He arrived in Santa María de las Piedras convinced that he was the most deserving. According to him, riches were waiting for him with open arms. He was brought up first by his grandmother, then by his mothers and some aunts who spoiled him rotten. In addition to whatever he needed, he could have for his pleasure whatever he wanted. Jorge Julito was young and very handsome, with a delicate presence and soft manners. Since he was from Hermosillo, the capital, he felt like a Parisian aristocrat among the lowly fortune hunters, and he often was deliberately outrageous. In order to look wise and superior, he always carried a set of pipes with him. If he happened to be with a group of people or at a social event, he would stick a pipe in his mouth, standing there in profile, hermetic, like he was Socrates. He pretended he was a historian, but in truth all he ever published were rehashes. He was a refined ass-licker of people in positions of authority. They repaid the favor with jobs related to culture with highfalutin names. The sad truth is that this pseudointellectual was as dumb as his backers. Everybody took it for granted he was a pansy. Nevertheless, about the time he turned sixteen his masculine hormones intensified considerably. His nature revealed a virility that demanded attention. No sooner said than done, his charms led him to Lucía Potosí. Lucía was the sun in a

99

feminine version—splendid, with more fire than a stove burning ironwood. Jorge Julito, now getting close to twenty-five, swooned over Lucía. Not even Saint Anthony could have helped him land her if his aunts hadn't gone to work on his behalf. They caught Lucía red-handed at just the right moment and married her off to Jorge Julito de la Flor. Everything was coming up roses for the middle-class couple, and with their income they were able to support a certain degree of comfort, although they envied the fortune of other people. They heard about the people who had gotten fabulously rich overnight in Santa María de las Piedras, and the phony historian was moved by ambition to emulate the leading men in the movies. So he decided to set out on an adventure, to Lucía's joy, for she was a dreamer ready for any new experience. Jorge Julito looked like a doll dressed up as a cowboy, with Lucía at his side like a camp follower in the middle of the tumult of mining prospectors. Within a few days their dreamy smiles turned bitter. Wherever they struck their pick they found plain, common dirt. It was all useless: the gold was hiding from them. They could not understand why others, in their tattered clothes, illiterate, ignorant of the pious practice of prayer, vulgar and dirty men who never made the sign of the cross, from low-class families, sinful and even criminal types, ended up with their pockets overflowing with the precious metal. It was decidedly unfair, since they were clean, refined, beautiful people with political influence. An Indian named Cachipachi was working right alongside them, and right from the start he was lucky. Wherever Cachipachi struck his pick he found gold. Lucía looked at him with hate in her eyes because he was uncouth and a dark-skinned Indian. Cachipachi went barefoot and he wore a short pair of rough cotton pants and no shirt. He was a young man of about twenty, tall, skinny, leathery, with stiff movements and small eyes that bored into you, and he was silent, as sparse with words as an anthill is lacking in plants. Despite the disdain the Indian inspired in them, they would watch him intently. Lucía was offended by having to see the Indian so unclothed and indecent. His parts that should have been kept hidden could easily be seen to be voluminous. And the worst part was they would stick out! What a shameless, savage, unworthy Indian. Cachipachi stopped looking for gold when he discovered that it had run out. Later he devoted himself to roaming the streets of Santa María de las Piedras. He went about with a knapsack on his shoulder in which he stored a large quantity of money and gold nuggets. Jorge Julito barely got a chance to touch any gold. Lucía, exhausted by the heat, the treading about, and more than anything else by her frustration, decided to remain in the hut they were living in. One morning as hot as a chunk of sun, well past nine o'clock on that Tuesday in the month of July, Cachipachi appeared in the doorway, which upset Lucía. The ugly Indian, in her words, looked even taller against the doorway. He was trembling slightly, and his nostrils were dilated by his heavy breathing. You could see by his eyes that he was hungry. He had smelled the female from a distance. Lucía was wearing a short nightie. She covered herself immediately, putting both hands over her pubis. A stiffling sensuality floated in the air. It grew painful and urgent. The Indian stood there entranced for a few seconds, fixing her with his gaze. He put his hand in the bag in which he carried his fortune, took out a few nuggets of gold as big as strawberries and held them out to the girl wearing the transparent nightie. Come on in, she said to him, stretching out both her hands. He put a strawberry in each of her hands. The girl turned away for a second and undid a button that left more than just the beginning of her breasts showing. Both of her nipples struggled to free themselves like pigeons taking flight. Cachipachi opened his knapsack and showed the restless girl all he was carrying in it. Cachipachi looked like a bronzed stag, lively and young. Her cheeks turned red, the nightie fell to her ankles, her breasts free, his member in flames. Like the power of a magnet their two bodies come together in a ready and violent thrust. It was not the diligence of gold that spread Lucía's legs, but the torrential urgency of her nature. Jorge Julito, obsessed with becoming a millionaire, had no energy for anything expect his pick and shovel. Meanwhile, his wife smoldered in a jungle of fantasies. Jorge Julito de la Flor lost one treasure without ever finding the one he sought. The Indian was only a pretext for Lucía to overflow. Later when the fleeting fortune of Santa María de las Piedras declined, the aristocratic nymph took off for Tijuana with Zenona. The madam opened a posh brothel there. Jorge Julito also gave himself over to the licentious life with vengeance, and he had women all over the place. Nevertheless, he ended up a melancholic poet, writing verses and composing songs that nobody paid any attention to. As pieces of art they were worthless, little more than the draining of his wounds. In Santa María de las Piedras he not only lost Lucía, but also his arrogance and a set of pipes. It was learned years later that Lucía Potosí was taken away from the brothel by a gringo twice her age. He took her to Los Angeles, where she got fatter and fatter watching soap operas and eating potato chips.

Well, Flor ended up the same way as Agapito. What Agapito, Güero? No one by that name has ever lived around here. But I've heard about him, don't tell me I haven't. Yes, it's said that that Agapito had real bad luck. How does it go, Paparruchas? Tell us, but don't drag it out because you'll keep us all there until midnight.

Agapito isn't from around here, nor does he even belong to this generation. But Lencho Morela came from Tepic to this town. Lencho himself knew how to laugh at his rotten luck. Many years later after Santa María de las Piedras's bit of good fortune, people used to refer to anybody with rotten luck as having the bad luck of Agapito. "He's lucky like Agapito," they would say with reference to some poor devil. Lencho Molera told us about Agapito when he went back to Tepic without a penny, dying of hunger, with a suit of clothes with more holes in it than a piece of Swiss cheese, and barefoot. Lencho, like a lot of other wretches, saw good luck turn its back on him. All he ever found in Santa María de las Piedras during the gold rush was a lot of sweat; his prayers were in vain and he often swore like the worst. But he was jovial and a good conversationalist who inspired sympathy. The only time he found the gold that would have allowed him to dress decently and to show up in his hometown with some money, he was robbed and left without even enough money to buy breakfast. And they beat him like a dog. Lencho's memory survived as a popular story that he would tell visitors when he was recovering from the beating at the hands of the thieves. I'm going back to Tepic because I'm as unlucky as Agapito. Who is Agapito, Lencho?

Agapito was a poor devil, the subject of a powerful king. He lived on his meager earnings as a carpenter, although he was a musician held in high esteem. One day the king went on a binge. Accompanied by his closest retainers he kicked it up with the best wine and food, his favorite woman at his side and three more concubines just in case. I want music right away! To satisfy the king's demands, they hired a drummer, a violinist and a guitar player. They asked Agapito to entertain the king with his flute. He accepted unwillingly because he had never gotten anything good out of being a musician, except for his poverty and some kicks in the pants from unruly drunks. After three days of bacchanal, the king ordered the

102

musicians to be rewarded. I hereby order each instrument to be filled with gold coins! The drummer needed help in carrying his fortune. The violinist and the guitarist both ended up rich. But Agapito's flute would not hold a single coin. Agapito swore once again that he would never play his flute for money, and he even forbade his family and friends to mention the word flute. You never know what life will bring. Two years later it happened again: the king went on a toot and called for music. No. Why should I go? Agapito said. I'm better off sticking to my carpentry, which is what puts food in my family's mouths. Except for that, luck only spits on me. But they begged him and promised him a different reward, one better for him. Agapito accepted in a bad mood, and set out tuning his flute. The party was even better than the last one. Kegs of wine were drunk, the food was outstanding, and gorgeous girls were much in evidence. After three days of partying, the king exclaimed: now I'm going to reward the musicians. Guards, I, the king, order that you shove each musician's instrument up his ass. The drummer's would not fit, nor would the violinist's, nor the guitarist's. On the other hand, they did such a good job with Agapito's instrument that even the last key disappeared from sight. That's why in Santa María de las Piedras when someone has a streak of bad luck, people say that he's as lucky as Agapito.

I know you're going to find things wrong with the story I've just told you, but it's true. Don't look at me like that; I'm not lying. Güero, we'll let you off on this business about Lencho Molera because we do remember the boy. You've made up the whole bit about Agapito, but maybe there is some connection, anyhow. There's a thousand stories about the days of placer gold in this town, and each is as incredible as the last. It's hard to imagine how crazy people can get when they find themselves up against a strange circumstance. What are you talking about, Teófilo, are you going to give Güero a run for his money with a tall tale? You're snoring while you're listening to everything, Nacho Sereno. What an old liar you are! Well, let's hear it, because I'll ride herd on your memory, so come on. You must remember Lupercito, the kid about eight years old who wasted a whole fortune in cantinas and whorehouses? A child, yes sir, only eight years old. There's no question that the boy spent thousands of pesos on drink, but don't get carried away, Teófilo, because he never got mixed up with a whore. Well, just for your information, Nacho, I was in the Golden Honeycomb when he went into a room with Santa. No, if it was Santa, that was in the church, where the kid must have been saying his prayers. What do you mean, saying his prayers, Nacho? Why even you were a client of Santa's. Go on, talk bad about me. Santa was that dark girl with very mystical eyes. She was from Sinaloa and was very, very serious, like a statue. Now I remember, Teófilo, you were going to get blessed with her. Come off it. We found out he was involved with Santa because one night the two of them came out of her room real mad. She threw his shoes after him, furious. The kid—listen to this— eight years old, ran by like the devil into the street. Otherwise, Santa would have killed him. What set Santa off, Don Teófilo? Was she jealous, or did the little pocket-sized pimp refuse to pay for her services? You're laughing and looking at each other, I know, thinking this is all a lie. Well, now that I remember, I won't tell you a thing, just so you'll learn not to doubt an honest old man. Yes, yes, Don Teófilo, we believe you, tell us about Lupercito. Please, Don Teofilito. Well, give me room.

One morning, after many days of his journey, when Timoteo was coming down from the mountains, he suddenly came upon an immense valley covered with fruit trees, vineyards, and other plants that produced an unendingly abundant harvest. Thousands of men worked in this valley gathering exquisite fruits to delight the palates of millions. Such harvests would be the basis of the food industry and would generate fabulous profits. Men, women, and children of all ages were filling baskets with grapes. Other fields yielded in other seasons enormous shipments of oranges, peaches, and so many other fruits. The workers labored with nervous agility, their faces drawn by exhaustion. Men who watched over the workers were distributed at points the length and breadth of the vast fields. They never moved and were always rigid, watching, inspiring fear, spurring them on to work harder, frozen in place like pillars of solid glass, hard, like cement and iron. The guards were blond with clear blue eyes. The harvesters would glance at them apprehensively out of the corners of their eyes. Not only did they inspire respect, but deaf terror ingrained in the harvesters' minds pinched their nerves. The faces of the unmoving men, like pillars of glass, bore traces of extreme hardness. They looked on with hatred, disdain and the threat of death in their eyes. Timoteo Noragua went up to one of them and asked him who the lord and master was of such a rich farm. The guard neither answered nor even seemed to notice him. Then Timoteo went up to the laborers. They laughed openly to see the burro and his ridiculous-looking rider. What a sight! The workers were Indians and mestizos like his own people. One of them spoke, while at the same time he gestured constantly. Heh, fellow, what's up? You look like a piñata. Say, are you looking for work, brother? Are you on vacation? Fellows, what are you doing here? Who's your boss? Ursula! Take a look at this guy. You know what, mister? These guys are really on their last legs, brother. Don't you know that all this belongs to the gringos? We work our butts off, and they pay us just enough to keep us from dying of hunger. We work for him from dawn to dusk, and we are still as poor as lizards. We go from one place to another, and the kids never get any schooling, and on top of it, they put them to work too. It's hell. We live in hovels while the gringos rule the roost with their lovely homes, soft clothes and cars you wouldn't believe. Excuse me, mister, I was only asking you who the boss is, the owner of all this land.

An ancient toothless woman with a very wrinkled small face, dark, all stooped over and bowlegged, answered Timoteo in a thin voice. The Indian felt sorry to see the sunken, watery eyes of the old woman. I, sir, came from Michoacán when I was a girl. My husband, who is already with the Lord, was from Sinaloa. That's my grandson you were talking to. He was telling you that we work for the Americans. We break our backs working from daybreak to sunset and things never get any better. They pay us very little, just enough for us to get by. My grandson was saying that we are always on the road, from one place to another. The children hardly get any schooling and all they do is work. He also told you that we live in very humble houses and that they, the Americans, have a lot of money, pretty houses, new cars, great food. You see, sir, our children hardly speak Spanish. Their speech must sound funny to you. We came to the U.S. because things were even worse there—no money, no work, no hope. My old man was a revolutionary. He was with General Obregón and he made the rank of lieutenant. His superiors got very rich, but nobody remembered him. When he asked them for a job, the best they and Obregón would do was to hire him as a laborer on their huge estates. He was so disillusioned to see himself in such poverty that he said to me, it's better we leave, woman, and go work for the gringos. He died dreaming about his village, my sweet old man, always dreaming about returning to his country. Ah, how he loved Mexico! Who are you and where are you going, sir? You even look like you're from my village. By the time the old lady had wound down, there was a large number of people standing around Timoteo. They listened in surprise, with smirks on their faces, to what he had to say. Just listen, ladies and gentlemen, to what I'm going to tell you: I have come from roaming the countryside and the cities in search of Huachusey. And who is this fellow? Huachusey is a god! For your information, he lives in this country. He is the one who has made ships that fly. He has put boats in the sea. He has built entire skyscraper cities, and you should see the bridges. Are you aware of all this? You know what, brother? Your head's screwed on loose and your gears are a bit stripped. What are you saying, sir? That you're crazy. The only Huachusey around here is the burro you're riding. I will find him, I will find him. I will speak with him, and I will beg him to help you and all the poor of the Earth. He's a mighty miracle worker. Everybody was laughing at Timoteo and his jokes, but he was looking at them innocently.

The peasants felt a jabbing sensation in their necks, and they noticed that the looks of the guards, standing there like pillars of electrified glass, were focused on them, hard and penetrating. With nervous haste they went back to work. An old man with a limp shook his head, smiling. You can't believe how crazy some people are . . . Huachusey, Huachusey, where the devil can he have gotten such ideas?

Salomón disappeared in the distance, Timoteo on his back.

Faith destroys the impossible and overcomes barriers. Later, when Timoteo found Huachusey, he was dumbfounded: it was as though he had known him always, even though he had never met him before.

Desperate, anxious, feverish, Timoteo gave himself over to finding the mysterious being who left his mark on everything that was grandiose. His burning eyes were fixed on one goal, a basic compelling obsession: to find God somewhere on the planet and to speak with him. The burro carried him along, and he seemed to be possessed by the same desire. This animal, who had once been so strong-willed, became the humblest of animals since that day long ago when his back carried the beloved man of justice in this glory of palms and laurels, with his forehead bearing the tragic epilogue of purple drops and the cruel flashes of red shrouding his body. Was it possible that Noragua's little burro had an instinctive memory, an atavistic recollection of the honored back that served as the throne of the sacred rider? In truth there was no great difference between Timoteo and the ass, as the two of them were both good and guileless.

The forests, mountains, rivers, lakes and farmlands gave way to populated areas. First, paved roads, lights in the distance and lanes going in both directions filled with fast, noisy, racing, souped-up cars. Then the teeming city and its outlines, filled with gas and smoke.

Timoteo was now on the outskirts of a monstrous city, traversing elegant suburbs and wandering through poor neighborhoods. He went up to the people he met like a beggar or he knocked on doors in order to inquire of poor and rich alike or the unemployed bum as to how he might find him and tell him about his faith, his love and his desires. All he got were blank stares, men who shrugged their shoulders or shook their heads with indulgent smiles when they weren't scornful, mocking, indifferent. Nothing, nothing, nothing that could guide him, until the time he came across people of his same origin and condition. That day, a pilgrim on his mission, he came to a very poor neighborhood. You could smell hunger there. The people's bitter faces were scarred by their many cares and that attitude of submission combined with a hard, distrustful look with which the poor realize how they have served as the fodder of war and industry. He knocked on the door of a dirty wooden, fallen-down hovel. A young girl answered, and she called her mother. Two children and the grandmother also appeared. He looked with great surprise at that living pastoral image: an Indian with rough cotton clothes standing next to a starving little burro with sad eyes whose enormous exhaustion was more than eloquent. With his hat in his hand, his manner humble, the Indian spoke in the same language as those who listened to him. For the love of God, I beg you to tell me where a very famous man lives who has a lot of rich and great property. He makes bridges on the water, just imagine, tall houses that reach to the stars, and boats like floating cities and others that fly. Oh, sir, I live shut up here with my grandchildren and my daughter-in-law. My son is at work over at the factory right now. What is the name of the man you are looking for? Ah, the whole world knows him and everybody speaks his name. He's Huachusey. Modesta, do you think that's the name of your son's boss, the Huachusey that this man is talking about? I don't rightly recall . . . Huachusey . . . Huachusey, that name sure sounds familiar to me. But I can tell you that they call the foreman Bulldog, but maybe that Huachusey is the owner of the whole place, because my old man says that the boss's got all the things you mentioned: tall buildings and airplanes, and who knows what all else. Seems to me that he must be the one. What did you say the name of the man you're looking for is? His name is Huachusey, ma'am; he is like a god on Earth. Well, who knows, my husband says he's a real bastard who works them to death and pays them nothing, see, and then runs them off when they're too weak and useless to work anymore. Do you want him to give you a job, mister? He must be a good boss. If you can, try to get my old man in, so he can work for Mr. Huachusey. Huachusey, ma'am, is a very good man and very powerful, and he can do the grandest things. I'm seeking him to speak with him, I need to see him. I think I know where Mr. Huachusey lives. You're only nine years old, my son, how can you know if you don't work or go outside? He came to my school, mama, two days ago. He pulled doves and rabbits from an empty hat, then he put his hand in my pants pocket and took out handfuls of money, and I didn't have a cent on me. Now that I remember, they had us all go to an auditorium and the teacher called out: boys and girls, this is the great Huachusey. And, mama, he made things disappear and then he would take them out of the kids' ears. He performed miracles, Mama. Mr. Huachusey is a boss; he's a man who does miracles. Yes, yes, yes, that's Huachusey, child, that's him. Tell me where he lives, in which direction. Tell him, my son, tell the man where Mr. Huachusey lives. Over there, a long way over there. That's where I'll go look for him, then.

The stones reflected with an intense brilliance the force of a sun that in its trajectory split the sky in two, like an ax of fire. A dozen workers were tilling the earth behind horses bathed in sweat as they dragged on Egyptian plows with metal tips and wooden handles. You could hear the rattle of the teams' chains and the crunch of the clods of dirt breaking up. Zanates and crows circled around close to the ground, descending to eat the worms turned up with the recently tilled earth and filling the air with their strident screeches. Güero Paparruchas approached the group mounted on his horse Barrigas. Both rider and animal were bony and long-limbed. Look, there goes the liar. You mean that Güero is not on his way to sow corn? He prefers to go around telling his little lies. Yeh, wasting everybody's time. Let's stop for a while and give the horses a breather. Let's see what Paparruchas has new to say. Hi, fellows! It won't be long before we're eating roast corn, right? Come on over, Güero. While we're having a drink of water, come tell us what new story you made up today. No, sir, I'm very truthful. Why should I tell you what just happened to me if none of you will believe me in the end? Come on, man, tell us. I, for one, believe you. If you won't laugh I'll tell you something really incredible that just happened to me. Just remember that what I'm going to tell you is serious and quite true, I swear by the body of Christ. You devil, Güero, you are already swearing in vain. I've just come from the woods. My spotted cow got lost three days ago, and I've been looking all over for her day and night. I'm still upset. I was looking for her on earth, but the fact is that I found her in a way so strange as to make you wonder if things like that can really happen. Ah, Güero, you big talker! Now you're going to tell us that you found her dancing the mambo. I told you doubting Thomases, and now you're already laughing. She was just getting ready to calve when she wandered off into the woods. Well, I said, you'll come back with your calf in tow. But no, she wasn't about to come back. So I told Barrigas here this morning, come on, I'm going to saddle you and we're going into the woods to see what's going on with that cow. It's so hot the devil must be hiding in the hills, because, with this sun, friend, you wouldn't find hare or hound to save your soul. I looked for her all morning for hours and hours, and not a sign of the calf or its mother, who I was sure was dead. But that's funny. There are no buzzards, dogs or coyotes to be seen.

They'd be at her carcass by now. Now, here's the good part, fellows. You're going to tell us that the cow snuck up on you, dammit, Güero. Tell us that the animal chased you. You're going to tell us you found the cow singing a lullaby to her calf. No, but just hear this. I had already lost hope of finding her. I took my handkerchief out to wipe my face, and while I was doing it I saw something far off flying toward me. What the heck is that? I doesn't look like a bird. No, it's not a bird. It doesn't have any wings. Hot damn! It's my cow, coming right toward me. Careful, she's going to smash into us! Ssssst, I saw her out of the corner of my eye. That damned cow was laughing, laughing right out loud. Then she knocked my hat off. She swoops back up, then comes planing in real slow. Hell, she's coming toward us! She's going to squash us this time, Barrigas, let's make tracks for home. Then I saw the animal land, and I thought, "I can get rich with this cow; I bet a circus'll buy her." Then what happened, Güero? Did the cow have wings? Is she still laughing? You're getting better and better each day. Nobody's ever told me about a flying cow. Was the calf also flying along behind her? No, just listen to this. There's an explanation, because the cow was already dead, and what it really was, was her spirit that was flying around. So, now get this, I went over very carefully, just in case. . . . Damn, the cow was dead! She looked like a drum, all swollen up, and you could hear noises from the inside. I go to look. Ah, of course! I kicked her in the stomach, and then I saw a buzzard came out her behind. I kept kicking her until a whole bunch of buzzards came out. For a moment I thought the cow was giving birth to buzzards—there were seven of them. Then I realized what was going on. The buzzards had already eaten the cow's innards and were picking the bones clean. Just then a coyote comes up, sticks his head up her rear, and lets out a loud yelp. Well, with the fright that gave them and the fact that they were stuck on the inside, those buzzards just flew off still inside her, and there they were circling all over the place, carcass and all. Now, tell me, who in his right mind would have believed that it was a flying cow. The devil's going to get you good for being such a liar. Enough tall tales. Let's get to work! Well, so long, fellows. So long, you old liar. Let's see what kind of story you have next time.

At sixty-five, Lolo Bruto had the mentality of a dazed young man. He was all wrinkled up, but his sight was nevertheless very good. When he was fifty his teeth all fell out at the same time. That happened because of the faith healer who lived in a hut down by the river that he went to see about something for his chronic toothache. The old woman prescribed the urine of a deer in heat, and the fool misunderstood her about the amount. The Saragozas lent a hand with the deer their kids had raised. At the right moment, they gave Lolo a small vial filled with the deer's piss. He swished it around in his mouth real good, and a few days later he was completely toothless, not a one left. Since he was a glutton and poor, he was always looking for something to eat. His guts took the place of his brain, and he would eat anything in sight. At first when he would chew tough things, his gums would split open and bleed, staining his mouth and his guts, and then his mouth would swell up. After a time he grew callouses on his gums that were like horseshoes, capable of grinding rocks. Lolo could crush walnuts with a real nice crunch. He looked like he had been born with a rolled cigar stuck to his upper lip. His reputation as a rowdy drunk was well established. A wag, always singing, foulmouthed—these were Bruto's salient characteristics. He worked as a day laborer on whatever he could get, whether it was making adobes or running errands, splitting wood, or getting rid of dead dogs. He had no need for shoes, and the souls of his feet were tougher than cowhide. Once when he stepped on a burning coal by mistake; he only realized it when his charred heel smelled of smoke.

Lolo Bruto had married Tilinga Lucas. By mutual agreement they had given birth to a gang of kids. With time, these in turn had paid them back with a gang of grandchildren.

The rocky fields turned brown with the gold diggers hugging the earth like ticks. Lolo Bruto had spent five days digging, and his hole was as deep as a grave when a stone hit him on the neck. It was gold. He saw in effect that the golden riches had been uncovered with the first blows of his pick. He came home with a knapsack improvised from his shirt filled with pieces of gold, and it really gave Tilinga a big surprise. Thus, Lolo Bruto became rich overnight. Nevertheless, the ones who spent the Brutos' fortune were not old Lolo or his already grownup children, but rather an eight-year-old kid: Lupercio, his grandson, who was the son of Felizandro, his firstborn. Lolo Bruto found himself rich, and spent his time going from one cantina to another "to wet his whistle," as he used to say. Lupercio was always at his side, and he was a real brat. He was Lolo's favorite grandson, and he had spoiled him to such an extent that he would have made even Beelzebub pale. Lupercio's hair stood up like the bristles of a brush. His face was a dirt brown, and one of his incisors was so long that it stuck out between his lips. The young fellow knew every dirty word that ever existed, thanks to his grandfather's sense of humor and a legion of willing teachers. His poor grandmother Tilinga, despite her aches and pains and her doddering age, saw the satanic kid as nothing more than an old witch or a black devil. The old woman would wipe her tears with her apron, while Lolo Bruto and his daughters-in-law laughed shamelessly. One morning, the foul-mouthed child was talking to Doña Tilinga with feigned tenderness: "Grandmommy." Trembling with emotion, she asked him, What do you want, my child? I want you to eat shit, Grandma. Lupercio would do the same thing with his parents and uncles, calling the men billy goats and the women whores. Lolo Bruto was in seventh heaven with the daily tricks invented by the little reprobate. If someone tried to get after the brat, Lolo Bruto woud jump to his defense, and God help anyone who tried to touch him. He was the boy's mother, father and grandparent. Naturally, he was not exempt from the kid's foul mouth. The last straw came when Lupercio went to the bathroom in the dining room and spread shit all over the stove, the table, the chairs and the dishes. His natural state was to be soaked with pee and covered with snot, and more than just being dirty, it was to bug people.

So when Lolo Bruto got rich overnight, he dragged Lupercio around to the cantinas and the whorehouses. One time, when the two of them, grandfather and grandson, went together to the brothel Prickly Pear Honey, they found themselves a place at the bar next to the black Siboney and her client, a venerable old man whose white hair glowed more than virginity itself. The astonished gentleman asked, What are you doing here, young fellow, among so many drunks? The boy spit on him like an animal. What's it matter? Slobbery old man, with your grimy old hair. The drunks and the whores egged him on just to hear his filthy talk. The only person who ever slapped the viperish brat was Misérrimo García, the dwarf who several months later would kill Romerazo with a pistol the size of a thimble. The fact is that, as always, Lolo Bruto had been making his rounds since early that morning. They went into the Sleeping Dove, because between the sun and being tired, Lupercio was acting impossible. The old man was standing up, drunk from "wetting his whistle with mezcal." He had sat the child down on a stool that reached as high as the bar. Misérrimo would pull the hair on the back of his neck and then hide his hand, which made the boy as mad as a wet hen. All of a sudden he caught Misérrimo in the act. There were a few minutes of expectant silence. Suddenly, what nobody would have believed possible came spewing out of the little boy. Who the hell's been fucking around with you, shitface? Both the old man and the kid ended up getting slapped and kicked all over the place.

It wouldn't be inappropriate to mention what happened the night the precocious child Lupercio spent with Santa, a whore who'd really been around, although she still was a lively number.

The Pitolocos were making their instruments bray with an earth-shattering music. The Golden Honeycomb was bursting at the seams with the sinful and the priestesses of Eros. Teté, the French girl, was dancing with a tough guy who looked like a dinosaur from out around Trincheras. She took her blouse off and let it fly. Her queenlike tits, on their own and set free, brought roars from the crowd. She also shed her skirts to wild shouts. Before Lupercio could gaze upon the plumed mystery Teté, in her liberal generosity, was about to show, Santa grabbed him from Lolo Bruto's side and carried him off to her room in a gesture of moralizing humanitarianism. It was not Christian to corrupt the soul of that boy to its hidden depths. There, with the most tender of accents, she showered him with advice. She showed him the saints that decorated her walls, and the statues on her dresser. She advised him to remain chaste and to persevere in the innocence of his childhood. When Santa wasn't looking, Lupercio grabbed the hose she used to wash herself with every time she'd been with a client and started blowing on it like a horn. Chasing the boy, the lady tripped and knocked Saint Martin of Pores over. Kneeling, she started to cry. "Don't cry. My Grampa Lolo will buy you another damn doll." Nevertheless, a few minutes later, Lupercio was running like a dog being chased, with the kindly whore wailing after him and hitting him with her shoe. The pint-sized devil made it to the street, hollering for help from his Grampa Lolo Bruto. Santa, somewhat calmed down, rubbing her pubis, was relating how, while she was changing her clothes behind the screen, the damn snot snuck up and pulled a bunch of hair from her snatch.

She didn't know whose idea that had been, whether it came from the mezcal-ridden mind of the old man or from Lupercio's little brain. Whatever the case, the event ruined any chance the Bruto family had to redeem itself. Kiss prosperity good-bye. The bonanza fizzled out, and there was no more food in abundance, no new clothes, and no more joy; only hunger, rags, exhaustion and ill-will. Lolo Bruto crawled from one bar to another, followed by Lupercio. Overcome by maguey liquor, he sprung his springs. Lying with his head to the side on Lalo's chest, the child would sleep with the angelical look that sleep gave him.

Whenever they entered the dives, the crowd would pick at the kid like always just to hear his mouth run off. Only his hands weren't empty now. He carried a sling around with him, and his pockets were full of stones in place of the pistol he couldn't tote. Seated at the bar in a strategic place, he would wield the slingshot. He positioned the projectile on the piece of leather, stretched the bands back as far as possible, aimed between the two ends of the fork, and zap! his shot sped out with cyclonic force to smash the belly of a bottle. When the bartender saw the fragments of glass all over the place and the contents spilling out, he would say to the little barbarian, "No shit, you son of Lucifer, I'll kill you before you spill all my booze and send me begging in the streets." But Lalo Bruto, his mouth brimming with thick and brutal speech, muttered with a slobber: my grandson has permission to do whatever the fuck he wants, and if any glass gets broken I'll pay for it. Just so you'll know, I pay for even bad looks.

The first day, the little brat broke fifteen bottles, and the atmosphere was thick with the smell of rum and tequila. The bartender, a sneak like all men of his type, charged Lolo Bruto two and three times what each bottle was worth. Moreover, this indulgent grandfather had to indemnify three or four drunks zapped by Lupercio's target practice. Such was the case with Churi Cordero, who, as was his custom, shouted to the boy: Lupercio! Shitty little queer! A few moments later, his mouth was bleeding, with a bloody wound where his teeth had been.

Lupercio's habits and Lolo Bruto's stupidity became big business for the bartenders, who lined their shelves with bottles of imported liquor: whiskey, champagne, vodka, premium wines, and so on.

Thus, the projectiles that Lupercio launched drained the pockets of the Bruto family.

The day came when Lolo Bruto, having spent many thousands of pesos, did not have enough to mitigate his hangover. Out of inertia, Lupercio continued the routine of his hunt. Since there was no one to support his bad behavior, he came back home with his butt a sizzling piece of meat, bloody and black and blue from the whippings that he had coming to him for good cause. Old Tilinga died from a varied collection of ailments, the worst one of which was sadness. Lolo Bruto gave up the remains of his humble brain, sighing for a bowl of chicken soup. The rest of Lolo Bruto's descendents were for generations a good example of the damage done by hereditary malnutrition, and more than one sought calories and the invention of dreams in drink.

Years later, Lupercio, now grown up, would say, while "wetting his whistle with mezcal," that he was not a Bruto like the others. Thanks to lacking the character of his parents and the stupidity of his grandfather, we would in the future call himself Lupercio Rebruto. What is most interesting is that as a grownup he avoided bad language. When he was sober he was like a rock, melancholic and quiet. When he was on a binge, he would go around cursing poverty, denouncing his grandfather, and crying for what he could have been.

God, Timoteo Noragua, you're as stubborn as you are dumb! The only thing that inspires is that one absurd name. It sprang from your mind and has taken you over completely, making you dance like a puppet. Your simple fantasy wrought it from nothing, and now it is your master. Huachusey. I can't stand how you can be so foolish. Not satisfied with feeding that stupid being with your smoked-filled brain, you're trying to find him in the flesh with a soul and thoughts, and you believe with your whole being that he is a god whose kingdom is of this earth. All you have left to do is build a temple in his name, kneel down, and pray to him, and in the process infect other fools like you, the simpletons and weak-minded, and form a legion to adore Huachusey, to sing and pray to him as a choir like the toads in the water holes, imploring him with your eyes closed, imploring his power and strength in order to acquire riches and attain worldly pleasures. Are you also going to establish a ritual? Ignorance is infinite, and there'll be no lack of fools to follow you. You will be a multitude, a procession of pilgrims. Hierarchies will be established around your fantasy. The great huckster will reign from his pinnacle with the complicity of a gaggle of little hucksters, structured in terms of an industry that will turn the credulity of your great simplemindedness into gold. Your face is that of a hunted animal and it makes me laugh. Just look at how your cheekbones stick out and how sunken your eyes are. The only living thing that moves you is in your eyes, which are two black bugs that look as if they want to jump out so they can find for themselves that god you are giving form to. When you were in the forest, you burned like a taper, consuming yourself with a phosphorescent fire in a sustained delirium. That ridiculous animal you're riding makes me laugh. His laughter sounds like he's making fun of you. His look is malicious, his teeth stick out, and his skin can barely contain his bones, as though he were dead and nothing but a figment of your mind. I see you everywhere, always in motion, craning your neck, invoking his name, inquiring where he lives. You don't eat, moved by faith in his existence, and you believe with all your will that you will find him. What can he give you if you do find him? Who are you, insignificant man, to seek him? You own no skyscrapers. You don't have one red cent. Politically you're a nobody. Timoteo Noragua, you're nothing. No, you are something: an illiterate wretch. On what basis is an omnipotent being going to hear you, if you are not a lawyer, a professor, an engineer? Do you have a doctorate? What kind of doctorate could you have, if you're nothing, a nobody? You have no importance whatever as a person, and you expect Huachusey to listen to you. What are you looking for? Why don't you die? You and those like you were born into this world by mistake. You are worthless in the face of the rest, you are nothing to those who govern in your country, and there are no laws made in your name. They only make you promises in order to laugh in your face. Anything you've ever had in your whole worthless life is drunk by the sons of the public officials in a single champagne toast. And this is how you wish to see God, you slob . . . Yet, I suspect you'll find him, also for me . . . You should know that whoever finds him cannot understand him. I tremble to think that you will go on living until you find his abode. Then, you will lose your tranquility forever, perhaps even your hope . . . Well, yes, the one you seek does live in this world. But listen to me; if you do find him, you will also find terror and the worst kind of sadness. No one can stop you now; your strength is the only energy that no one and nothing stops. Eventually you will stumble on Huachusey, a pity, since you were doing so well in your world of innocence.

You will have already noticed, Salomón, that the stones are silent and that they neither shout nor move. They are capable of staying in one place for centuries, millennia. Better, for millions and millions of years. You must look upon them with respect because they are so old. There are many, many stones here, which is why this town is called Santa María de las Piedras, Saint Mary of the Stones. I like to study them. Each one is different in shape and size. They are so pretty, and they have taught these people to be silent. People here are like the stones. They withstand the heat without fleeing, giving the impression that they never budge. Everything is in suspension in Santa María de las Piedras, everything in silence and stillness. Where do the old men in the plaza get so many stories? They get them from nothing, maybe from the stones themselves, because here, Salomón, nothing moves. If someone wants to know about what the stones do not discuss, he will have to go out beyond the immensity of the sands. I must be a poet, Salomón: I have seen the dry, colorless desert, and then I have dreamed that it was covered with fountains bubbling with polychrome letters that cover the area all around them with beautiful poems, and that it is a miracle when they flower, transforming everything into a meadow because the water takes pity and once again floods the fields that it forgot about so long ago. This silence is beautiful, Salomón, this riotous peace where nothing stops the voices, which die in the distance, evaporate and turn into nothingness. You and I will go out beyond where the voices succumb. Remember that the sands hold their echoes. Come, Salomón, let us go find the echoes of the words.

Don Rumboso Noragua was very loved and respected in Santa María de las Piedras as a just and honorable man. When he was sane, he was the most judicious and the wisest of counselors. He was even treated considerately during his attacks. He would himself say that when he was out of his mind, he felt like he was drunk and that was what made him do such crazy things. When violence took hold of him, he lost all notion of himself and of things around him. On more than one occasion his madness was brief and even funny. Then he would cut up like a good-time drunk. The day he showed up in Santa María de las Piedras's plaza dressed like the Virgin was enough to make the stones smile. Wrapped in a pure white sheet, crowned with flowers, his hands devoutly joined, walking with slow and measured ceremony, he made the sign of the cross at everyone with sober gestures. A shouting group of kids surrounded him. The grownups exchanged startled looks. If they didn't break out laughing it was only because they were afraid they would be committing a sin. Father Hilario! Father Hilario! Come quick! The Virgin is outside in the street. Father Hilario runs out, his brow furrowed. He sees the people and makes his way through them, fascinated, coming to a stop in front of the madman. He freezes and looks with his mouth open. The man in the costume comes out of his trance, turns his head, sees the priest, raises his eyebrows and smiles slightly: Hilario, my son, I am the Immaculate Virgin herself. The priest turns on his heel and hurriedly reenters the church, his hand over his mouth to keep from laughing out loud. Don Rumboso returns home. Why were you dressed like that, Papa? I played a joke on Father Hilario, poor fellow. He never laughs.

You shouldn't get the idea that the Noraguas had a monopoly on being crazy in Santa María de las Piedras. You could find all sorts of outrageous people there. Perhaps they made up for the absence of a circus or the theater. The young people would get together in the plaza in the afternoons and on Sunday. There they would imitate the speech and manner of some old man, bursting out in laughter every now and then. A very popular sport consisted of making fun of the cripples. They would yank at the jacket the deaf man Pérez wore, and this would drive him wild with anger. Then he would throw stones at the young punks right and left, cursing their mothers and grandmothers. Things really got out of hand with the deaf man Pérez when they began to touch him on the ass as if by accident. He would start to cry, and he wanted so much to kill one of these creeps. The blind man Rosendo was the victim of some really bad jokes. All decked out, he used to walk down the middle of the street with his keen sense of direction, and they would stretch a rope across his path and make him fall flat on his face. Rosendo had a real talent for dirty words, and he would make up insulting jokes with them. He was so good at it that he could have been a great poet. This blind man Rosendo was so mixed up that he even fell in love with the shadows, which caused the youngsters to pass him messages from make-believe women. He would suffer the consequences when he tried to go pay his formal respects as a lover. Crazy Aguilar would strut down the middle of the street calling down the rain at the top of his voice. We want drops of water, he would say, drops of water is what we want. He was red-faced and puffy-cheeked, and the heat made his eyes look like they were about to pop out. When the heat was at its worst, he would cry to the saints for a few drops of water. There was only one crazy woman to be seen in Santa María de las Piedras. This madwoman was a nomad who just showed up from time to time like the comets, always with a big belly like she was in an advanced state of pregnancy. She would always be carrying a large load of bundles, and she never paused. She had a hard look in her eyes, and she trekked across the desert better even than a camel could do. Existence for women in Santa María de las Piedras has always been a silent affair. You can often see them playing as little girls in patios, and they appear fleetingly in dances and out on a walk. They make themselves up, comb their hair, find a fiancé, get married, and then bury themselves in their homes. You can see them at wakes and at church, wearing long sleeves and covered by their shawls, praying for the souls of the men and the salvation of the whole family. In their homes they wash clothes by hand by rubbing them on large stones, they carry water and kindling from great distances, they grind their own nixtamal, make meals, and beget children. Nevertheless, all madness and frustration vanish when death appears. Then they join in the sorrow of all of the inhabitants of Santa María de las Piedras to bury their withered and emaciated dead. They do not need to make the sign of the cross in ashes on their foreheads to know they are of the earth, for it is their own tears that stain their faces when they cry and roll down through the layer of dust that always covers their faces. They are also accustomed to protecting each other when drought or famine weigh down on them like the plague. In the afternoons they stand against a sun that hides from them, and they shroud themselves in melancholy and rose-colored illusions because deep down they thirst for a life without suffering for their descendents. People in Santa María de las Piedras move and act like senile actors who must perforce invent their own characters daily. This is why they act crazy.

Time passed inperceptibly, and Noragua the Indian talked and talked to himself. With his sunken eyes he scrutinized intently the distance and everything around him. The same obsession filled his thoughts and occupied his soul, Huachusey. . . Huachusey. . . . He had to find him, to seek him as best he could, and for that he counted on his enormous willpower. He could do anything, he was capable of everything, and his creative hands would also be prodigious. Huachusey would shower him with gifts, and he in turn would with love and charity bring good fortune to the others. He could; of course he could. Who could doubt it after knowing his works? He could make abundance spring forth, provide many gifts, make the afflicted very, very happy. Thanks to his grace and his works everyone would march toward a sublime destiny.

Thus Timoteo continued to seek Huachusey in every place. One day in the midst of his bliss, he was struck by the memory of his land, his wife, his children, his goats and his dogs, his chickens and his cats, and the forbidding wasteland of Santa María de las Piedras. He felt the urge to return in the deepest fibers of his being. Despite his deep, unwavering faith, he was tormented by the concern that he would not find his way to Huachusey. The roads had become many, and each one he had explored had been the wrong one. Every attempt to find him had been in vain. The strength of his spirit grew hour by hour, but his flesh was succumbing. His skin and his bones hurt him like burns, and his two eyes glowed like two beacons of fire. He decided to make a supreme effort, and he would pursue him in a direction that would lead him toward his own people. From the farthest reaches of the miraculous country, in a journey that retraced his original trajectory, he began his march backwards, knowing in the depths of his heart that he would find him. The brilliance of his passion erased any doubt he might have. All signs of uneasiness turned into certainty. Despite the fire of his spirit and the feverish joy his task inspired in him, his bony face showed the outlines of anguish and a slight shadow of uncertainty. He knew, nevertheless, that he was near, very near. . . .

It was a day when his resistance was weakening under the inhuman effort he demanded of his body, neither eating nor drinking. He had come by chance upon a place where mercy and consolation were distributed to all the unfortunate who requested it. It was a very large town, a city both of very ancient and also modern buildings, with a heavy traffic of cars and people, an ostentatious display of rich and beautiful things, bejeweled people, toothy smiles. The precise place of his meeting with charity: a plaza filled with flowers and grass, benches to rest on, venerable trees, and in the center a broad circumference brimming with legions of individuals, the majority bereft of joy and down on their luck. Hundreds of them, all with glassy stares, withered, wearing masks of coldness, transparent suffering and profound disillusionment. They wore threadbare clothes stiffened by dirt, so foul-smelling that they appeared to be rotting carcasses, but yet death did not inhabit them. It was misery personified; each face a cemetery of illusions, of absent looks. They walked by slowly in a procession of the hungry, and compassionate-looking men distributed bread and hot soup to them. The poor walked away with their food, silently and slowly, to revitalize a body whose alienation from its spirit was evident. Unnoticed, like strange apparitions that troubled no one, Timoteo and his noble beast found themselves in the same line as the down-and-out. A bowl filled with soup, bread, a spoon, along with some words in a strange language, God bless you brother, greeted Timoteo. He also asked with a smile, Who do I thank for this charity, sirs? What'd you say? Timoteo Noragua ate his meal, deeply moved by the compassion in evidence and by the miserable condition of those men who were morally defeated. He smiled at the idea of a generous Huachusey. But it was strange that he failed to ask, as he usually did euphorically, if Huachusey lived anywhere specifically. Thus Timoteo Noragua did not know that it was the last time he would be serene. From then on, the traces of the man he pursued would denounce a closer and closer presence, his feverish admiration would lapse into a terrible state of suffering, his usual calm would turn into anguish. He could sense that sought-after meeting with Huachusey was only a matter of days away.

The city was a square with a million lights that marked the avenues through which another million lights flowed noisily and swiftly in both directions. The Indian fled among the multicolored shards of the night streaked with the imitations of the rainbows and moonbeams.

He knew that he was far from his village, but he was spurred on by brief thrills of pleasure at knowing that he was homeward bound from his exploration. He came to at another city dotted with skyscrapers, a replica of others that he had crossed, eternally spewing out cars and filled with high screeching noises as if, mothers of iron, they were cursed with never being able to rest for a single moment. A street, the broadest and most central, was overflowing with people marching in a procession. The multitude was made up of uncountable thousands of persons. There are so many of them that the front and back of the procession is lost in the distance. The multitude is shouting and yelling, and their cries resound against the walls of the buildings. They carry banners with various slogans: "make love not war," "halt the manufacturing of bombs, criminals," "powerful thieves never go to jail," "Hispanics, hold your head up high," "down with racists." That current of men and women flowed like a flood, and the protestors shouted with their fists in the air. There's nothing like a human river whose cry of indignation whips the glass of the hundreds of windows along the faces of the buildings. The single cry fills the canyons of the streets, spreads over on the cement, until it is swallowed up by the sky in a spiral of lamentations, laughter, curses and a bellowing filled with desire that explodes with the urgency of sex. The marchers head toward the nerve center of government. Like a crazed herd, they reach an open field that serves as a square facing imposing solid and ornate constructions. Facing them are improvised walls of men interspersed with rifles, submachine guns and clubs. They wear face masks to protect themselves against the gasses that they will turn on the crowd. The action takes on the appearance of a children's game. The police are firing and several young people began to fall. In violent, stumbling waves, they cry, enraged and panic-stricken. You can make out the husky, meaty-fisted policemen in the middle of the smoke produced by the tear gas. They chase the dispersing people and flay at them, raising their clubs effortlessly, striking home with force. The blows of the clubs strike young girls and boys, breaking noses, smashing eyes, killing. The dazed, bloodied man stumbles. There is a woman whose hair is damp with red. A beardless youth is now down on all fours, bathed in blood. The representatives of law continue the slaughter. The side streets are swallowing up the fugitives. Now calm descends; the faces of the dead, those who are dying gasping; the moaning wounded are stained with violence. It is a strange calm, more harmful than the collective cry spewed out by thousands of throats. A peace hovers in the air and stifles the spirit of all the sharded glass in the city. A cold silence floats like the iron innards of all the skeletons of the buildings. The harsh passivity of the cement that covers the urban surface.

Dusk speaks of another dying day enveloped in the layers of icy air. The wind which never ceases to blow on this city makes its usual rounds in a hurry. The footfalls of a man who walks down the middle of a street alongside a burro sound like heartbeats. Timoteo Noragua contemplates the strange city, his hat in his hand, reverent, humble, sadness matching fear and anguish. From the hollow eyes of the Indian two large tears fall on the spilled blood. A hundred bodies lie on the pavement. Beautiful young girls who only recently bloomed like flowers lie with their eyes still open, devoid now of ideals and romantic illusions. Handsome youths who dreamed of justice and good fortune lie with their heads bashed in and bullet holes in their bodies. The cement absorbs the reddish flow. Timoteo Noragua is crying. Brigades of body collectors arrive in trucks and ambulances. Timoteo Noragua goes up to a tall, very serious man in uniform. Sir, who is responsible for all this barbarity? What'd you say? The Indian repeats his question once, twice, three times, many times, until there can be no doubt as to the identity of the criminal. Now the man seeking a god continues on his way, dejected, downcast, until he is swallowed up by night in a barren, empty space.

That night Timoteo Noragua camped under the stars and called them his sisters. He would have liked to embrace them, to cry on their breasts. If he could not do that, he could look upon them with profound tenderness. They, his sisters the stars, comforted him with their loving gaze.

Timoteo Noragua's brow deepened with the tardy pain, profound ridges as though drawn by claws. The ass also seemed to be afflicted. Noragua hugged his animal and rubbed his face against Salomón's. The quiet suffering of the humble mount had the taste of the tears of human suffering.

Timoteo Noragua sought his way home, treading down roads and devouring distances. His pleasure at drinking in the landscape disappeared, and he allowed the little burro to find the way himself. Then he plunged into the thick of a jungle so alive, as profoundly rooted as doubt itself and the anxiety to replace ignorance with understanding. Timoteo Noragua began to enmesh himself in ideas, and the more he struggled to free himself, to come to a clearing of comprehension, the thicker and more labyrinthine they became. He tried to soar from the solid earth he trod toward an endless cosmos.

126

He wanted to penetrate his mind, to explore. The "whys" and the "who is Huachusey" acted like bats, and they flew into his face and hung by their claws from his ears. Who is Huachusey? Maybe a child god? A child god who learns to create by destroying and rebuilding? Is he an apprentice god who molds his clay with blood? My God! Have mercy on this being.

When the old gabbers get together in the plaza, they plant themselves on the benches and get to yakking, dozing, or losing themselves in their own thoughts, swimming back to the past. They forget their ailments or hide them under proud boasting about their toughness and their manly pride. Men don't cry; only old ladies, babies and sissies do. Nevertheless, every night they fight a battle that takes a little bit of life from them. Protests become a serenade of complaints. Between the scoldings, attentions and remedies of their women, they survive as though by miracle the rigor of the dawn. The sun comes up with the crest of luminous roosters. Dogs and children bark and shriek together. Hunger turns skeletal ribs into marimbas. Father Hilario rings the call to mass: ding dong, ding dong, come on you bastards, come and honor God. There the old men go like disobedient children to join other kids. Their guts are bleeding, their pipes are clogged, their hearts beat now and then, followed by long pauses, and every step is a drum beat. They bear their fleeting souls on a derailing train. Good morning, Don Teofilito. Good morning, daughter, God be with you. You're getting to the plaza very early, Don Abelardo. I'm late, boys, because the sun lay in bed all morning. How do you feel this morning, Don Nachito, where are you off to? To my grave, gentlemen, unless a miracle happens. Help me up the curb, that's it, thanks. Your comrades beat you, Don Güero, they're already in the plaza. What do you mean beat me? I've already been to the cemetery. I spoke to the dead and also to the sahuaros and with a buddy of mine who turned into a tecolote some years ago because his old lady slapped him around. Come on, Don Güero, it's too early. Bless yourself before you get going with your stories. Are you suggesting that I'm a liar? The old men have already taken their places. An unexpected guest appears.

Look who's here, someone who doesn't talk, only writes. What a drag. He spends his time shut up scrounging around in books and talking to himself. Hi, there, it's about time you got some sun. You're right, Don Teofilito, I've come to say hello to my friends. You've come to see what you can pick up. Come on, we'll teach you how to tell stories. I'm sure, Don Nacho. Maybe I'll turn into a liar just by listening to you, friend. Let's hope not, Paparruchas, that would be a shame. How are you, Don Abelardo? Well, we invited you to be a part of this group of old yakkers quite a while ago. But if you prefer to stay closed up between four walls, that's your business. You're a little younger than we are, but age is getting to you and your hair is turning white. Sit down next to Paparruchas and Teófilo and tell us something, man. I like to write and that's all. I'm one of those writers you find in the woods. I don't publish a thing because I'm not known, and I'm not known because I don't publish. Besides, publishing is all a mystery to me. Do printers really exist? It's like when a dog bites his tail and turns around. What a hell of a comparison, Güero. I'm talking to the owner of the tent, not to his clown. You old goat, Don Nacho. Here's Don Nacho, you bastards, great grandfather to more than just a few. You all look like spoiled brats, heaven help me. It's better for you not to publish anything, man. You'd just get criticized by those guys who'd like to be writers but can't. Some of them know their job, but the majority think with their large intestine. Writing fiction is like talking from afar without seeing the faces of the people. You never seem to hit the mark. It's like buying curlers for someone who's bald. That's right, Teófilo. There's nothing like straight talk. And, speaking of straight talk, Paparruchas? It just means let's get down to brass tacks. Look, fellows, that means "let's call a spade a spade," with all due respect to the reader. Well, I don't give a fig for the reader. Hold on, Güero Paparruchas, where're your manners? I've never met them. Once I went over to the university there in the city to ask for a job as a janitor, but the sons of bitches said no to me. You're hopeless, Güero; even if you were born all over again, you'd still be a mess. But Güero wasn't born. His mother shit him out. I'm going to kick the shit out of you, you old fart. Give me my walking stick back, Paparruchas. Ay, damn it, you got my ear. Shape up, gentlemen, shape up, or that's the end of the session. Well, you didn't really hurt me. Next time you'll end up like Agapito and his flute. A few days ago I sent you "Huachusey," the story I just wrote. What'd you think about it? A lot of stuff and nonsense, with some comparisons that are a bunch of crap. Those are called tropes, the metaphoric use of language. Metawhat? Metaphoric, that is, symbolic, using images. Well, maybe, but I don't swallow that story. Nobody'd believe anyone could be as stupid as that Indian Timoteo, looking for God in Gringoland. Well, if you don't think there are guys as stupid as that Indian, you're the dumb one. You're crazy, and one of your screws is loose. You drag that Indian Timoteo around from one city to another mounted on his

129

burro. You know that that's impossible. In reality, the animal would fall flat on his face the first time around. The gringos have guards all over the place, and you have them going into the most absurd places without any trouble whatsoever. Just tell me where's the logic in that? If your goal is to portray the human essence, rationalistic logic is out of place. You fellows also dress your talk up with fantasy, isn't that right? Look, what happened to the child Fidencio when he got to Culiacán? Well, there were so many people crowded together waiting for him that the faith healer walked on the heads and shoulders of the fanatics casting handfuls of wheat around so they would be cured of their ailments, and everybody believed him. Then you stick the Indian in a world of magic with ghosts and trains that fly. Well, there's a place like that in Los Angeles. That's Disneyland, in case you want to know. You don't need to tell me. Do you think I don't know? Maybe it's the fevers you get. A crazy old man started a church in Mexico, in the capital. He said he was Alcalá the god, and half the people signed up. What's so strange, then, about an Indian looking for God in the United States? He's right. Right here in Santa María de las Piedras there was Brother Trini Brown, and he threw the whole town in the river to baptize them, all except for Father Hilario. We're just pulling your leg. That story is interesting to us, so why don't you come and tell it to us? We're here every day. It's just that it's one thing to talk and another to write. If you write it's as though you were telling the same story over and over again, year in and year out, without having to make an effort. Well, we don't make an effort here, that's the difference. Here we talk because we like to. It's all a matter of taste, and one form is just as good as another. Maybe the two ways complement each other, and if one way dies the other disappears, too. Thanks, Don Abelardo, you always encourage me. I have just finished the episodes in which Timoteo wanders enormous cities flattened by atomic bombs, and I am going to write now about when the Holy Father says mass for the dead Huachusey and Timoteo disappears among the galaxies. So long, gentlemen. So long. Good luck. Keep on writing novels. The Pope, galaxies, bombed cities; this guy is nuts, really, brought up in a poor village with only a few years of schooling, and he wants to be a writer. What's that about him wanting to be a writer? He's a writer because he writes and has a reader, me. If I don't read it's because I can't see the letters because my eyes are no longer any good. They've never been any use to you to read because you don't know how to,

130

you silly old goat. You don't know how to read either, you old mule. Everything is possible. This man writes and writes while he ignores the world around him. His family, his friends, and women have all laughed at him. They say he's lazy, ignorant, and crazy. If he does get anything published and it gets read, it's certain that those who have criticized him will find they're the real fools, crazies, and incompetent ones. That's right, Lalo, there are a lot of stupid people as far as serious things are concerned. They're happy to gossip and spend years doing nothing, saying dumb things and withering away in vain. But if he wanted to publish his things he would have to go to the big city and from one publisher to another like a poor beggar. No, wanting to be a writer isn't worth a hill of beans. And in the bargain, he'd be read by people with the minds of merchants who think more about money than the merits of the manuscript. How do you know that, Lalo? Because I've been out in the world. Then booksellers don't know anyting about books. Oh, they know a lot, but they are blinded by ambition and can't see beyond their noses. On more than one occasion they've rejected works because they believe that they won't sell, but these works get published by someone else and turn out to be gold mines. In other words, there're jerks everywhere. Just like wise people, Nacho; that's called mankind. This pipsqueak of a writer has made us waste the day. Tomorrow we'll talk about something juicy. Come on, all I know is that the longer you live the more you eat and I'm hungry.

The wind reappears on the horizon like an advancing pinzer attack. It is a phantom horse brigade whose gigantic steeds raise the dust to the sound of their hooves, now pounding down, now flying up. Forward and upward, the area all around becomes saturated with dust, covering the face of the sun. Not only can you see the air filled with sand that whips, blinds and turns into shadows and silhouettes everything standing still or moving. Time also bumps, spirals, and crashes against rooftops and doors. The hurried swirl of the wind suddenly pushes along the bodies of the dead hours accumulated during long periods in the static setting of Santa María de las Piedras. The earth, atomized into minimal fractions of seconds, acquires the fluidity of time. The hermetic intimacy of the cracks is violated, and the winds rattle angrily. There go the old gabbers on their way home. They wander off confused in the dust, the wind beating against them mercilessly, time moving everything and dragging it along.

That morning there were no stars in the sky of Santa María de las Piedras. They had turned to liquid and ran in torrents, just like Pomposa's eyes. I was at that time a child of six. The familiar sound of the carts was accompanied by the clattering you only hear at the crack of dawn. Full of fear and curiosity, I looked out the window. My father placed a hand on my back, but offered no explanation. The procession of people humbled by suffering and by the water streaming down from heaven followed behind. Tall and thin, dressed in black, her hair finally undone, head held high, Pomposa marched in front. The figures followed the cart pulled by two sleepy oxen. Although they were still at a distance, I could hear the cries and murmured prayers and a dull treading of feet. The dogs and roosters burst out barking and crowing. They're going to the cemetery, my father told me in a soft and very gentle voice. They're burying Nacho, Pomposa's boy, killed yesterday by a lightning bolt.

Where are you going on that horse, Ignacio? Into the woods, mama, just like the men, well armed and on horseback. Don't go, foolish child. Can't you see the clouds are coming in early? A flash of lightning might kill you. I'm going to fight death, and if you want me to win, kill the rooster so I can eat it and be strong. Forget that. I'm not going to leave my chickens widows just to believe your foolishness.

Pomposa never quit crying over the fact that she didn't kill the rooster for Nacho to eat. He was the only son she had left.

Well, for your information, Lalo, I remember back then. How could you not, Nacho, if you were riding dinosaurs when you were six? You're an old goat, you and your dinosaurs. When I was six years old, Teófilo Paparruchas, you already had crow's feet all over your face. By the way, where have you been off flying, Güero, with your famous cow? You look a little peaked. I'm just thinking about when I was a child and I saw death face to face. Tell us about it, but no nonsense, or we'll throw you right out of Santa María de las Piedras. Come on, you have to see just what kind of things do happen, right? I was in the woods and night fell. I was riding a horse we called Barrigas, herding some animals. I fell fast asleep. Damn, but it was dark! Where am I; these trees are so huge! Where'd this forest come from? There's nothing but cholla bushes around here. Giddyup, Barrigas, stay close by and eat what you can while I take a little nap.

Time went by. I slept soundly, and the sun was about to come out. And all this? Where am I? What thick trees, what heavy shadows! Then I heard a heavy, strange clatttering, and I started to hightail it out of there. I ran like the devil out of the forest. The sun was already high. All I could see of my horse's back there were his flanks and hind legs. A tarantula was eating him! She was trying to get to me, devouring me with her gaze. Not even my mother-in-law looked at me like that. I got up and stabbed her in a leg, and she let go. How mad that tarantula got! I left her choking with anger. I think I flew that day, because I was home quicker than a wink. From there you ran straight to church so Father Hilario could wash your mouth out with holy water. It's too bad the tarantula didn't eat you. If she had, you wouldn't be such a yakker, I bet. If you don't believe me, I'll take you there and you can see Barrigas's bones the tarantula spit out. I went back later with a rifle to get her. She must live in a cave up there. You're the one should be in a cave. Maybe that'd cure you. All that's left is for you to tell me that you've flown, too. Well, if I'm not mistaken, Don Nacho, for your information, I have flown all over the world and beyond. Oh, really? Bring me a needle and thread, Lalo, I'm going to sew this guy's mouth shut. Don't believe me, then. Sometimes late at night my friends the Martians come to see me in a large ship with lots of lights. . . . Shut up, Güero, majority rules, shut up; once you get going no one can stop you.

Time moves slowly in Santa María de las Piedras because it is bound by fire. Morning wraps it in a spiral of roosters who are all upset by yet one more sun to rise from the shadows. The sheep intensify their lowing, and the ridges and hills join in with the sheep. The cows moo their love for their penned-up calves, and the latter answer back with long onomatopoeic monosyllables. The piercing barking of a dog announces his splintered ribs, his back arched and his paws a jumble. The shouting of the children sounds like noisy birds against the heavy voices of the adults. Along the horizon saturated by the daily assault of the dust storms, the sun is born with an explosion. Gold and purple take over the sky.

The miracle of the fish is repeated every day in Santa María de las Piedras. The cracked and wavy sidewalks bear the shaky outlines of people passing and greeting each other with vague smiles. They go into the small stores and come out with scrawny packages. The kitchens lie idle, their utensils hardly used. The younger kids go out on a mission. They go from one home to another, a cup in their hand, begging "a little bit of sugar," "a few beans," "do you have some flour—my mama says she'll pay you right back." Santa María de las Piedras lives by miracle. The women see the men go out in search of bread, just as if they were going off to war. Some fight the snakes for metal: the gold overlooked by the avid in bygone years. Others water the dry land, aching for a harvest with their sweat. There are those who'll rent themselves out by the day in exchange for a few coins. The children gather at school, nurturing there their minds with basic studies, their stomachs empty, between old walls, taught by a sad teacher who loses himself now and then in deep thoughts and gets drunk on Sunday because of his lack of drive and his powerlessness. In Santa María de las Piedras, everything is silence. The roofs of the thick-walled houses are tombs where marital squabbles, riotous joy, ill feelings, the illusions of the young, the imperious desire of the flesh, the mysteries of sex, and the savage outburst of the wailing for the dying all fester. The grandmother knits there in her corner with the skein of generations. She hangs traditions from the children like scapulars. At times she prays; at times she lights the fire of fantasy in her grandchildren. When sleep overcomes them, they are covered by the beating of wings of doves and guardian angels. In Santa María de las Piedras you can hear the silence; only the wind goes by, dragging the ragged tail of time sleeping with the sloth of the oppressive heat. No one here remembers a single thing; comments are useless; words sleep like rocks. Time cuts stories off, burying them beneath the useless piles produced by the spinning of the earth, making them disappear in the ephemeral condition of memories. There are no complete stories, only the absurd invention of the logic produced by minds that hold time prisoner. Lost words like pollen disperse in the air, settling on the back streets of the past. Minds discharge a matter that fades, fleeing like mad. But the stories do not come from the mouths in the same way they entered by the eyes. They come out full of dreams, madness, laughter, and constellations of tears and stars. I don't follow you, Abelardo, I don't understand you. But your words are making me sleepy. They keep me awake, and I don't understand them, either.

The wind and the dust storms cloud the atmosphere with the sandy mist of the barren waste. The human beings who walk through the streets of Santa María de las Piedras turn into useless silhouettes. Inside the homes, the women dust in vain a never-ending layer of dirt from their stoves, tables, and every other surface. Only the clearness of their eyes shines through dust-covered faces. The presence of the stones is obscured, and now the wind and dust take over the whole setting. Words and enchanted stories and the breath that one day will bring the dead back to life travel on the wind. The old codgers of Santa María de las Piedras have given up the plaza. Cornered in their houses, they hear the voices that the air mutters through the make-believe mouths of the cracks in the doors and windows. The words of the narrators of all people strike their ears with the sand, forgotten words of languages swallowed up by time. Striking furiously against a sealed nature, the voices also travel with the wind and sand that one morning will tell thousands of stories about Santa María de las Piedras, where everything is unchanging and where nothing ever moves. One clear day, between the blue of the sky and the ochre of the earth a procession will bear Don Nacho Sereno to be buried. With the passing of his friend, Don Teofilito will bewail the death of his youth which figured in Nacho's jokes and funny stories. During the many winters, the earth will cover the grave of Don Abelardo, and with his body, his thoughts, and the presence in the world of a wise man will disappear, a man all the wiser for having gone unheeded. The last to go will be Don Teófilo.

Immobile and blind, he will yield up his shell hardened by the years. Other old men will persist with the same old story. . . . In Santa María de las Piedras nothing happens. Everyone remains silent. What is told on the street corners and in the plazas are murmurs that transcend the stones, fleeting stories that have gotten loose, girl-friends of the old men who hold their memories in their recollec-tions.

Now I am going over this golden night. Against the golden sky the glitter of the blue stars runs the gamut from the faintest to vivid irridescence. I wander among the stones of Santa María de las Piedras. They are of a nacre that is so pure that only the moon fragmented in a piece of sharded sea can equal it. The cactuses sharpen their red whistles in order to slice the wind. From the hills to the river, I row across a barren waste whose current descends in rocky crests crowned with pebbles to die on the floor of the desert in a festival of sand. The ground trembles under so many eyes. Now the sahuaros, the prickly pears, and the viznagas have hidden them-selves, and all green has disappeared. A marbled dawn covers every-thing. With the land hidden there is no longer any glittering purple or yellow. Alone, I am completely alone before the stones. Resentful of being ignored, they cry and moisten the atmosphere. Eternal stones, stepped and spit on by the animals, never caressed, at the mercy of the winds and the time that weighs on them. After several million years, the stones now reach the rock cemetery, the desert. If it were not for us stones, the first amphibians would not have laid eggs, for our shape existed before theirs did. I am not a stone; touch me; see, I am round, I am concrete water. I am flat like a coin, so that the blind may feel my rainbow between their fingers. I have sharp edges; I hurt like recently forged words. Are you a writer? A stone spoke, hunchbacked with the accent of a very old woman. No, no, I only gab on the streetcorners and in the plazas. You speak of forests that sing and rivers of silver, of skies of poetry; you say beautiful things about the seas. But you forget about us because the poets do not love us. It's that . . . It's that . . . Now the stones feel soft under my footsteps, although they are only petrified hearts. Murmurs can be heard in notes that only spring from the soul of the stones. Say that you love us, say that you love us: the voices of young women. I caress their smooth and stony faces. I hold in my hands various small stones, warm like tears. I come to the edge of the river. It roars with water that fell from clouds up by Claro and Santa Ana.

Ochre water, earth-colored water flows; liquid earth flows, the waters of all time, celestial and subterranean traveler, the dust of every corner of the planet and of every region of the cosmos. I caress the stones with my naked hands and I contemplate the flour of the water and of the earth, both passengers in the river. From within my breast, I hear the jubilant beats of my heart. My God! Time and space flow together with my emphemeral beating, and concrete matter combines with my own.

You sometimes come up with the strangest things. I am intrigued by the soul of this world of stones. At times I think the stones have stolen our souls and that we wear their faces. Is it the result of age? Maybe, maybe so. Maybe you're turning into a poet. Here in the desert? No, I don't think so. Poets spring up on the edge of forests, mountains, rushing rivers, beaches, there where nature sings. No, man, you're mistaken. Poetry springs up where imagination, feelings and words are to be found. Forget all that, gentlemen, I don't understand a word you're saying. How can you understand, you're such an uneducated lout. You and your studies are old goats. Tell us about the time you saw the cow fly. I don't want to. Tell us, you old ignoramus, about when they were going to hang you and they pardoned you because you started screaming. You and your screaming are old goats. Well, this has become a goat pen, so I guess we'd all better get home. Tomorrow is another day.

People are really bastards when they set out to do each other harm. We are, said the other. Shut up, Teófilo. When they say chamber pot, hold up your hand. You and the chamber pots are old goats. Order, gentlemen, you look like kids fighting. Of course, Nachito, that's the way we human beings are. We grab onto some-one worse off, weaker than we are. How else could we avenge ourselves, by letting people stronger than us do us in? That's sure true, Abelardo, and if there isn't some other poor devil to kick around, there're always the animals. What does that have to do with anything? Nothing, but we've been serious for quite a while, and I don't know why I thought of that guy who made his dogs talk; maybe because they had something to say. You mean Silviano? No, he's the one who would pee in school when they asked him to read. I'm referring to Bullán and his family. Ah, yes, yes, yes, we used to call him the Dumb Monkey because his face would hang and his eyes always looked crazy. He was a real bastard with the animals, and he liked to kill chickens. What's that business about him almost mak-ing the dogs talk? He had a lot of ways of going about that, as you'll see. He collected about a dozen dogs one by one and took them out to a vacant lot on the outskirts of the city, out beyond where the Noraguas live. What do you think he'd do with each dog? He would bury them up to their necks sitting down. He buried all of them with a little room between each one. All you could see were their heads. They would stretch their necks and open their eyes wide like little old men who've lost their glasses. They'd all start barking up a storm together. Then Bullán rounded up his seven cousins, the Chindos they were called. They were all on horses and galloped at full speed between the dogs. They got off to look at them, and they said the dogs were trying to talk. They would open their mouths just like they were forming words. With their eyes they were saying, no more, no more, because we're very scared. One of the Chindos said that they did talk, but in a foreign language, and you can just imagine the brutes bursting with laughter. That's not right, Nacho, that's pure savagery. Maybe so, Teófilo, but if we don't even respect each other as human beings, what do you expect? You're right. Poor hounds, their ribs show how people have thrown stones at them. All you have to do is reach for the ground and they arch their backs. That Bullán was evil. He'll come back a dog in his next life, I promise you. But I have another story for you. Well, toss the roosters some corn, Teófilo, it's your turn. You probably remember that slob we used to call Chicharrón from Cochi because he was all pockmarked and had a few hairs on his chin. His last name was Pérez, I think. Of course we remember him. He was still a pain in the ass at eighty. He's that blind man they lead to church on the end of a halter. He's blinder than the feet he walks on. That's the one I mean. He was a real bully when he was younger, more evil than malaria, and he has good reason to pray a lot now. Well, I saw that animal in human form running over the dogs in the middle of the street with his horse. How they would howl, trying to get away but not knowing how to. And then he would charge them again! And again they'd start yelping; it looked like their tails were getting stomped on. What a strange way to act. Those old hounds were so faithful and never bothered anybody. They were deep into their lovemaking just fine. But he acted real indignant, claiming at the top of his voice that he was teaching them a lesson for being sinful, immoral in public, and exhibitionists. Even after having separated them so violently he was still going on to himself about decency and what proper behavior should be. Come on, Paparruchas, tell us. You're not smiling for nothing, you old rogue. Well, here goes, but don't call me a liar because it hurts my feelings. I have a dog I love like a brother and an old horse I take care of like my father. I love animals, but I had the misfortune to see a bull tortured. Do you remember that big bull Don Clemente Ruedas had? Of course, the one they called Policeno. It was a huge bull, bad-tempered, with eyes like firecrackers. That animal really liked the cornfields. Over toward the river, there wasn't a patch of corn that he didn't trample on and gobble up. He had no use for fences, and this despite the fact that they made a yoke for him from fresh-cut mesquite logs. He was a giant of an animal, and nothing could stop him. Don Clemente got complaints from all sides. Policenos was ruining all the farmers. Well, one day but it didn't occur to that bull Policeno to stomp the fence down and charge into the cornfields of reckless Toñón. He had been ready and waiting for the bull with relish. He hopped up on his flea-bitten dappled horse, with the smile of the devil on his face. He lassoed the bull and managed to get him tied up to a stubby iron-wood tree, keeping out of the way of his horns and his legs. He took a bag containing a kilo of chilepiquines peppers out of his saddlebag. Don't you mean chiltepines peppers, Güero? Call them whatever you want. The important point is there's no pepper hotter. Go on, then. Toñón grabbed up a bunch of those peppers and rubbed them in the bull's eyes. Hot damn, you should have seen the look on the bull's face, like he'd just smoked marihuana! He rubbed his ears with the hot stuff, stuck a quarter of a kilo up his nostrils, and the rest he shoved the length of his arm up his tailpipe. Toñón loosened the lasso and then ran off just in case, and you should've seen Policeno. Here comes the cannonball! He looked like a circus bull. You can't believe the acrobatics. He did summersaults in the air, then he'd squat down to rub himself, then he pranced and ran around; it was a ballet, friend, snorting like a locomotive. Truth is he never did any damage again, and Policeno would look at the fields from afar, wrinkling his nose up real sad. Well, that was a great remedy, Paparruchas, a real lesson for human beings. Don Abelardo, you don't seem to have any misadventure to tell us about. You're lucky if you've never seen an animal mistreated. I'll tell you something just so I won't be left out. It's shameful an cowardly to mistreat the dumb. There is nothing lower, my friends; it's really unpardonable. Tell us, Don Abelardo, there can't be any harm in that, since the one who tells about such things cannot have taken part in them. This neighbor of mine, whose name could be Santiago, is such a religious man that he goes to bed with the Bible by his side and wakes up clutching onto its teachings. I had already suspected there was something strange about this learned hypocrite who was always talking about the punishments of hell. He preached to relatives and strangers about pillars of fire, red-hot coal pits, lakes of boiling oil, and all sorts of fires in the depths of hell. There is no human sin that this guy couldn't point to, along with its corresponding punishment: adulterers would boil in oil, gluttons would roast on a slow grill, drunks would drink tongues of fire, and so on. You could tell right off that his greatest joy was to dream of fire. Well, one day Mr. Santiago was busy about noon serving himself a tasty stew, surrounded by his family and his sainted wife. He prayed aloud to the Lord, blessed the meal, and gave the sign to begin. With both hands, he picked up a meat bone by each end, and half closed his eyes in ecstasy over the treat. At that moment the house cat jumped up and grabbed the bone out of his hands and made off quick as a wink. My neighbor chased him until he cornered him, bathed him in gasoline, and set him on fire. The cat turned into a streak that disappeared forever. Not even light moves as fast as that cat afire. I challenged my neighbor. How can you explain what you just did, friend? Why did you do it? This guy answered me with a twisted smile. I can assure you that pleasure leapt from his eyes. So, what did he answer, Abelardo? Ah! He answered, "I'm doing some experiments with rockets, you know, I've just invented a new one, and you can see it's different."

It's not hard to see, friend Abelardo, that in these villages sometimes we don't behave like civilized persons, whereas in those great countries there is protection for the weak, whether human or animal. God save us, Don Teófilo, from acting like those supercivilized people. Tell me why. Because those modern countries are the cruelest and the bloodiest. They kill without getting their hands dirty, my friend. They invent infernal weapons, they raise armies well-trained in the science of war, then they kill millions of human beings. And they turn around and invent excuses and false concepts, like liberty, honor, glory, and love of the fatherland. Pretexts to control other people and to steal their livelihood! Do you know how they do it? Well-dressed, very neat, wearing a tie, with exquisite language, a smile on their lips, cold and determined, fully conscious of their crimes. No, friend, I don't approve of what these men of instinct do to animals and to themselves, but there's a big difference between this sort of inhumanity and the massive crimes of the so-called polite and developed countries. We always learn something from you, Lalo. You haven't traveled all over so much of the world for nothing. And I from you, gentlemen, because as old men now we are moved by humanistic passion to want to bear witness to horrors and injustices so those who listen to us can see the point and make this world nobler and healthier. I believe we're talking this way, Lalo, because it's gotten late and we're tired. That's right, it could well be because of the approaching dusk. Tomorrow we'll talk about ghosts. You're crazy, Nacho, that's a bunch of stuff. Maybe so, if that's what you think, but just as long as there's something to talk about, because if not it'd be too bad.

Güero Paparruchas was the youngest of the old narrators, and he couldn't have been more than sixty-five when he died. That day, the old men didn't trade stories or tell jokes. They only exchanged a few words, and when it started to turn dark each one disappeared on his own way. They didn't form part of the funeral procession, but they saw when Paparruchas's body was carried into the church. After the funeral mass, they saw the coffin on the shoulders of his friends and

142

relatives as the procession disappeared from view. That day they didn't buzz with real or invented stories, but they did take note of things that they hadn't seen in detail for years. They looked at each other with great curiosity without making any comments: seas of wrinkles and watery eyes in very old faces. They looked at their hands, fingernails, their scuffed and tattered shoes. Their canes looked like strange objects to them. The benches they usually sat on were a faded green. They had lost their paint in part, and moreover they were made of wood. For the first time they noticed that the eucalyptus trees that surrounded them were tall and that—strange thing—there were birds in them. The birds flew back and forth, singing. When some person walked across the plaza, they followed him with their gaze, intrigued. They looked at the people who walked by them as intently as though they were laboratory specimens. A four-year-old got away from his mother, and stopped dead still in front of them. The old men stood frozen with surprise: that small-sized person was in effect a new object full of energy, running around on all fours, waving his arms, shouting, dynamic, tireless. A few tears escaped from Teófilo's eyes, and he pretended he'd gotten something in his eyes and wiped his face. Don Nacho looked dumbly out from his bitter face of an old man with rusty pipes. Old Abelardo took the hand of the child with reverence, looking into his youthful eyes. It was a day of few words. The old gabbers gave their words up to the streets, to the sidewalks, to the trees, to the surrounding landscape. For a moment they contemplated ecstatically the two peaks that jutted up from the hillside on the brief mountain range that runs along the side of the village, the ones the Spaniards called the Cathedral and the Indians before them knew as the hill of the Twin Tits.

It arrived in Santa María de las Piedras in 1915 on horseback: war, death, revolution, fear, hunger. Dogs, wolves, coyotes and vultures stuff themselves on the fallen. Desolation prevails and no one can predict what will happen. There are signs among the revolutionary chiefs of the metamorphosis their spirits will undergo. Men whose school is war and who attain the highest levels of military rank spring from among the despised and hopeless youths who formerly had nothing. The aspirants to power arise from among those who were once young, furious idealists and fanatical ideologues. Social justice is the guiding theme of their speeches. With extremely rare exceptions, they are moved now by the ambition for power and wealth. The passion for vengeance materializes as a weapon of death at the beck and call of the conquerors. The bulk of the revolutionaries follow their leaders blindly. The very clear objectives of the revolution become abstract, distant, incredible, strange. The peasants crush the forces of Victoriano Huerta. The army of marihuana-smoking soldiers succumbs.

Before the revolutionaries turned on themselves, hungry for power and wealth, the revolution came to Santa María de las Piedras like a wave surging up from the center of an ocean. It came like a whiplash. General Isaías Gallardete faced two thousand conscripts on horseback, half naked, sunburned as black as skillets, shrimpy in stature, their faces like stone. He sent an advance party to reconnoiter from the top of the Twin Tits. Water! Or we're in a fuck of a mess. The bladders of men and beasts are parched from lack of water. The May sun had drunk up even the breath of the stones. The rattlesnakes and gila monsters, heroic and rabid, haughtily contemplate the heavens from their lookouts of fire and sand. A blanket of a million cicadas intensify their cry to the last vibration of their sirens. General Gallardete, sir, this village has about three thousand souls, but you can't see a single one. I suspect they're all sleeping. Lieutenant Cuchillo! Take your people and form a flank to the east. Colonel Machetazo! Take your braves to the west. Those with horses stay with me! We will take the town, get provisions, rest a few days so the horses can get their strength back, and then we'll leave this hell as quickly as possible. Don't go too far with the women. Shoot any rebels or suspicious-acting citizens. We'll conscript the young men. Forward, march! Let's go. They had arrived like ghosts, as though a crack had opened up in the desert like an enormous vagina and given birth to horses and men. All because the bigwigs were squabbling. Colonel Rosario Cuamea, a fierce revolutionary, was hot on their heels. For the last three months the dreaded colonel had been pursuing them without letup. "General Maldonado, sir, please do me the favor of allowing me to go after General Gallardete to catch him and his men and beat the shit out of them." Well, everybody knew that this Colonel Cuamea was hot for Death herself and, moreover, that he always got his way. The feared Yaqui Indian had learned his own brand of Spanish in the revolution. General Isaías Gallardete and his men had lost their way, more concerned about escaping than fighting. He didn't realize he was coming up against a labyrinth. With no notion of the weather or the terrain they were traversing, they were swept toward the unknown like a ship adrift. What General Gallardete least expected was that the defenders of Santa María de las Piedras would keep him at bay for three days and three nights. When he finally did enter the town, he left more than 1500 of his soldiers on the ground. The federal troops hastened to heed the order to attack that their general shouted. No sooner had the contingent commanded by Lieutenant Cuchillo reached the outskirts of Santa María de las Piedras than they ran into a group of strange warriors. They were children! A few kids dressed in blue. They fought with flying slingshots. Guns or subma-chine guns claimed no victims, but the stones felled instead the tattered soldiers, hitting them smack in the middle of the face. There they lay for all eternity with their mouths sagging open toward one side. Their eyes were turned up but open, as though giving a signal to the buzzards. Have you ever noticed how they go first for the eyes? Well, there goes Colonel Machetazo in the other direction, where he runs into a guy wearing a tunic with his hair standing on end, claiming to be the commander of some fifty guys fighting with clubs. I can't deny someone must have gotten shot, but there was not a single casualty. Just imagine, these scruffy guys only had to hit once with their clubs, but right in the neck, and one blow was quite enough, putting the soldiers out like a light. Well, what can I say, fellows, there was General Gallardete with his cavalry, if you can call those scrawny nags they were riding on horses, because they were nothing but bags of bones. They came upon a boy about eighteen years old, riding a handsome white horse. You should've seen that horse strut. The boy was dressed like a Roman, but without the knee pads and without a helmet. The young man was very pretty, with long hair and no trace of a beard. The truth is that he looked like a young woman or a pansy. The boy had five companions with him, male or female, who knows? According to the testimony of the federal troops, they just stood there. But then like magic, General Gallardete's troop was decimated. He saw with terror how his men fell off their mounts, spurting foaming blood from what was left of their necks. The fury of such accurate swords resulted in only a single beheading. After that encounter there were fewer than two hundred conscripts left, terrified because the mysterious army had disappeared in the direction of the plaza. Some said that it vanished behind the church that forms an alley between the wall of the Bichicoris' house. Finally, General Isaías Gallardete entered Santa María de las Piedras followed by a group of beaten and muttering soldiers. He entered in defeat, not as a vanquisher, but on foot because the horses had been left lying among the cactuses. They threw themselves under the ash trees in the plaza. The buzzards grew fat from gouging eyes out and picking bones clean. The townspeople locked themselves up in the farthest reaches of their houses, from where they could smell the stench of the carcasses. If the priest had not gone out with fresh water to revive the soldiers lying all over, they would all still be there. Even at that, several died. No, it wasn't Father Hilario at all. His mother would have just started looking for a husband about that time. It was Father Cosme Auxilio. Who wouldn't remember Father Hilario? It seemed like only yesterday he took up with Susana, Lazareto the coalman's little girl. Gossip, Teófilo, pure gossip. Father Hilario was a man of good intentions. He was a man like you and me, but he tried to lead his flock on the road of righteousness. He never refused to give bread to the hungry nor at any time to help anyone who needed to die in peace. If he had not been firm in his religious and moral convictions, what would've become of this town? The fact is that priests are victims of evil tongues. He was a worthy pastor of his flock. Sure, Don Teófilo, but he separated the she-goats. Shut up, Güero Paparruchas, you heretic! Evil tongues said that Father Hilario gave a bag of money to Rémulo the sacristan to take care of the virginity of the little fifteen-year-old. Rémulo said that out of revenge against the priest for having stopped him from taking a cut from the alms money. Well, for your information, Rémulo said in the Golden Honeycomb that the priest got her down on the desk in the sacristy with her legs up in the air. Sure, and you were the pillow for her, you liar. If you start up again with your pack of lies, I'll baptize you with my cane, Güero, you liar. They call me fighting ready, Don Teófilo. That's enough, gentlemen, let's get back to what happened to the soldiers. Father Auxilio, try as he might, couldn't convince anybody to be a good Samaritan and help the conscripts. About four in the afternoon, he had already given each one of the buggers something to drink. He realized he was obliged to feed them. Otherwise he would have a pile of bodies in front of his church. He sat down in the middle of the plaza on one of the benches that surround the bandstand. His gaze wandered, leaping from one bunch of rocks to another, then it flew over the cactuses until the distance came out and swallowed it up with its ash-blue jaws. At five o'clock Father Auxilio was still in the same spot, except now he was crying like a child because no one offered to help him calm the chorus of wailing coming from the hungry and the wounded. Then night fell with its dull step, like a mother who bundles her suffering up in a black shawl. Father Auxilio continued to cry quietly over his powerlessness, looking up at the sky. All the stars, timid and kind, converged in his eyes. The wailing cut the waves of silence and wounded the distances. Father Auxilio fell into a drowziness like a dream, allowing him to sleep and to keep watch while barely conscious. The miraculous child appeared on one of the paths, walking without touching the ground. As in a shared dream, everyone felt his presence. The holy child, who seemed like he had sprung forth from phosphorescent clouds, stepped among the dying, his footsteps blue. It was then that gangrenous purple regained the whiteness of happy dreams. He was a youth so beautiful that he brought the day with him, to judge by the light shining around him. He wore a black hat like the one the Holy Father wears. He was wearing a habit the color of poetic blue, a short brown cape tied around his neck with white tassels, and sandals on his feet. He carried a staff in his right hand, and in the other a piece of bread. There was a gourd of holy water tied to his waist. He went about treating everybody at the same time! It was enough for the wounded to barely moisten their lips with the miraculous water in the gourd for thirst and suffering to yield to well-being. With a tiny piece of the bread that he proffered with his little hands, hunger fled and vitality returned in full force. Despite the fact that he suddenly disappeared,he remained stamped forever on the retinas of those exhausted soldiers. What a beautiful child! What a glorious smile!

After the shouts and cries had quickly subsided, the explosion of silence reached Father Auxilio. He ran over to the wounded, believing in his anguish that they had died. Not only were they still alive, but they were sleeping peacefully and were healthy, almost smiling. Father Auxilio knelt. It's him, the Holy Child of Atocha, who goes throughout the world taking pity on those who are down on their luck, especially wounded soldiers, no matter which side they are on.

A whole day went by; another night fell; hunger returned to General Gallardete's troops. He knew that in less than five days he would have his pursuer on his back. The mere mention of Colonel Chayo Cuamea's name made him grind his teeth. Since everyone in Santa María de las Piedras was on the side of the revolution, no one came to Father Auxilio's aid on behalf of the soldiers. General Gallardete was striding about the plaza at midnight, his stomach empty, his heart overflowing with worry. Like a dream, the procession of campfollowers arrived along with dawn. They had been delayed in the desert, even though, as usual, they had left a day early to get to the place first in order to be ready right from the start to serve their men. They lost their way among the dunes because of a storm that even sent the sun into hiding. They roamed around in circles for a couple of days without resting and without water, constantly moving, dry, blackened, looking for their men. With short, firm, harmonic steps, they reached the plaza in Santa María de las Piedras in silence. They scurried along without letting out a single sound. They lowered to the ground the pots they were carrying on their heads replete with kitchen utensils, medicines and so on. Then they loosened the packs on their backs. They did everything mechanically like an often-repeated ritual. While some gathered firewood, others went for water, built fires, set beans to cooking, chopped dried meat, made cornmeal dough, and put their cooking plates over improvised stoves. Even with all that, they found the time to run their bony hands over the foreheads of their wounded and exhausted men. By the time the sun made the atmosphere burst with the dawn, the wounded had atole to drink and food in abundance. Yet they ate little, drinking calmly. Their stomachs had shrunk to the size of a fist, and the water made its way through almost-forgotten conduits. There was room that morning for a few tears and to give thanks to the Almighty.

The men were once again whole thanks to the presence of the women. In two days, as a consequence of the careful attention and

148

the kind good will of Father Auxilio, the soldiers were in a condition to continue their march. General Gallardete, seeing his soldiers well, proposed a plan: they would sack the homes and carry off as a conscript any child over fifteen years old. That Thursday morning General Gallardete instructed his officers to pretend to be retreating. But they were to break ranks suddenly and storm the houses. We are not Sisters of Charity. War is war and we need more soldiers. Colonel Machetazo and Sergeant Sangría had the troops fall into line. The campfollowers had been on their way for hours. They were about to execute their orders when they saw Father Auxilio standing in front of the door of the church. General Gallardete couldn't help but thank him for so much bountiful kindness. But the priest answered him that he owed him nothing. But they might come into the house of God, to whom they did owe their thanks and to whom they were obliged to personally pay their respects. General Gallardete, other officers, and half a dozen soldiers entered the church. In the house of God the contrast between peace and war hung heavy. They felt strange, afraid, a little guilty. They looked around and up at the ceiling, flustered. Suddenly General Gallardete stopped cold, and turned pale; he would have fallen if Sergeant Sangría had not caught him: right in front of him stood the wooden figure of the beautiful young man who had beheaded his people, Saint Michael the Archangel, the scourge of the devil! Colonel Machetazo, Sergeant Sangría, and the soldiers began to tremble, with their teeth chattering. There was the exquisitely carved figure of the long-haired youth in the tunic who had shown them their fate at the end of a club. They grabbed at their necks instinctively. Saint John the Baptist! They rushed head over heels from the church, jamming against each other in the doorway, and the General himself caught someone's elbow in his left nipple. Soldiers, let's get out of this town! Don't touch a hair of these people. We'll cross the desert, no matter who dies. There's nothing we can do against this race of warriors. There go the women with their packs on their backs and the pots on their heads. Between hell and the desert, there is no choice. It's the same flames, the same fire. The soldiers march by later, carrying the sun on their shoulders, their feet treading on little bits of sun. The shade accompanying them is none other than Death herself. So long, General Gallardete and your troops! Best regards to Neverseeyou!

Little or nothing was ever found out about the warrior children.

As much as they rummaged in sacred history, they could find nothing. The only thing they were sure about was the accuracy with which their little hands had wielded the slingshots and the dizzing impact with which the stones smashed heads. The soldiers and Father Auxilio deliberated in a circle about this very strange occurrence. They ended up going two hours without saying a word, lost in the world of ideas, seeking some sign over and over among the atavic constellations, no matter how uncertain. Suddenly it struck Father Auxilio, and his lower lip stretched in a slight smile. He spoke with a learned voice: they are ghosts of the children of the Holy Crusades. They were children made to swim the sea to save the Holy Sepulchre from the bastard infidels.

No sooner had the federal army disappeared than the inhabitants of Santa María de las Piedras filled the plaza, talking excitedly about the brief appearance of the conscripts. Father Auxilio cried as he talked about the divine defense by the holy. Everyone was moved and prayed contritely. They assessed the losses and damages. It became evident that nothing serious had happened to worry about. Ah, but cursed lust, the passion of the flesh, had invaded the moonlit streets of Santa María de las Piedras. There had been ten rapes, perpetrated with full premeditation, wickedness, and success. Everybody knew the full details of the sexual assaults. Morbid curiosity was thrilled by the retelling of these erotic events, and they became an obsessive topic of conversation for both men and women. The tragedy of persons who lose their virginity in such circumstances delighted everyone over and over again. But the victims were neither young girls nor married women, but a dozen men who tried unsuccessfully to hide their faces. The simple fact was that there were three campfollowers for every soldier left alive. Besides, the latter were so strung out that, despite the meticulous efforts of the women, they were unable to answer the urgent call of the flesh. Thus, silently wrapped in light clothing that blended in with the clear light of the moon, the women sneaked like silvery shadows in through windows, doors and back patios. Chibetito Cantoral, a sober young man destined for the seminary, was the first victim. There were four of them, and they led him at knife point to a corner of his own corral. When he tried to shout, one of the women, a dark-skinned hag, informed him that at the first outcry they would bury the bayonet in his bellybutton. They stripped him naked quicker than a wink. While three of them persuaded him to get his prick

150

going, the other was busy shedding her rough cotton clothes, including her mesh panties. Chibetito fixed his large eyes on the venus mound for the first time in his life and he became so filled with terror he started to stammer that he was scared to death of tarantulas. He collapsed in a faint, crying for his mother. They left him lying there, but not without first kicking him. Come on, we've ended up with a queer! Of the others they got, three were married. These were so deeply grateful for the assault that, not only did they fuck the women, but they later followed them across the desert. None of the six remaining victims knew anything about carnal love outside of fantasies and dreams, even though they were around eighteen and, by nature, full of vigor. The six were turned into lovers before they knew what was happening. Thus, by being raped, they became acquainted through the desperateness of their aggressors with the storm of sensual passion. They wanted intensely to get married, that is, if they could be excused for not being pure on their wedding night. In reality, there were dozens of men in Santa María de las Piedras who engaged in erotic acrobatics with the camp-followers camouflaged by the light of the moon. The former had found out about the adventures of the latter, and by pretending to be naive, they managed to get themselves in the path of the rapists. Thus they were able to succumb by design while pretending to be taken by force. Later it was discovered that, because of a full moon, they had coated their bodies with flour. Naked and invisible, they sneaked about the streets hoping to be assaulted. The home-loving women of Santa María de las Piedras also report (they tell it with their fists clenched in fury) that the thousand and one playful and spasmic screams of pleasure that arose from every corner and alleyway were taken to be the cries of the wounded in the process of yielding up their souls and on more than one occasion to be the yowling of cats in heat.

Twenty-four hours had not passed since the departure of the soldiers led by General Isaías Gallardete when Colonel Rosario Cuamea, dark and smooth-skinned, thin, with a mat of hair, entered Santa María de las Piedras with ninety-three Yaqui Indians on horseback. Some of the horses were shod. Since it was getting dark, you could see the sparks fly from each hoof as the metal struck the stone pavement. They set up camp between the church and the plaza. The terrible Cuamea immediately assembled the principal citizens of Santa María de las Piedras. Don Hilario Noragua, Father Auxilio,

Don Exaltación Rodó, the police chief, and a few other patriarchs were there.

Okay, first I want you to tell me in which direction General Gallardete and his men went off, when they left and how many there were. There were about one hundred and fifty of them, sir, with about two hundred campfollowers in the lead. That's strange. Where'd they get so many women? We've only got seven. Did they have a lot of weapons? Colonel Chayo Cuamea, sir, when they reached the edge of this town, General Gallardete had something like a thousand soldiers on foot and about two hundred on horseback. You should know that, in fierce combat, they were defeated in three days and only a little more than a hundred survived, hungry and wounded. Ah, yes, and who reprovisioned them, then? Just tell me that. The government troops themselves are witnesses, Colonel, that they were defeated by the saints. You don't say, now. Yes, sir, Colonel Cuamea, that's what I'm telling you. They stumbled on the archangel Saint Michael and some angels of his legion. I want you to know that they put to the sword those who were not left dead. Then Saint John the Baptist and his men with clubs bashed a lot of federal soldiers. You should've seen them; they looked like startled hares. The children of the crusades, colonel, fired rocks at any enemy that got in their sights. I'm not a child, so don't go telling me stories like that, God damn it! Saint John and the angels and the children of their mothers, I'll be damned. Do you think I'm a stupid idiot? And who tended their wounds, then? They certainly were able to get away in a hurry. It was the Holy Child of Atocha, may God be blessed. The Holy Child of Atocha, my balls! Hunger must really be getting to your brains. These are nothing but pipe dreams! I fought with Gallardete for barely a month, up in the Chihuahua mountains, and I left him with a hundred men and we took his old ladies away from him. Where do you get off telling me they were more than a thousand? This is really strange!

The revolutionary, a pure-blooded Yaqui, ordered food for his troops, stressing that there'd better be meat and pinole and quelites. Espiridión, a sickly old man, a comet with a tail many years old and eyes whose irises had only a sliver of blue left, spoke in a thin voice with a tone of distant echoes. And how are we going to get meat for you, seeing as how we don't even have it to give to our children, much less for us old people and the women and anybody else? Can't you see we are all skin and bones here in Santa María de las Piedras? You couldn't find a fat person here to save your soul. As soon as we scrape a bit of food together, the government soldiers show up and take it away from us. The soldiers leave and you arrive and take the food from our mouths. Shut up, old man! If I don't shoot you for being such a nuisance, it's because time has already gotten you. Can't you understand I'm a revolutionary officer? Whatever we take now will be paid for by the revolution. You, priest, get us the money for tomorrow afternoon, five thousand pesos. But, son, I do not have that kind of money. Well, get it! Either you get it right away or I'll break you. You don't mess around with the revolution! I'll pay you back twice as much when we get it from the reactionary forces. And don't forget, we want meat for us and hay for our animals. By next week, we'll have beaten the shit out of Gallardete. Don't give me that stuff about the children of the crusades and little angels, with or without long hair and armed with clubs. Whoever heard such a thing!

In Colonel Rosario Cuamea's troop there were more pure Yaquis than mestizos; maybe one or two sunburned and shaggy whites who looked more Yaqui than the Yaquis themselves. Everyone knew it was no secret that the Yaqui Indian Cuamea inspired terror with his boldness. Blood led him on, and as soon as he smelled it, he fought like a dog. Nevertheless, he inspired more fear for his lust: any woman he set his eyes on ended up plastered beneath his bellybutton. It is factual knowledge that he came down from the mountains of Bacatete looking like a barbarian. The war was his school, and he learned Spanish among the troops. It was also in the heat of battle that he fell so passionately in love with Death that he swore to hold her in his arms and love her with all his might. In the thick of battle, when flesh and bones were being crushed beneath a rain of blood, the Yaqui Indian Cuamea spotted Death out of the corner of his eye as she was carrying off souls from among the dead bodies, and the libidinous fellow would sneak up on her with his machete drawn. She got away twice by a hair. But the dove really fell asleep on him. Thinking that the soul of the wicked man had been set free, she climbed up on him in order to blow out the small lights barely left flickering in his eyes. That's when the Yaqui stuck it to his rider. She was so enraged that she grabbed on to the bundle of roots that grew in his breast for centuries back to yank it out but good, dragging

153

it off like it was a tangle of snakes. Before something that unusual would happen in the savage Yaqui's old age, many things were still to take place in his adventures.

The women of Santa María de las Piedras had the great fortune that Chayo Cuamea arrived newly married to Macuca Topete Q. Otherwise, he would have been messing around with young girls as well as with old ladies, even more so with those ripe to be picked or ready and willing. Macuca Topete Q. was a bony frame covered over with leather, with breasts as flat as a plank, buttocks with no padding whatever. The ridges of her pubis were as aggressive as the forehead of a goat ready to charge. That's why Rosario Cuamea loved her, because he saw in her his skeletal fantasy, his beloved woman of death. Mucuca Topete Q. was a first-class campfollower. Not only did she give herself body and skeleton to her Chayo Cuamea, but in addition to carrying on her back the cooking plate and other kitchen utensils, she also toted a pick and shovel. Colonel Rosario Cuamea, recently Christianized, did not like to leave lying around on the ground the dead he had created by dint of the grace of his 30-30. He felt compelled by devotion to bury them. His humble and faithful companion took charge of this task. There were days when Macuca dug more than a dozen graves, all with the prescribed depth unless she was digging at straight rock, in which case she only went down three feet. But her lord and master had to give his permission first. Then she would prepare her man's meals: beans, dried meat, freshly-patted tortillas and something to drink, all this in the moments between burying perforated bodies. On top of these activities, enough to do the toughest sort in, Macuca Topete Q. gave herself with Dantesque passion to her Yaqui Colonel. The two of them filled many a night with laughter and the catlike shouts of their lovemaking, mixed with the moans and groans of the whores and the dying soldiers. The next day, when the second hand crossed ten in the morning with the rhythm of a waltz, there was no sign of the provisions of meat that Colonel Cuamea had demanded nor of the five thousand pesos that Father Auxilio was to lend the revolutionary cause. The townspeople of Santa María de las Piedras trembled in hiding in their houses of stone and mud. The majority of those who walked the streets were Cuamea's own warriors. Suddenly, from one of the houses next to the church, the one belonging to the Paredes family, to be exact, Oralia ran out shouting. Alarmed, Father Auxilio rushed out of the sacristy, as did the other townspeople, among them those commissioned to provide the meat requested under pain of death. Doña Oralia's nerves had snapped, and she was screaming and pulling at her hair. Colonel Chayo Cuamea and various soldiers joined the scene. What was happening to this screaming woman? A revolutionary climbed into my house through a window! Quick, save my children! Various soldiers knocked the door open and ran into Oralia's house, followed by Colonel Cuamea. There they found the soldier Nandino Colorado seated at the table devouring beans from a pot. He was shoveling them in his mouth in large quantities with the help of wheat tortillas. Shoot this man right now for insubordination! Nandino Colorado looked at the Colonel with the eyes of a whipped dog, and asked him for a final wish: permission to finish his banquet because he was very hungry. I couldn't stand it any longer, Colonel, sir. You son of a bitch! Shoot him! Nandino Colorado was placed against the side of the church, facing the Paredes house. Oralia and Father Auxilio threw themselves on their knees before Colonel Chayo, sobbing and begging for mercy for the hungry peasant who had just joined his ranks as a combatant. The execution took place before half a dozen terrified townspeople. Nandino Colorado was shot by six of his comrades. Ready, aim, fire! was shouted out by the Colonel himself. Moments later the figure of Macuca Topete Q. could be seen on her way to the cemetery, dressed in black, looking taller and thinner, stooped, walking slowly under the weight of the pick and shovel on her back. The very small amount of livestock owned by the starving townspeople yielded a sacrifice to the revolutionaries of ten goats, three skinny cows, five calves and about twenty chickens. Father Auxilio gave the five thousand pesos to Colonel Chayo in silver coins, trembling, his eyes red with circles. With this money he said good-bye to the restoration of the church's façade. The edges of the niches were eroded; there was a headless Saint Anthony; another saint was so disfigured that his identity was no longer clear, not to mention three angels with missing and damaged wings. The church needed hands and money for its preservation.

As was the custom, the women left first on foot. By the time midday was becoming afternoon, they entered the desert enveloped in the burning pyre. The only thing that resisted the intense thrust of the flaming atmosphere was a deep silence and its millenary faces sculpted in granite. Hours later, when the sun stretched itself out with large wings along the peak, Colonel Chayo Cuamea left Santa

155

María de las Piedras, haranguing his troops: General Gallardete will pay for this.

Once the darkness and the distance had swallowed up the outlines of the troops of the wild Chayo Cuamea, all of the parishioners of Santa María de las Piedras met in the church to thank God for mercy. Nevertheless, their faces betrayed an enormous exhaustion; they were so overwrought that their eyes filled with sadness. The priest said in his sermon that God often puts the faith of his followers to test, and more than once he emphasized that God's plans were inscrutable. Father Auxilio could not help but see the hard looks the men and women cast out of the corners of their eyes at Saint Michael the Archangel, Saint John the Baptist, and even the Holy Child of Atocha. It was certainly strange that they had fought with such verve and diligence the hosts of General Gallardete, saving the women from dishonor and the boys from being conscripted. But yet they had refused to even try to staunch the barbarianism of Colonel Chayo Cuamea. God's plans are inscrutable, Father Auxilio was repeating. The people left the church a little angry at the saints. When had Churrunga Alemán ever kept her mouth shut? She was shouting at the top of her lungs that the saints had taken sides and that they were a pack of Pancho Villa's supporters. It's just great that they've become revolutionaries, but they ought to stop and take a look at the others and do something about that damned animal who was worse than the Huerta supporters. That guy is taking advantage of the revolution to do whatever he damn well pleases. Liberty and justice, my ass! Shameful creature, cheating shepherd, fuck-face. Meanwhile, dumb little miraculous captains are hiding in the church, oh yes, with their holy swords, their divine clubs, and the stones of the blessed kids. Shit! What really happened is that they were afraid of that Yaqui stud. They were scared shitless of him. Just shut up, Doña Churrunga, you act like the devil's gotten into you! Your fucking mother is the one the devil's gotten into! Let your grandmothers do the praying from now on, damned saints.

Rosario Cuamea had been pursuing General Gallardete for seventeen months. Every time he came upon him, the two armies would lock in such fearsome combat that they ended up sharing defeat. They even came to forget why they were fighting. The passion for revenge both inspired and enraged them. They seem to move in an eternal circle. According to General Gallardete, he pretended to flee as a strategem to exhaust his enemy in the pursuit.

Meanwhile desert and time were devouring everybody. Chayo Cuamea and his soldiers came in their raging madness to believe that the Sonoran Desert was endless. General Gallardete, for his part, with intimate sarcasm, perfected more and more the circle that he drew with each turn about the wasteland. Back and forth, little by little, the two leaders were left without troops. If the combatants did not desert, it was because they fell in battle. And what was not accomplished by hatred and bullets was executed by the passing of time. Both officers, with a few faithful followers at their side, continued to circle about the desert. They occasionally reached the edge of a town to reprovision. More than anything else, they persevered out of inertia, until the day came when amnesia drove them completely mad, not for reasons of war but as a consequence of the effects of the intense heat which had, little by little, drained their memory. In the final days of the absurd campaigning in which the two warriors were locked, strange things happened. Since they continued to go in circles over the sand, they followed each other's tracks, each accusing the other of being a coward and afraid to stand up and fight. Not only did they get lost among the dunes, but also in time. What was a couple of weeks' action was registered by them as the heroic operation of years. The month of August turned out to belong completely to the sun, who took up residence with all its flaming raiment.

The men of Cuamea fell that morning into a very deep sleep, so unusual that they failed to awaken to the dawn as was their custom, but to a blazing sun. The rain of light given off by the sun flooded the atmosphere with fiery waves. Macuca Topete Q., who would go weeks without saying a word, spoke: we no longer live on earth but on the sun itself. The Yaqui Indian Cuamea and Sergeant Sangría laughed secretly while pointing at the others. Then everybody whispered in each other's ears and burst out laughing. They began by trying to figure out what color their skins really were, and they thought that was a lot of fun. With their bones sticking out and their skin extremely burned, they could pass for any race. The fact is that they started kidding each other about being so dark. Cuamea yelled at them, choking with laughter: laughing like that, you all look like you have a piece of cheese in your mouth, you poor bastards. You look like you've got a corncob stuck in your face, slob, Bichi Buitimea answered back. Everybody's hair had turned white, and they all looked like photographic negatives. Suddenly there was silence. Then they all began to ask each other their names, where they were from, and where they had been. They discovered they couldn't remember a thing. In reality Bichi Buitimea was the worst off of the group. He had been sort of an errand boy of the officers, assigned to the task of helping the women cook. When there was no water, he would scrape off the cicadas and the bits of snake that stuck to the bottom on the pans. The Yaqui Indian Cuamea started to ask him to tie his shoes for him. When he was in a bad mood, he would abuse him to the point of slapping him. Bichi Buitimea was able to pass himself off as retarded, although the campfollowers knew full well that he was quite shrewd. He knew how to take advantage of situations by keeping his mouth shut. The questions were all the same. Who are we? What are we doing here? It was then that Bichi raised his voice with great strength. We're muleteers, then! And where are our animals? We can't see any horses or mules. Of course not, because we ate them, we were so hungry. Ah, right! And why are we carrying weapons? The federal army has ordered us to take them to Santa María de las Piedras because there's a gang of traitorous bandits in the desert that's rebelled against the high government. The Yaqui Indian Cuamea approached Bichi and shot him two questions. Who's our leader, then? Who's in charge? Bichi rose up on his heels. I'm the boss, you fucks! Cuamea, out of sheer instinct, answered by sticking his face in the other's: I don't like you as chief. Bichi Buitimea landed such a heavy slap between Cuamea's jaw and ear that the latter got up spitting sand and blood, crying like a baby. There was no further argument, and everything was jokes and laughter.

In General Isaías Gallardete's camp, something similar happened. In the middle of the anvil of solar heat, the soldiers wandered about like phosphorescent hulks, their skin wrinkled from being so dry and their bones sticking out because they were so emaciated. Their appearance coincided exactly with that of mummies, with the difference that the eyes of the ragtag soldiers looked like insects lodged in their hollows. The general carried his pants over his shoulder, looking half-naked for them among his other things. A group of soldiers improvised an orchestra with the kitchen utensils. Two of them were imitating the sound of the bugle by holding their closed fists against their mouths. They claimed to be playing "La Adelita." The necessary questions rang out. Who are we? What are we doing in this oven? Where have we come from and where are we going? Clarification came from an exaggeratedly short soldier whose name was Circuncisión Tanilo Aldrete de la Rinconada. We are members of a scientific expedition that left Aguas Calientes a few months back. We have come to Sonora in search of a town lost in the desert centuries ago. So, what's the name of the town? It's the town of Santa María de las Piedras. Bah! As far as I'm concerned, that town is a legend, Chon el Golondrino said. Folklore, nothing but damn folklore, seconded Analítico Cantú. Maybe it's a novel. That idea came from Guavesi the bugle boy. Everyone started to laugh until their eyes turned red. Then why aren't we wearing explorer clothes like in the movies? As far as I know we're dressed like soldiers. Ah! That's because the government doesn't have any other kind of clothes. Everybody accepted completely what Circuncisión had to say, and they continued to goof around happily. It seems they understood deep down that they would no longer have to beat the shit out of their fellow soldiers, and that made them happy. At no time did they argue about rank, but yet something very strange happened. They started to call General Gallardete "Papa," Colonel Machetazo "Son," and Sergeant Sangría "Uncle."

It happened one day when the ashes of the blistering air were flying about. The rival troops happened to stumble on each other in the middle of the immense wasteland. With fewer than twenty soldiers in each group and something like three women, they set up camp a little ways apart facing each other. They visited back and forth, they traded their poor rations, they drank juice made from cactus meat, they conversed with great curiosity. Each asked where the other was from, what they were doing, where they were going. They answered back silly things, and they began to laugh until they were doubled over. The federal soldiers did not call Isaías Gallardete "General, Sir," but they did call him "Papa," wrinkling up their foreheads. Among Cuamea's men, it was Bichi Buitimea, a buck private, who gave orders. They claimed to be muleteers whose mules had all died. That same day Bichi Buitimea had kicked Chayo Cuamea in the butt for fooling around with the cooks. Colonel Chayo Cuamea asks General Gallardete what he's looking for. Something, he answers, clenching his fists. He could intuit the presence of the hated Yaqui Indian. And you? he asks in turn. I think I'm looking for a . . . a . . . and then he quickly changed the subject. Chayo Cuamea, with his eyes shut from laughing so hard, asked the general if he knew where women have curly hair. You already know where, Gallardete answered, playing along with the

159

joke. No, that's not right. It's in Africa where women have curly hair. They laughed like they were lifelong brothers. Then the most extraordinary thing happened: they started playing ring-around-the-rosy. Men with faces hardened by hatred, cruelty and exhausting marches, with scars made by bullets and machetes, with ears missing, mutilated, and lame, started acting like innocent, tender, smiling children. Holding hands, they started to play games like "Doña Bárbara," "La pájara pinta," along with "Mambrú se fue a la guerra." They didn't look like the bloody combatants who scarcely nine days ago had clashed in a battle that took more than thirty lives on each side. The bodies had left a mass of guts, blood, shit, curses and moans so penetrating that even the coyotes got goose bumps. Now they were playing "Los encantados." When someone was it, he would stand in a comic pose to make the others roar with laughter. They were all laughing because of the fun they were having. At midnight they separated. But first they offered each other the provisions that had allowed them to survive in such an inhospitable environment. The revolutionaries presented the federal troops with two half-filled sacks of dried crickets and one of locusts, telling them to flavor them with chiles for better taste and that for protein there was nothing like these delicacies. They also gave them some sweat beetles, which, despite being dried out, stretched like rubber when chewed. The federal troops responded with three bales of rattlesnakes, delicious roasted over coals, a bag of dry rodents, hares, rats, and so on, along with some burro bones that, despite already having been used on various occasions, still could flavor a pot. They said good-bye to each other with shining eyes, happy and sad at the same time. The soldier Bichi Buitimea told them to be careful. There were rumors of armed bandits in the desert. He stressed that these bandits were led by a Yaqui Indian who was very bad and ugly. There was only a little bit of trouble that night when the Yaqui Indian Cuamea put his hands on Verónica, the favorite of the Creole Gallardete. Gallardete looked closely at Macuca Topete Q., attacking the Yaqui Indian and yelling to him that he was a bastard, abusive, and ready to take advantage of any situation. Two days later came the irremediable confusion of the breaking up of each group of warriors. Now they were looking for themselves, lost in an enormous inner desert.

So it was that one day by mere chance, the two enemy officers ran into each other in the plaza in Santa María de las Piedras without even recognizing each other. General Gallardete asked Colonel Cuamea, taking him for someone who lived there, to tell him where the telegraph office was, because he had to send an urgent communiqué. Colonel Chayo Cuamea asked in turn where the brothel was located. When each saw that the other was a stranger in town, they both laughed, saluted each other with a slight bow, and never saw each other again.

Magic and myth, outstripped by the overbearing nature of the unknown being, weigh with their enormous pressure on the mind of the simple man who had suddenly jumped from one realm of time (fixed in remote centuries when man made the will of his mind prevail with rudimentary techniques) to another one, separated by centuries of distance, even when it coincided with a single present. His whole curiosity turned into fear. The pleasure he derived from discovering the unknown and the certainty of witnessing the presence of a great architect now turned for him into abstractions in which only a strange fear surfaced, a fear as great as all the fears together of all men of all time, He no longer invoked the name of Huachusey! Every time it came to him, he hid his face, as though he wished to rid himself of it as he undertook his return or to cast it from his thoughts forever. He no longer pretended to see him at all. He fled from his encounter. Nevertheless, destiny meant for him to come face to face with that mystery: Huachusey and he would come face to face. Finally he would meet him. Death would be better!

Salomón's quadruplicated steps resounded on the cement, while Timoteo's dragged behind. You can feel dawn coming. The moon has traced an arch from one ocean to the other, and now it is a ship about to enter the sea cautiously. Another enormous city can be seen before the pilgrims, one whose soaring constructions are giants that reach up to the very clouds. There was no light to be seen around it. Not a single light can maintain its glow in such vast spaces. Dawn gives way to the morning, and the masses whose roots extend deep into the ground turn golden. In the sky there are signs of blood and gold. The highways are abandoned tracks. There is no traffic, and there is a complete absence of human beings. Something has happened, something unusual: there are cars, thousands of immobile cars distributed on the freeways, alone, without apparent owners. No one is around them, no one claims them, there is no mind to make them go. The sirens and ambulances and police cars that cry and scream in cities lie quiet, dead and buried, squashed by a marble silence. The ships that make the sky howl when they thrust themselves dizzyingly in the entrails of the firmament fail to appear. As extensive as the city and as gigantic as the buildings is the silence of the city without voices, without souls, without the screeching and the braying of cars being cut off or the howl of tires being stripped by violent braking, or the wild scream of women being viciously raped, or the contagious fever of television sets spitting out one stupidity after another—knives, tits, asses—or the metal screech that impregnates the air with the bloody spirit of glass and granite surfaces. It is daytime, and man and beast cross the heart of the city. Timoteo stops every now and then to examine the growing silence and solitude. Suddenly he is gripped by anxiety, his face wrinkles, his eyes feel like they are going to jump out of his head. It's a trap! It's him, it must be him! The only inhabitant of the ghost city. He has led him to his abode in order to make him pay for his audacity and for having evoked him so many times. He evoked his presence and asked after him so many times. He dreamed of knowing him. Huachusey! He was surrounded by the light of hope. Now, right now, that he can feel his presence near, he chokes with fear. He's dragging Salomón along with the urgency that gives wings to anxieties. Come on, Salomón, let's get back to Santa María de las Piedras right away. Back in our village they will never find us because no one knows it exists. At each intersection he looks about carefully. He looks both to the right and left, one after another, the stockade of skyscrapers crowned by a wisp of thin clouds. Heavy breathing and the sustained thumping sounds in his chest, along with the secret prayers and the pounding of the little burro's four paws on the concrete, bouncing off the iron and the solid walls like the crash of a rockslide. He feels his presence, knows that he is close to meeting him. He hears the noise made by a heavy flow that carries along objects colliding with each other. Is that him approaching? It is a windstorm that bears bones along with it. Then he sees groups of skeletal forms here and there. He looks in the windows of public buildings, and what he sees makes his hair stand on end. Good Lord! What a horrible fright! The skeletons of once beautiful cashiers seated at the cash registers reveal their full bony structure. On padded seats around tables, happy people, whose flesh has been devoured in turn by other mysterious customers, pretend to enjoy each other's company. Timoteo notices the holy cross in stone that stands out on the face of a building and the carving of the Savior alongside the doorway. He hurries in, and sees human figures of all ages in the interrupted mass. They are nothing but skulls set on sternums and rib cages. In the cars paralyzed in the middle of the streets there are also dead people holding onto the steering wheels with hands reduced to claws. There is a moment when the Indian goes from sobbing to convulsive crying, praying with his arms spread. With his gaze on high, he shouts: Leave me alone! Leave me . . . ! Leave me in peace, I don't want to see you. Terror forces the man and his ass to hurry their pace. He runs, gripped by fear, collapses exhausted, kneels, hugs the animal and tells him sobbing, trembling, I'm afraid, I'm terrified of finding him. They continue on their way. Silence is the absolute master of a world formerly replete with noises. Suddenly, clouds of what seems to be birds arrive in bunches from massive nearby constructions. They cast green shades, but do no harm. They lack beaks, and their whipping about causes no damage, as they are inoffensive. Timoteo examines closely the bats that have fallen around him. He's amazed and incredulous. He picks them up. They are millions and millions of dollars in bills. Bills! Money! Bills of a hundred, a thousand, ten thousand dollars! The wind plays with them, some are blown on high to come down far away, while others form small piles. Salomón goes over with deliberation and begins to eat large mouthfuls of paper money. The whole area of the city through which they are passing is full of bills. They plow through millions. Salomón stops to piss on an enormous fortune.

It's growing late. Every now and then you can hear an explosion in the solitude and silence. Imprisoned echoes burst from the nothingness with the roar of daggerlike locomotives, the feigned cry of a hungry baby, the moaning of the souls of the suffering dead, the massacre of colliding pieces of iron. The skeletons, with their eternal, faceless grins, unredeemed fools, sarcastic by nature; hah hah hah hah, their morbid jaws laugh. The silence expands to swallow the laughter. The burro Salomón and Timoteo Noragua are now crossing through a field where some children had been playing, so many that they cannot avoid stepping on bones and plastic toys. It's all only playthings: little skulls, little tanks and machine guns, fragile ribs and spinal columns, dolls and toy soldiers. The tiny forms of children playing at war. At dusk the outlines of the huge cemetery without gravestones or monuments took over. They reached a vacant lot that had until recently been the site of a shady grove. The Indian and his ass lie down to sleep like logs.

Days later, Timoteo Noragua came upon the city that he would have wished never to know. It was at the moment of a sinister fall of night that outlined the shadows of the fateful city. As he drew near the edge of the city, he was stopped by a feeling of anguish that came from deep within him. Intuition kept him from continuing forward.

The silent city in the dark seemed frightening. He camped at the edge of the ghost city because Salomón, wiser than the human, like all animals where death is concerned, became terrified and refused to go forward. The Indian Noragua did not sleep a wink, filled with fear and curiosity. At midnight his hair stood on end as though being drawn by the power of a magnet. The wailing of women filled the air, the cry growing until it hurt the ears, crawling along the ground like a wounded wolverine. As a counterpoint he heard the crying of men, weak, monotonous, husky, like a spring of blood reduced to intermittent bubbles. The chorus of cries bespoke such despair that even the hardest soul would have been moved to its very core by hearing so much hopelessness. They were praying and begging for mercy in hushed tones. The voices reached him amplified in the dark, filling him with terror. What terrible mystery that city held. He felt as though his roots were being pulled so hard they would burst. A presentiment zigzagged down his spine from head to foot. Could this city be the home of Huachusey? It was a night that lasted for centuries. At dawn the moaning began to fade with the stars, as though the latter had been responsible for it. It was then that he saw the evidence of what never, never should have happened. Man and beast were witnesses to the most frightening tragedy ever.

The skyscrapers of the enormous city that had numbered hundreds, rising triumphant like assertive babels, the wonder of the whole world, resistant to hurricanes and airplanes, lay destroyed. Opulence and solidity had become misery and ruin: mounds of pulverized bricks, heaps of dismembered concrete, here and there the remains of mechanical instruments, broken desks, refrigerators. Automatic vending machines for cigarettes, soft drinks, and candy had ceased to function along with a large number of small objects. Towering buildings whose foundations reached into the depths of basements were nothing more than overturned, twisted skeletons, half shorn off, while others were completely collapsed. Glass and plastic had melted together. Beneath that gigantic heap lay the bodies of millions of dead persons, in addition to others who had melted away, leaving no more trace than perhaps a shadow on a broken wall or a tiny bone fragment. Nevertheless, of those who had come from other neighboring cities and the survivors of remote residential areas that had resisted the impact, hundreds wandered around among the ruins in search of their loved ones. They were crying and praying with one voice, breaking into unintelligible monologues, their faces blank, their minds wandering, crazy from fear and suffering. Their faces and their clothes were nothing but dust, as though they were earthen figures. Their hair was falling out, wafting away on the wind like ashen flames of fire. The sun in the sky was hidden behind a black screen of particles and fragments. The hazy days seemed like nighttime, with dark blots instead of bright stars.

Timoteo was no longer laughing, nor was he dreaming, lost in his startling world of marvels. He was no longer the gentle, calm madman who drove the vagrants of his village to cruel actions. Now his sorrowful, somber, stony face showed no further sign of happiness, enthusiasm, or cheer. Timoteo left the edge of the city behind and prepared to cross the cadaver of the city of Fate. For hours he traversed the zone of death and silence. Astride his mount, he had no other goal except to reach his village, Santa María de las Piedras. Finally he crossed the boundaries of total annihilation and came once again to the frontiers of crying and lamentation on the other side of the ominous circle. The torture of the burns and wounds of death made the air quiver with suffering. The flayed, bleeding, gangrenous, dismembered, and the grieving who came to save them were the center of horrifying scenes. Fear and suffering provoked terrible shrieks from the deepest part of their being, as though there were atomic bombs exploding in the middle of their souls. Trying to escape that setting which afflicted him to his core, the Indian and his noble mount were crossing through an enormous space when he saw in its center a woman sitting in the middle of the cement, as the whole area was covered by pavement.

The woman was so beautiful that she could be called a celestial apparition. Alive amidst solitude and barbarous extinction, she was still beautiful. The woman's hair was clear like water, her eyes seemed made from a crystal that held the blue-green tints given off by the sky and the sea; her skin had the color of light, her forehead was sublime, her face was nobility itself. She was crying with her lips closed, without a sound; only a flow of tears altered her condition. As though lost in herself, she caressed the hair of a young man stretched across on her legs. He was a skinny boy, shirtless, barefoot. He was wearing army pants, and muddy boots were at his side. He was no longer a child, and he would never be an adult. There was a hole in his chest, another in his head The woman was bathed in blood from her waist down. The streaks of blood stretched over the pavement like lines on a map.

You do not need to tell me who was responsible for the terrible destruction of this world and the death of your son for me to know it. It can only be him. But tell me anyway. Who was it? I want to hear it from your lips. The woman did not answer. Timoteo asked again, moving his lips slowly. The woman smiled slightly, barely. A tiny sigh of lucidity penetrated the dense thickness of her shadows. Then moving only her lips she uttered the name, that name: Huachusey. . . .

The demonic force had leveled the heart of the city with total destruction, with a decreasing impact as it reached out. The dying, dismembered, incinerated bodies gave way to a circle of wounded who might live at the cost of horrible suffering. Even farther beyond, those saved from physical damage were caught up in the worst kind of hysteria, fragmented from within, weighed down by their terrified souls. Hospitals had been improvised, and in many cases the doctors operated in the open air. Hundreds of volunteers brought the wounded in from the half-standing buildings. Voices in familiar and strange languages mixed with moans, the howling of dogs, mysterious canticles of roosters, and a constant crying that penetrated iron and pavement.

Timoteo Noragua helped out with the bodies. He strung them across Salomón's back and carried them to first aid stations that had been set up. A very old man with a distant look on his face was rushing about nonstop. Possessed with a strange energy, he sought out the victims. Among clouds of dust he fearlessly entered buildings on the verge of collapse. There were fallen beams, mountains of bricks, glass projectiles, and metallic objects, but nothing could stop him. People could see him entering burning buildings, but he walked right through the flames. When it seemed as if he had been buried beneath the ruins or devoured by the flames, he would return carrying some poor unfortunate in his arms if not on his back. He no sooner would leave him in the care of the medics than he would return to his task with the same measured step. But you could not help but see the tremendous fatigue that afflicted him. No matter how exhausted, he kept on going night and day. In the midst of all the confusion, he began to arouse curiosity. They offered him water, but he refused. I do not deserve it, he would say, his eyes filled with tears. They begged him to rest in the shade. I don't deserve to, he would respond. Suffering showed in his face. The man realized that the others were whispering among themselves while he wandered about, never resting, never taking a break. Then he lost himself by walking through the fallen city, moving off in that direction. Those who saw him go said he was crying. He had been walking for thousands of years, and who knows how much longer he would walk in his eternal pilgrimage.

Under such circumstances not only did the spirit of compassion emerge, capable of overcoming fear and advancing in the face of danger, suffering long days and nights without sleep, but the materialistic human condition also manifested itself, vain and ostentatious. A lame old woman who collected multimillionaire husbands dug around among the ruins searching for jewelry, which she would hang around her neck or place on her fingers and arms after ripping them from the dead. Small groups of human vultures gathered together the money that remained scattered about the streets, even though they were now scraps of paper as insignificant as toilet paper. They gathered the coins together by poking around among the decaying bodies with sticks. Obsessed to the point of sickness with wealth, deathly contaminated by radioactivity, they smiled at the very sight of gold and money. They forgot to eat, they did not sleep, they smelled like carrion, but those orphan vultures dug incessantly.

Another unusual individual who did not participate in the activity of the others, always looking for someplace to set up a stage was Brother Trini Brown, religious preacher by profession and as a vocation. Now quite old, wrinkled and shaky, he still showed signs of having been a husky man. His face was a universal compendium of all races: very dark, with oblique green eyes, Indian and European features, and a voice that sounded everywhere like thunder. Among those who fought to put out the fires, those who tended the sick and those who ran from one place to the other crazed by the terror, Brother Trini Brown shouted from his tribune the virtues of mankind and those of the Eternal Being: I told you, the ancient damned of all continents, refrain from starting wars. You, with your faces wrinkled, your flesh mummified, raised your voices hidden in subterranean rivers to order the destruction of the human race, for gold and dominion, out of ambition for power and wealth. Where are your cursed corpses now? Where are your perverse spirits? They burn in eternal fire! I have preached everywhere the need for you to repent, pernicious sinners. I have stood in the middle of this destroyed city and shouted my head off, Repent! Renounce sin! Not only did you turn a deaf ear to my preaching, but you saw me as someone demented. You grown men, men who are robots, men who live only to amass money, you hocked the souls of your children in exchange for comfort and luxury. When the massacre appeared before them, you ordered them to respond with their own blood. You who have ignored the natural laws are like dogs which feed on their own vomit. You women who go about these streets half-naked and provocative, spreading lust like cats in heat. You government officials and corrupt judges who have spat upon and ignored the laws of the Bible and the constitution, who have built more and more prisons in order to do away with crime while stealing the money meant to build schools and to ensure our daily bread. You who have made criminals and fornicators of children. You who have paid your servants with hunger and are the salt of the earth. Damn all of you! May all of you be damned who have not had eyes to see nor ears to hear the eternal verities. Damned be you who have ignored the word of God because you were in a hurry to join your lovers and to give yourselves over to every vice. Damn you who have killed, for nothing will save you from the second death. Damn you who plotted the death of your brothers born of the same mother's womb. May you sinners be damned who denied the path of God. You will now go to inhabit the eternal shadows, there where there is wailing and the gnashing of teeth. Your raiment will be columns of flames. Above you all will be fire and you will walk on burning coals. Heed me, those of you who are just! Rejoice! You will arise from the ruins, from the grave, from the very oceans, and you will form the new kingdom of God, our Lord forever. Here on this very Earth you will be the chosen for your humility, your compassion, and your obedience to His precepts and laws. Rejoice! Because the day is coming when He will bless you.

Timoteo continued his journey in the direction of Santa María de las Piedras. The moans continued to resound in his ears and the horrible scenes to burn in his eyes. The dilemma gnawed at the deepest roots of his judgment. When the evidence seemed the clearest, so much darker did the shadows of his doubt become. Confusion took hold of his spirit. He felt a strange fear that at times became terror, and he knew that it would not diminish with time. Thus he urgently covered the distance, to see if distance and the warmth of his own people could help him recover a little peace, because he could never forget, nor could he even laugh or hope to dream surrounded by tranquility.

Although he was leaving the fatal circle behind, for several days he still bore witness to the incredible damage of this cruelest and most aberrant and incomprehensible of situations. Here and there birds fell motionless from the sky, while others lay dying on the ground. Even the eagles dragged themselves along with their useless wings, and the vultures covered the surface like a black blanket. The lightning speed of the deer which leaped and flew over plains and rough ground had become a total lack of movement. Beasts and reptiles had lost the glow in their eyes. The light of the sun, the air, and the water were poisonous. . . .

Only a false idea with a thousand faces remains of true history. Santa María de las Piedras never had an official historian. The shreds of history of this village of stones, sun, sand, and cactuses that survive pass from thought to tongue dotted with spit. They are base rumors told by drunks that circulate like counterfeit money, the tales of senile old men, and God knows who else, ladies and gentlemen. The Nacho Serenos, the Teofilitos, the Churrungas, the Paparruchas and other street corner and plaza storytellers have thrust senseless stories on us by the ton. Moreover, they have done it as the crab walks, by moving backwards. Instead of beginning with the dawn of the seventeenth century and moving toward 1985 in the present, they have inverted the order. Poor fellows, it's just that they are so old, and each new day for them is another step backwards. It's been a long time since they looked toward the future and followed it step by step. Now they live on memories stained with ashes, at times with the unconsciousness of the unborn, the ingenuousness of children, and on occasion the vivid bits of the glorious moments that have sunk into the past. Besides, they are village narrators, and if they talk it is to hear themselves without the least consideration for whoever is listening. They must be excused; what can they know of literature? In the first place, they never went to college; hell, they never even went to high school! In so many cases—would you believe it—they have to dip their thumbs in ink to sign something. Something, nevertheless, can be discerned in the chaos in which the days flow in a horizontal direction, turn corners, move vertically, collide, overlap, and at times spin and disappear in the unknown spaces of the mind's cosmos. These people do not know, nor do they wish to know, whether the days come or go or if time remains static. They are faced with a succession of dawns and dusks that give the false impression that something is coming, when it is only we and the globe who are going like machines outfitted with little hands and a continuous tick tock, machines which will one day burst a spring like a cheap watch, God help us!

I can't understand you, Don Abelardo. It doesn't matter, my son, I understand myself even less.

As for the story of Timoteo Noragua, it would be difficult to attest to its authenticity. Timoteo Noragua ascended in 1999 with only a few steps remaining to finish out his odyssey. He missed Santa María de las Piedras by a hair. His incredible adventure takes place in the fourteen years following the present. Nevertheless, it has all the earmarks of reality, and it is confirmed by its correspondence to eternal facts. It doesn't matter if you say, as has been said, that Huachusey was a Jew, a Russian, an Arab, a German and so on. What is certain is that by the same token that he's an Anglo-American, or better yet, a gringo, he might as well belong to any race: Chinese, African, European. What cannot be denied without running the risk of bearing false witness is that the man who went to see the face of Huachusey was born in Santa María de las Piedras, and is thus a Mexican. So then, in the eighty-four years that have been covered retrospectively in the life of Santa María de las Piedras, there are periods that have been leaped over. History is as faithful as human memory, which is the same as to say that its cells are in the process of dying throughout its existence. Santa María de las Piedras, like so many other impoverished villages that do not attract the greed of high dignitaries, was like a miniature country lost in the Sonoran Desert and abandoned in time. People lived in Santa María de las Piedras as in the most wretched of exiles. It is not inappropriate to mention that, with the triumph of the revolution, with Carranza and Obregón in the lead, social justice came to Santa María de las Piedras. Zapata's theme of "Land and Freedom" took shape there, and more than a hundred communal landowners took possession of property that the government assigned to them with the appropriate documentation. The government also opened the Rural Bank in order to facilitate the resources needed to farm for a future filled with the sweet promises of hope. Previous sessions have not dealt with the facts that will now be expounded upon, simply because there is no record of them and they must, by necessity, arise from the fragmentary recollections of the old men in town. The daily concern of these old men to reconstruct the history of Santa María de las Piedras explores labyrinthine corners where some episodes have gone astray and others manage to dislodge themselves imperfectly, more like something brought forth by a fever than concrete facts. Despite the fact that chaos overcomes all chronological order in the narrations of these old men, the essence of life in Santa María de las Piedras rings true. The muddled minds of these people are history consumed by the land. Only dreams remain that dissipate with time. Among the peasants who benefited, there were mestizos, more than a few creoles, with a majority of Indians. They were given seven hectares per head and three thousand of open range to be held in common. There, now you can get rich. The land belongs to those who work it: plant cotton, corn, wheat; plant whatever you want, that's what the land is for, for it to yield crops. Make it yield, with affection, with effort, with love; cultivate it. They opened channels from the river to irrigate its edges and then, beyond, its adjacent fields. They lost themselves in the earth, digging wells until they tapped hidden springs. It never really rained in earnest. They felled cactuses, they leveled the land, they sowed and awaited their bounty. When the river snaked through the pallid world of the desert pushed along by a sporadic downpour, it looked like a stream of boiling chocolate. Although the river did not flood the lands of the farmers of Santa María de las Piedras, it did streak them, leaving in its wake a wet blanket of lime that added patches of green to that colorless geography. Thus was born the deceit fed by the demagoguery of stupid if not dishonest politicians, plunging the peasants in an illusory dependence, hunger and constant ill health. The local Rural Credit Bank faced the plaza of Santa María de las Piedras. The peasants would go there to receive their part of the money set aside to stimulate agricultural production. Such money was like the current of a river whose parched bed causes the flow to lessen as it advances. The peasants received only a few drops of spit from the money set aside in the capital. The despotic and corrupt bank employees would give them a puny credit as though they were handing out alms, and humiliate them in the bargain. The farmers would depend on that to eat a few beans, to get drunk on mezcal, and to buy the boards to build coffins with relative frequency. The streets of Santa María de las Piedras at that time were shaded by dozens of somber individuals with large straw hats, torn clothes, and clumsy remnants of shoes. Some of them would arrive early to line up at the door of the bank, while others waited, sitting on the curb or walking around the plaza. Finally Lutero Santana would come out to tell them that the assistance had not arrived or that it had run out. Then the peasants would leave for their poorly built huts of mesquite and ocotillo branches, where their families waited, hoping day after day. Luterito was a stuck-up young man, skinny and prissy. He worked as an assistant to Maximino Ruelas, an engineer who had graduated from Chapingo, according to his own account. Maximino was also assisted in his work by a young secretary: Cronilda Portales.

Luterito took pride in his typing skills, pecking out the letters with his index fingers as though he were poking out the eyes of sleeping children. Whenever he said anything he stressed each word with a studied gesture. Since federal employees always followed the example of the president of the country in office, whether in his speech, his clothes or in some form of posture, Luterito was for his chief Maximino what Morones had been for President Calles: a pimp. He organized bacchanals in the Sleeping Dove, a whorehouse whose madam at that time was the famous Marietona. Maximino Ruelas, head of the Rural Bank, ordered the brothel closed to the public, but provided free drinks and women for the exclusive use of his friends and employees. Later, during the days of the gold fever, this same brothel changed its name to the Golden Honeycomb. El Sarahuato's orchestra and his rubber trumpets blew their brains away, playing for all they were worth. During the high point of one of these orgies, Luterito, paired up with some plump little chippy, had danced in the nude, acting like a clown. He handled the scene to the delight of his boss. Ruelas paid him well when he obtained inexperienced girls for him. The bonanza of the employees in the Rural Bank was in scandalous evidence. They dressed like millionaires, they came to own automobiles, their houses shone with fine furniture. Despite the fact that Cronilda, the secretary, got only a small portion of the loot, she always wore a hat and high heels and she had become haughty, looking down on anything vulgar. She denied that she was from El Bebedero, a miserable collection of huts where she had milked cows and had to sweep the chicken shit out of her home every day. Cronilda went to mass dressed like a queen and paid no attention to her suitors, disdainful and rigid, waiting for a prince worthy of her stature. Finally, Maximino Ruelas covered Her Majesty Cronilda with a parasol of stars. One night he lowered them to her feet. Cronilda's panties fell with the lights. The proud secretary came down pregnant. The chief of the Rural Bank, terrified by the brothers of his young conquest, married her off to Lutero Santana, and things went on as before. The representatives of the federal credit devoted themselves to vice, to the extent of not sharing with the communers a single cent of the funds set aside for the development of agriculture. With very few exceptions, they received the capital without distributing it among the farmers. As far as they were concerned, the most natural course was to stick it in their own pockets. The Indians rebelled and sent three communers on a pilgrimage to the capital itself to find out what was going on. Once in Mexico City, they planted themselves like statues in the waiting room of the agrarian agency, until six weeks later they were received by a bureaucrat. He pretended to be indignant when he found out about all the treachery of the people under him. After first treating them to a harangue full of revolutionary clichés, he promsied to take care of the matter, forcefully if necessary, no matter whose head rolled, he shouted as he pounded the desk. Seven months later an engineer by the name of Fulgencio Suárez arrived in Santa María de las Piedras as an inspector. He examined the situation and met to deliberate with some peasants. He turned red and clenched his fists and shouted in the middle of the plaza that for the supreme government the rights of the rural citizen are sacred and that justice would descend like a flaming sword on the throats of those who had cheated the people. The revolutionary cannot tolerate or pardon those who hold it back. Luterito and Cronilda were quaking, but Maximino was smiling calmly. When Suárez thought the moment appropriate, he entered the cubicle of the Bandidales. He shut himself in for two hours with the thieving employees and came out singing a different tune. About a hundred peasants were waiting for him in the middle of the plaza, already satisfied that the constitution would impose its laws and would see justice done. Fulgencio Suárez faced the peasants and shouted to them indignantly that the only reason why they had not made any progress was because they were beggars looking for a handout, rather than working the land like real men instead of acting like drunks and assholes. Teo, the one whose face was pockmarked, was the first to open his mouth. Well, they must have greased this guy's palm. The rest looked at him with a smirk on their faces because there's nothing to be said about the obvious. I don't know any rivers that flow upstream, and problems always flow downstream. Teo went on talking to himself while his comrades dispersed. Later, by strange coincidence, the Rural Bank abbreviated its name to RurBank, but as far as the people were concerned, its real name was Bandit Bank. The majority of the employees of said institution have gone on with business as usual, although they have refined their cynicism. Demagoguery, like Teo said, runs downstream. As an epilogue to these facts not contained in the unschooled versions of the old chatterboxes, who have no other occupation except to entertain themselves with memories which time, like a leafstorm, has left hidden, it would be appropriate to note that Maximino Ruelas died in a hospital in Tucson, Arizona, one torrid summer in which July was a ball of fire. A young man just about to turn thirty, he gave his body up to the worms. From tip to root, his tongue was covered with sores. His nasal cavity was filled with gonorrhea.

Well, it was certainly interesting how that guy Sacramento González set us straight. What do you mean, there were no official historians, only gabby old men? Bah! So-called historians are nothing more than people on salary with a boss. Güero Paparruchas was more of a historian than they are, no matter how much you might claim he was a hoaxer. Anyone who wants to know the history of Santa María de las Piedras only has to go over to the plaza and pay attention. What you don't know there you make up. Sacramento González pretends he's smart because he's always glued to the books and knows about the lives of the Greeks and Romans. In the final analysis, they were just a bunch of queers and sissies. They'd lost their guts and didn't have the foggiest idea what they were doing. By contrast, Don Nacho Sereno, Don Atilano del Toro, Don Teofilito and that whole pack of old men who lean against the walls in winter and drink the sun in with their bones are the ones who have seen things.

Yes, sir, I was there, I saw it and others saw it, too, men who are also old like me. But Don Atilano, don't you think you're going a bit too far with that business about the dance? No, sir, old bowlegged Román danced with the Sorrowful Mother and Tavanico, the one they call Dumb Ass, danced with Mary Magdalene. So that means there was a dance in heaven, Don Atilano? No, that's not the end of it; just hold on. The night the people call the "night of the devils" really did have Luzabel wandering about the place. Did you know Tostado, Don Atilano? I tell you I knew them all, you'll see, just let me search my memory.

Almost all of us old men who are close to eighty were there when Tostado came with his people in the back of the church, some of them on horseback. Some of them are still alive today. Tostado wasn't from around here, and only God knows where he'd come from. What is certain is that he was a schoolteacher, very devoted to eradicating the traditions that, according to him, had kept the village backward. He was supported by the constitutional authorities and by Cárdenas, who was in his first year as president. This was a little after the business of the Followers of Christ down there in Jalisco.

We got the tail end here in Santa María de las Piedras. Cárdenas was no sooner settled in as President when, by official order the school children were singing the "Internationale," which is something like the Russian national anthem, every Monday morning. "On to battle, workers, on to the final battle, may the human race be an international soviet." Among those who went into the church on horseback was Cacharpón Montaño. He was riding a draped stallion, which was rather dark, almost a roan. Cacharpón was wearing chaps, a Texan-style hat, boots, and a white silk shirt. That devil of a Yaqui Indian, his hair like the quills of a porcupine and his hat hanging on his back, held in place by his scarf, twirled his lasso and let it fall over the Holy Sacrament. He wound the lasso around the saddle horn, gave an animal cry, spurred his horse, and exited at a gallop, dragging the divine symbol behind. The other two riders spurred their horses onto their hind feet at the alter itself. All this amidst screams, neighs, and curses so horrible as to scare the devil himself. That set off that night's wild party. Among the crowd, those who were dancing with the Sorrowful Mother and Mary Magdalene sneaked into the church. Zas! The band started playing "El Pagaré," and everybody started dancing with the saints. They were whirling around this way and that. Then there were six couples rather than just two. "El Pagaré" came to an end and the musicians struck up "Jesusita en Chihuahua." Tacha Ramonera and Tarrosa Guzmán were some of the old gals who participated in the bash, wearing boots, leather skirts and wide-brimmed northern-style hats. Tacha took a bottle out from between her boobs, downed a real slug, whooped like an Apache, and to the strains of "Jesusa" grabbed Saint Anthony off his pedestal. She was followed right behind by Tarrosa Guzmán, who was hopping around like a frog with Saint Joseph. Both women were among those who wholeheartedly supported the campaign against the Church that had produced frothy rivers of blood in Jalisco and neighboring states and whose echoes had been a scourge throughout the country. Flaca Pereira ended up stripping the Sorrowful Mother, and, lo and behold, she dressed herself in the beautiful black dress of the holy figure. The old drunk everybody called Tragacharcas jumped up on the main altar and began to knock holy objects to the ground: the main crucifix, which was very large, three small angels, and a Saint Martin the Horseman that he had hauled over. He was shouting like a deputy obliged to destroy the instruments in the exploitation of the people. The musicians had been contracted by Tostado, and there were four of them: a guy from La Sangre was on the tololoche bass, someone from Las Polvaredas played the drum, someone from El Tecolote the violin, and a fellow from Bacamechi was on the horn. From that night on they had a permanent job at Satan's parties.

Tostado and his pals had been doing their thing for about three months. They would go to homes at a time when the men would be out working, whether as goat herders, storekeepers, or farmers. They were accompanied by four gunmen who weren't from Santa María de las Piedras and whose real names nobody knew. All four shared the same nickname: the Shock-Headed Devils. The women would cry for them not to search their homes for statues of saints. Tostado and his devils added to their collection in any event. Doña Lola del Cid fell to her knees, crying for them to return to her a Virgin of Guadalupe that they had stuffed into a sack, along with Saint Judas Tadeo and Saint Benito. The roundup of saints ended with a bonfire stoked by the saint-burners in the middle of the plaza with dry cactuses. Tostado stood there in the middle of the plaza so no one could miss his words, shouting until he was hoarse that the priests are not fathers but pimps. He swore to them that religion was the opium of the people and that the priests tricked their women in the confessional and took them in the sacristy. He called the representatives of the church all manner of bad names: accommodationists, ass-lickers, assholes, freeloaders, exploiters, hypocrites, the spawn of Lucifer, drunken souses, sex fiends, jackasses and dozens of similar compliments.

The next day, several women recovered their statues among the ashes. It was interesting to see how all of them looked as if they had been canonized in the very heart of Africa. Which is why Raimundo del Cid and his seven brothers, well armed and with good horses, once they found out what had reduced their mother to sobbing in her shawl, went off to get the firebugs for their deed. The del Cid brothers found them in front of Doña Cholita Ceniceros's house about to execute another raid. They had no trouble disarming them on the spot. Raimundo dealt Tostado a blow between the eyes and smashed him in the face with the barrel of his gun, all the while cussing him out with the worst language anyone had ever heard.

Tostado's haughtiness dissolved at Raimundo's feet. He screamed and begged for mercy. Raimundo gave him such a kick in the mouth that his face became a fountain of livid purple. He told him next time he would kick the shit out of him, and that wouldn't be all. But under the cover of the devil's night, Tostado, accompanied by an ugly crowd, is back at his old tricks, and it would leave a mark forever on the life of Santa María de las Piedras. It was known that four youths definitely had danced with holy figures, in addition to several men who had danced with virgins. The women ended up real religious old ladies, always crying and full of moral virtue and performing the humble tasks required to keep a church going. Moreover, when they were not praying, they kept the saints' clothes looking nice. The strange part is that they ended up not marrying any of the bullies, and, what is more, they all suffered from the same problems in their lower extremities: corn-encrusted feet, bunions, warts, varicose veins, pinched nerves, ingrown toenails. And if that weren't enough, they suffered from hemorrhoids as big as grapes. And, to top it off, they gave off a stench like a dead cat that not even the strongest stomach could stand. We only know what happened to two of the men: Román, who danced the polka with the Sorrowful Mother, and Tato, who danced the tango with the Most Blessed Conception. As far as we know, they only danced with the statues and not with the holy pictures. Both dancers became drunks and could always be seen dragging their asses through the mud, consumed by fear, jumpy to the point of going cross-eyed out of fear of God's punishment. By the time their bodies ended up in the cemetery, their legs were dried out, twisted roots. Tragacharcas died one Sunday after downing a half gallon of mezcal in one gulp. When he died he was singing an old tango whose lyrics go: "I dragged my shame through the streets. . . ." As for Cacharpón Montaño, he died in a fight in a way that was more grotesque than funny: his best friend stuck an awl through his bellybutton one morning in December. Happy and with their arms around each other, Cacharpón and Chololo were returning to their huts. They had drunk so much that Cacarpón passed out with his eternal chaps still on, drunk down to his toes. Chololo took his chaps off, then his pants and his underclothes, until he was half naked. With premeditation and malice, he laughed his head off planning his bad joke. He proceeded to play it by redressing him with only the chaps and boots.

Chololo was careful to carry off the underpants and pants of his passed-out friend. Cacharpón was left lying on the ground to sleep his drunk off. With the sun high in the sky, Cacharpón jumped up ready for a shot of booze to warm his blood, followed by coffee and some food. He started to walk through the streets of Santa María de las Piedras, alongside people of all ages on their way to mass. He ran into people on their way home with things they had just bought and people just out for a morning stroll. He was headed himself to Doña Lina's place to buy something. He noticed that women would cover their faces when they saw him. When Doña Susanita covered the heads of her two nieces with her shawl, it was too late: the girls had seen the whole show. Those with children turned around hurriedly and told them not to look back under any condition. The men would point, some shaking their heads and others writhing with laughter. Some people said afterward that the morning was so cold that there was steam arising from Cacharpón's butt, as though he were smoking with his ass. When he walked into the store, Doña Lina looked him up and down, wrinkled her nose, and her full-moon face turned red. Then she struck him with her shrill voice: That's the last straw, you stupid Indian. What the hell is going on? Did you buy mezcal with your pants? From behind you can see your gorilla's ass, and from the front your dong's swinging all over the place. Did you lose the little shame you had left? Cacharpón looked down at his chaps, saw himself in plain sight, and took off terrified. With each bound, his rage grew and he swore he'd kill Chololo a thousand times as the lowest of hounds. Chololo woke up with the noise made by Cacharpón throwing himself over and over again against his door like a wild goat. When the door crashed in, the nudist entered like the wind, holding a huge club over his head, ready to bash Chololo's head in. Before he could, Chololo, who saw him coming, plunged the awl in up to the handle. And that's how life ended for the man who had dragged the Blessed Sacrament out of the church tied to the horn of his saddle.

As for Tostado, the orchestrator and executor of those nights of the Devils, we have it from a good source that he died in the grace of God. He had time to say his confession and to receive the last rites. By that time he was an old man eighty years old who was afraid of the dark, acted like a spoiled child and went often to church to kiss the hands of the priests.

Pain and longevity combined to curse Timoteo with the first signs of old age. His eyes, smaller and sunken in their sockets, sought in the distance what he did not know in his heart. He passed by cities, settlements, strange machinery, sumptuous marvels, and gave up his idea of finding the extraordinary being that had the power to satisfy his every whim. He no longer sought him, he did not understand his duality, he could not explain why if he was capable of forging the dignity and happiness of the human species he would undertake its horrible destruction out of hatred and cruelty. No, he no longer wanted to see him. He preferred to flee and to be ignorant of his existence, to forget his name, not ever to be bothered by him. The mere idea of finding him terrified him and made him tremble. He hid his face in his hands and sobbed deeply. He suffered with the pitiful appearance of the nostalgic old who have been deceived and have no room left to heal their wounds, encourage their faith, revive their illusions. The idea that chance might bring him to meet him made him hasten his pace, as though Santa María de las Piedras were an impregnable refuge closed to this terrible being. Nevertheless, there would be no accord between his will and his fate. Huachusey the enigmatic was waiting for him. The more he tried to avoid him, the closer he got to the moment when he would see his face. That face! That face that would make him tremble, touching the very fibers of his spirit, the deeper the more sensitive, the very fibers of his ancestors, beyond his being.

Forests, rivers, mountains, and lakes were left behind. He left behind the symphonic thrill of thousands of birds, the full measure of the woods, and entered the silence of the desert. The thirsty howl of solitary coyotes and the rhythmic rattle of the snakes spoke of vast vistas of isolated and skimpy vegetation. As he came to new landscapes, his heart was filled with joy. He looked with reverence upon the first cactuses that announced the area where he had been born: barren wastes, seas of humpbacked sand and the barbarous sun, his homeland!

From above, very high above, where the stars follow their trek, there are lookouts for studying the celestial bodies. The distances observed from those heights are humbling, but one can see the worlds like globes, spheres, and sands that inhabit the universe. There are so many and they are so huge that the imagination has no room to hold them. In a miniscule point in the infinite expanse of the universe, there is a star that governs the circular travels of various planets. One of those is the Earth. To be sure, all of them are beautiful, and they radiate light. They are the sign, the truce that destroys any doubt as to the creation. No creation can exist without a creator. God also created the Earth, the beautiful planet where we live, the one privileged among the celestial bodies that surround it. The blue and noble Earth, prodigious nature, all-bearing mother, fountain of life, the channel of the rivers of generations of spirits that travel in the genes that flower as flesh during one instant. The cocoon whence springs the ethereal, undying soul. One can see the Earth from on high enveloped by the blue phosphorescence that exalts the green of the forests, the pale yellow of the deserts, the windows of existence. From the sky one can marvel at the perennial whiteness of the poles in the shape of enormous circles that cool everything. An enormous storehouse to warehouse the foodstuffs produced by the seas and fields. What a beautiful and generous world is the Earth. Seen from space, the rivers shine like arteries that move through the valleys, giving revitalizing life. The rivers and the seas are mirrors of space, fountains of beauty. The lakes are like pupils seen from vantage points beyond the planet. Earth is a beautiful, generous abode, the masterpiece of the Supreme Architect. The seas, enormous and dominant, can be seen from distant crossings beyond the borders of the planet Earth. They are the onomatopoeia of the rain that falls, moistens, flows, rejoins, evaporates, and rises, traveling through the atmosphere to fall again, overflowing river-beds, flooding fields, flowing through the rivers, returning to its very source. Water is the confluence between spirit and matter. It goes underground and does not perish, is reborn in subterranean currents, and comes together again in a continual flow that gives life and does not die. This is how the spirit is, surviving on buried matter. Earth is very beautiful. It has the breath of life and it spins to receive the warmth of the sun that makes its nature grow. Nature sustains its own life and the life it produces. Earth feels, speaks, sings, cries, loves. Love is the greatest feeling, love is the word, love is the divine clue. As long as there is love on Earth, she will not perish, because love and God are one word. From the vantage points of space, Earth can be seen, multicolored, exalted by the light blue, the loving hand, the tranquil gaze, the smile, the desire for peace. From boundless space, the stars and the sky tell of the glory of God. Rivers, valleys, mountains, and seas all attest to the work of His hands. The generosity and the beauty of Earth attest to the love of God, just as His laws and designs are the light that guides. Everything is disposed to make our stay on Earth happy, we whose spirits inhabit the flesh temporarily. Do you hear, Timoteo Noragua? I feel sorry for you. You've been sitting still there for hours, crying to yourself. I feel terrible for the way your eyes look. I see before me a bag of bones with some pieces of hide attached. Did you love him like a slave? Like a friend? Maybe like a brother? Yes, there's no doubt my friend Salomón has died. I don't know, Timoteo, if burros have souls or not. What you and I do know is that they feel pain and get worn out under their cruel burden. Sometimes they get to enjoy pasture, water, and love, Timoteo, because they love in their fashion. I just told myself a moment ago that death is grace, it frees the soul, cures the fatigue and the suffering of the flesh, erases afflictions and worries, and it does away with the solitude of those who have only their shadow for company. It also provides dignity, for you will have seen how people take their hats off before the dead and mumble prayers, with no concern as to whether the dead person has been a saint or a devil. Now nothing can harm my burro, not thorns or brambles, not hunger or thirst, nothing. I, Timoteo Noragua, rise up. Santa María de las Piedras is very near. He is also very near. You will soon meet Huachusey.

The revolution was undoubtedly a tremendous scream that rent the silence of centuries. A silence of choked tears, of killing hunger, of fatal resignation, of hushed conversations, of murmured prayers in which rage was mingled with fear. The inertia of one day after another was a single petrified tragedy. Death, dispensed in daily doses, became a bloody stampede, a truceless holocaust in which both the just and the sinners fell. All in the name of a titanic effort to pull down inhuman social structures and to change the course of history for the better. Nachito, things have gotten a little better. Of course they have, especially for the politicians. You can find everything in the garden of the Lord. Including fools, which is what we are for putting up with so much corruption. You've noticed how they paint the rocks along all the roads for election day. They could build houses for all the poor with that money, rather than ruining the countryside with the names of coyotes. You talk that way because you are old, Nachito, and you've already lived overtime. Shut up, Teófilo, I can still whip traitors. I think that's more of a boast than a fact. Just mind your Ps and Qs. Okay, fellows, that's enough. Calm down.

In addition to the present cemetery located on the level plains around the hills shaped like a half-moon that the inhabitants call the Cathedral and the original dwellers call the Twin Tits because of the two points that stick out, there were other cemeteries. They are effaced cemeteries, the tombs swept away by the action of the elements. Small mounds of stones scattered by the passing of animals, the wind, the sand and time itself, which gnaws and consumes. They are graves that time in turn has buried. Although it's still possible to make out a few graves, the crosses have disappeared. They are cemeteries in which lie those who in earlier days worked along with their whole families as slaves in the mines of Santa María de las Piedras. Little or nothing is known of these dead as far as details of their lives are concerned, nothing of the world of anecdotes that they peopled. The whereabouts of these cemeteries is known because the old people point to their whereabouts and also because of the discovery now and then of a skeleton by the frequent diggers. Here, friend, there are neither archives nor documents, nothing written. If someone wants to know the life and miracles of those who lived around here during the last century, let him go disinter the old people who died filled with experiences and the knowledge about the old days in Santa María de las Piedras. Maybe by digging around among the skulls you can find signs of their thoughts or some written record produced by a brain before rotting. Now, rumors are something else again.

They say that Don León Marcial de las Colinas established himself in Santa María de las Piedras around 1830, the lord and master of the gold mines that the first Spaniards had discovered in the hills of the Cathedral. The mines remained covered over for many years. They were very deep, and it seemed as though they had run out. Nevertheless, Indians and mestizos pulled out carloads of gold that were sent to the capital or even to Spain. In Santa María de las Piedras all that remained was the scarred land full of holes. Only the story of riches survives. Don León Marcial built a baronial house between the tiny village that fit in the palm of his hand and the semicircle of hills; that is to say, the hills that happened to spring forth to face the sands of the desert to the front and sides, and the level plains behind filled with cactus, random bushes and skimpy trees behind. Don León Marcial's wife and children lived in the capital and visited Santa María de las Piedras only occasionally. He, on the other hand, spent short periods in Mexico City and spent most of his time watching over the working of the mines. The enormous house with its thick and solid white walls was home to the silent rich man, an old servant, two Indian girls, and a wild Indian who never spoke and barely moved his head. His wife, two daughters and a son traveled a lot in Europe. Old León Marcial, like all men of his type, had a heavy hand. If one of his slaves tried to escape, he would have him tortured by his overseers, if he didn't have him killed. Otherwise, let the wind tell about the life and miracles of those people, unless I decide to make them up.

That's enough, Don Teofilito, that's enough. As for providing information about that world, what about the saintly priest that built the church in Santa María de las Piedras? Yes, sir, that was in the second half of the seventeenth century.

Father Encarnación's eyes seemed to grow larger with time. And the brighter they shone, the blacker they got. He never hid his bones beneath the flesh, and he treated the charms of gluttony with disdain. More than food he was fed by the passion of his spirit in the cause of God and the defenseless Indians. Wherever his image appeared, riding on horseback, the natives would give up their weapons, and hostility and danger would disappear. The voices in a murmured flow, reminiscences of streams of limpid and serene waters, would envelope him with affection. The Indians loved him. His passion for Christ became their passion. Their faith joined in a single goal. They built mighty temples, graceful and elegant with towers to embrace the heavens. Father Encarnación's eyes would glow with the mysterious phosphorescence attained by body and soul in its submission to the postulates of God. Skinny, restless, feverish, he would wander around the area on the back of his noble steed. He sowed the seed of the love of God so that it would bloom from one generation to the next for all time. He taught the Indians to work the stones, to make adobe, to mold the wood. He instructed them in the secrets of architecture. The Indians heeded his wisdom. Father Encarnación, his voice, his pointing finger, his extraordinary energy, his eyes of fire gave the Indians inspiration, spiritual awareness, and strength for their bodies. As opposed to the simple logic of limitations and scarcity of resources, the dynamic was born that would forge marvels. Santa María de las Piedras's church was built for the centuries to come, with the sweat and blood of the Indians, with the determination and the faith of the missionary. Father Encarnación built a rosary of churches. The spirit of Father Encarnación survives forever, by the grace of God. The memory of his name takes on new life with the passage of the years because of his love and his works. Santa María de las Piedras's church welcomed in the eighteenth century, receiving the remains of the illustrious man as his final resting place.

A little bit after the second half of the seventeenth century a group of men whose appearance made them look rather less than human reached what is today Santa María de las Piedras. They were Spaniards. They had heavy beards and were wrapped in leather harnesses. They stank, had an imperious manner, were irascible, devout, idealistic, proud. They brought with them a spirit of fire; they were courageous, daring, imposing, doctrinaire, pious, humanistic, despotic, humble, cruel, religious. They were soldiers, missionaries, liberators, black slavers, teachers. They were, nevertheless, haughty individualists, servants of God and the king. Nevertheless, in each one of them there existed a feudal lord, arbitrary, paternalistic, dominant, resilient, hard as steel. They were men who charged windmills and showy giants head on. There was no mountain they could not cross, no river too impetuous to ford.

They knew that life ends up a game of chance, and they played it with a will to win. They also gave their all to the deserts. They left their mark on the immense territories of America. They erected churches wherever they chose to and without regard for conditions. They dug up the gold and silver wherever they found it. In Santa María de las Piedras they dug holes in the hills and took out the gold. In areas where there were savage and warlike tribes, they discovered the Opatas, Indians who were the terror of the Apaches. If the Spaniards never got along with the Yaquis, they did form alliances with the Opatas, who were certainly great warriors. With the centuries a very strange mestizo population emerged in Santa María de las Piedras. The semidesert plains that surround Santa María de las Piedras appear immense. It is less than a day's ride on horseback to the enormous wavy sand wastes of the Sonoran Desert. The village emerges from the middle of the plains, next to the short chain of hills crowned by a hill in the middle and at its two ends by two tall peaks. This inhospitable place, where water is scarce, seems like a strange place to put a village. The bed of a rocky river lies near Santa María de las Piedras. It is almost always empty, except for those rare occasions when it fills. That is perhaps where the water comes from that the families found by digging very deep wells. In time, Santa María de las Piedras came to have a rudimentary agriculture, with a few shade trees along the streets and in the plaza. People arrived summoned by gold. Men and women begat others, who in their turn did the same thing. The town grew and its streets, plaza, and the imposing church were all established. This took decades that added up to centuries. On the broadest of its flanks, on a level plain, the cemetery is located, with its back toward the aforementioned hill whose extremities arise in elevated peaks like a sumptuous cathedral with no equal in all the lands of Earth. The cemeteries are roots, pillars that reach down deep, the solid support of the descendents of the dead, the deep foundation of the villages.

The fire of their spirit, their boldness, their overwhelming character, and their passion for great deeds petered out in the Creoles after several generations. The distance from Spain in space and time, the challenge of multiplying and making the species grow, the enormous vastness of the forests, the vast reaches of the deserts, and the separation and isolation of the villages from each other produced exhaustion and nostalgia. Nature in these inhospitable and vast regions was not to be subjugated. Rather, it imposed its own stamp. Santa María de las Piedras was left in almost total isolation for the space of years and years. The appearance of a stranger was a novelty, and the departure of one of its citizens a rarity. With time, Spanish became the language. Spanish brought values, customs, ideas. In exchange, the creoles adopted the manners and words of the Indians and their dialects and a good amount of the accent of the local languages. Thus Santa María de las Piedras reached the edge of the present century with a blended population in which the majority are mestizos, along with numerous Creoles and Indians. Time and the play of circumstances gave it its character. Society and economics were based on these racial elements. The mines of Santa María de las Piedras were practically exhausted. The majority of its citizens lived on stories and memories. Although Santa María de las Piedras was a poor village, there was a profound division of castes among its sons and daughters. The color of one's skin became an obsession. It was a stigma and an insult to be born with dark skin, and to be born with fair skin was the basis of a family name and preferential treatment. Conflicts of this sort occurred in the same family. By that time, no one knew the names of those who had planned and constructed the plaza, located in the very center of the town. It seemed as though the narrow streets had been cobblestoned forever. The houses joined one to another with no space in between and common walls were the handiwork of ghosts. The artisans and the architects whose hands had bled and who had lost sleep in the planning and construction of the town had died long ago. If perhaps Father Encarnación's name remains, it is because he built the church. If historical accuracy had faded with time, the legend remained, luxuriant, exuberant, as abundant and vigorous as a creeping vine. What tremendous upheavals changed the face of Santa María de las Piedras: the Revolution of 1910 and, in the 1930s, the burning of the saints and the persecution of the church by the atheists. Toward the end of the same decade, it was the extraordinary discovery of placer gold on the edge of the town itself. There were those who found gold just by digging with their hands, while others found it not very far from the surface. Like a cruel game of chance, there were those who found nothing. The inhabitants of Santa María de las Piedras also multiplied, and many of them had to leave their homes in search of new horizons. The tragedy of the descendents of Colonel Rumboso Noragua was a part of that same revolution. He was the grandfather of Timoteo, the very madman who, riding on the back of his burro Salomón, sought God in the cities of North America until he found him. Brother Trini Brown, the preacher of the Brothers of the True Faith of the Lord, swears that the odyssey of Timoteo Noragua ended a few months before the dawn of the year 2000. Trini Brown, the driver of pernicious sinners, is himself the one who followed Timoteo Noragua's itinerary throughout the United States: Tucson, Yuma, Los Angeles, San Francisco, Chicago, New York, possibly Boston and San Antonio, in addition to cities in between.

In 1650 Santa María de las Piedras does not exist as a village. Its name cannot even be imagined. It is like an empty theater, without an audience and without a stage. In the same space in which it would come to be only an instant of cosmic time, there are stones, cactuses, dwarf bushes, sand, the corpse of a river, a short swath of rocky hills, and a prophet preaching in the desert: the wind.

A pilgrim on his way, Timoteo Noragua reaches the inexorable day that has inspired so much worry in him. As the second hand breaks the bridge of four o'clock, he contemplates a singular, strange panorama: small mountains in a semicircle whose extremities rise up in two enormous peaks like cathedral towers. There is a shallow mesa in front of them that backs into the hills like a stage, with a cemetery that could be reached with a pounding heart and baited breath. He blinks incredulously. He can't believe it. Men clothed like priests of the Roman Catholic Church march up on the stage. They belong to every hierarchy, from the lowliest to the most exalted. In the very center of the group, officiating and looking heavenward with his eyes wide open and his hands in a prayerful gesture, stands the Holy Father. Suddenly, Timoteo notes that immediately next to the place where he is standing, almost close enough to touch—his ears are not missing a thing, even something whispered in secret—there is a procession as wide as it is long. They are men and women of all ages. They come from all over the world and belong to all epochs. In the lead, on the shoulders of the multitude, he can see a coffin of the same color as the shadows of darkness. The footsteps resound on the earth like the dull roll of drums, providing the background for a chorus of lamentations and the rhythmic wail of tearful notes. The low crying that comes from afar increases with each step to take on volume and force. The faces show despair and suffering so profound and wrenching that they cause tears to flow from the deep, eternal fountains. Timoteo Noragua turns into a man of stone from whose eyes flow parallel rivulets that dampen the ground. Now the Indian is praying, crossing himself and extending his arms in the form of a cross. He is unaware of his acts. The procession is made up of an interminable series of mosaics representing the races and various costumes. Horses and elephants pass by richly outfitted with blankets of vivid colors, embroidered in bright colors with pastoral scenes and images of war. The servants are on foot, while the great lords of the Middle East march by stiffly on horseback. British lords and ladies and passengers in gorgeous carriages show faces full of sorrow. Green and blue eyes fill with tears. Golden hair waves in the air. They have the steely look of those who kill to forge an empire. On foot, enormous and statuesque men and women from Africa, their faces noble from suffering, their black and glistening bodies glowing. The elegance and reserve, with no reduction in their suffering, of those in the procession coming from the very heart of Spain is impressive. The Spaniards demonstrate such nobility and strength of character that history certainly cannot claim any more worthy, handsome and valiant. The same is true for the mystery of the East as seen in the individuals whose faces are a metaphor of the thoughts and deep knowledge of human nature. The peoples of America are mixed in among those who arrive from faraway places, not only those taken over by the natives of Europe but also those proud indigenous races that had left their mark of grandeur as indelible evidence. Aztecs with rainbow panaches and Incas and Mayans with polychrome costumes advance in ceremonious procession and movements of awesome ritual. The children of Russia and Germany as well as France and many other different peoples advanced sadly to bury the man who had just died. That they are different in language and appearance and that they are separated by centuries and millenia provokes neither concern nor surprise. The majestic kings of bygone ages with their court of noble knights advance alongside the humble step of their slaves. Modern automobiles of powerful politicians and wealthy millionaires roll alongside what were once Roman chariots pulled by horses. Here and there, dotted among riders of proud horses, the cream of the crop of medieval knighthood, there are modern-day motorcyclists squatting on their bikes, each wearing his respective helmet. Despite the diversity of dress, origin and language, everything moves together smoothly. Nobody bothers anybody else, since everyone has his mind set on the same thought and looks straight ahead, the attention of the collective soul on the dead man. The afternoon brings out the glow of the cardinals' purple. Having reached the prominent site, the pallbearers lower the coffin from their shoulders at the edge of the cemetery that stretches out in a sea of crosses. Below on the level ground, the multitude stops and waits. The liturgy begins, with the highest dignitaries of the Church officiating. The word rings out against the walls of granite and is amplified. The voices in Latin, with all the solemnity and mystery accorded by the centuries, rise above the contrite throng. A canticle arises that begins in a chorus of minimal and low notes like the murmur of children or angels that imposes, prevailing in the distance. All of the voices are added successively as they grow in volume, until they join in unison in a single canticle, elevated and uniform. Once it reaches its climax, the chorus drops off, the voices fall silent, and now an absolute silence prevails. The Holy Father has raised his arms. Timoteo Noragua wishes to inquire after the identity of the dead man, but fear paralyzes him. It is not necessary, for he feels that the crowd, which until now has paid no attention to his presence as though he were invisible or did not exist, fixes him with its look. Then he notices a shape coming directly over to where he is standing. Timoteo Noragua holds his breath, as though his chest were a cage with the door open and his heart a bird. A presentiment strikes him all of a sudden. Who can the person coming toward him be? Timoteo sees that it is a woman coming toward him, dressed like the moon, tall and scrawny, hovering over the ground, covered with a spiderweb. He doesn't even have time to ask. Do you know who died? the woman asks, and before Timoteo can answer, she adds. It is he, Huachusey. He awoke smiling, making plans. They had taken a big breakfast to him in bed. He tried to say something, and the words froze in his mouth. Now he sleeps for all eternity. But, is it true you wanted to meet him? Timoteo's high cheeks are burning, surrounded by the scattered hair of his beard. His straight black hair hangs over his forehead, and in his half-closed eyes there is a strange light. Yes, at one time I wanted to meet him. Come, I will show you his face. The woman, whose very long ashen hair matches the color of her dress, signals with her hand in the air, and her extremely pale and very beautiful face smiles slightly. The whole world stands paralyzed in an extended instant. Everyone stands frozen as though bewitched. The high pontiff remains with his hand in the air, as do the priests, bishops, and cardinals, with the exact expression they had when surprised by the imperious order of the pale lady. The same holds true for the people around him, and even the tears and lamentations hang suspended in air. With the purpose with which one leads a child by the hand, the woman guides Timoteo. In a silence in which only their voices can be heard, they come face to face before the mystery. Timoteo sees the grave that awaits the inverted birth, and then he looks at the bier resting on a mound of earth that will cover the body forever. His gaze wanders over the religious and then down over the sea of people. He contemplates all of them as though they were wax figures in a gigantic museum. The woman studied the Indian closely. He was panic-stricken and pretended to ignore what was going on, trying to back off and run away. Lift the lid of the coffin and meet him; I order you to do it. I cannot, madam. Come close, then. He draws close, the man who had sought throughout so many days and lands, trembling with fear. The woman leans over, all her ashen hair falling over her body. She lifts the lid of the coffin, and with a firm, harsh voice exclaims, here is Huachusey, your god! Timoteo Noragua steps back in terror, unable to believe what he sees. He falls to his knees quaking, stunned, his eyes fixed on the dead man. Huachusey, the man who lies in the coffin wrapped in a white shroud, has Timoteo's own exact face, as though the inside of the coffin had turned into a mirror. There is not the slightest difference between the dead man and him, down to the smallest feature. It is him, it is him . . . he himself! He turns questioningly in anguish and sees that the woman who had been his guide is walking away from him. He tries to follow her, but at that moment he hears the powerful voice of the Holy Father praying in Latin as he lowers his arm. At that precise instant, the tumult begins to move again in time.

Requiescat in pace!
Rex tremendae majestatis
qui salvandos salvas gratis
salvame, fons pietatis.
Recordare Jesu pie
quod sum causa tuae viae
ne me perdes illa die.
Lacrymosa dies illa
qua resurget ex favilla
judicandus homo reus.
Huic ergo parce Deus
Pie Jesu Domine
dona eis requiem. Amen.

Each time the Pope sings *Resquiescat in pace* an "Amen" rises up from the people, like the notes that follow each other on a piano. They lower the body in its coffin to the depths of the grave, and then all present embrace and cry. The strongest console the most afflicted, and the sea of people becomes a sea of tears.

Timoteo Noragua emerged from among the crowd, looked toward the grave, mumbled a prayer, crossed himself and then went out into the field covered with stones. His steps erased the crowd and silenced its lamentations. He saw the towers of the church of

Santa María de las Piedras, and he ran swiftly like a deer ready to embrace his people, his hometown, his land, his longed-for country. He ran without tiring. He wanted to see his wife and his children. They must be all grown up, married, with children, his grandchildren. The sidewalks, the huts, the goats, the old walls of the houses, the cobblestone streets of his village, the bells pealing in succession like the beads of a rosary, the old men in the plaza, the embittered people. Timoteo Noragua ran without getting tired, his feet no longer hurting him. He could already make out the streets of his beloved village, and there in the distance atop an elevation the home he had missed so much, the stones, the grass, the outgrowths of prickly pears. He noted with surprise as he ran that his stature was the same as that of the sahuaros, and then he saw that the stones and cactuses were getting smaller and the hills were losing their bulk. His beloved village became a miniature made by an artist. He was still able to make out a surface whose details were not clear. He saw then an enormous ball enveloped in a blue color, its edges white, with extensive patches of yellows, greens, ochres and silver. The globe grew small in a blue and extremely beautiful phosphorescence, until at last it was lost from view.